SISTER TO BEAUTY

SWEET HISTORICAL FAIRY TALES BOOK 1

ROXANNE MCNEIL

SISTER TO BEAUTY

Sweet Historical Fairy Tales, Book 1

by Roxanne McNeil

Published by Butterscotch Books

www.roxannemcneil.com

Cover design by Blue Valley Author Services

See back page for printing information.

ISBN: 978-1-7356614-1-4 (e-book)

ISBN: 978-1-7356614-0-7 (paperback)

For Mom

With many thanks to Karley, Crystal, and Tricia

CHAPTER 1

Celeste

I sabelle was the first to meet our father at the door. She had an uncanny ability to sense when he would return from his travels, though it simply may have been her near-constant vigil at the front window. Her excited shrieking drew me to the entryway, just as Father stepped across the threshold.

"Are you all right?" I asked, walking forward as I wiped my hands on my apron. Business had been poor for some time, but I'd never seen Father with such deep worry lines around his eyes.

Isabelle didn't seem to notice. "Is it a new gown, Papa? More rose bushes?" she asked over my voice as she flung herself at him.

"Let him breathe," I said.

Isabelle made a face that contradicted her famed beauty. "You're just jealous because he doesn't bring *you* gifts." She turned back to Father, whipping me in the face with her long, dark curls, an impressive feat only made possible by the height of her hair style. I readjusted my glasses.

Isabelle always received a gift. It was true. My father used to bring me gifts too. I think he still would have if he hadn't learned I'd sold the last three to pay the maid. He was notoriously late in paying people. But then again, he might have stopped bringing me gifts anyway. I didn't demand them as Isabelle did, and she wanted enough to satisfy ten girls. Even someone as extravagant in his expenditures as Father knew better than to double that kind of spending, I suppose.

I tried to ignore Isabelle's barb. "Please tell us what the matter is. Do we need to sell more furniture? We can always move into a smaller house."

Isabelle pinched my arm. "Hush, Celeste, you know we could never leave here. This is our home." Whenever the subject of selling the house was broached, Isabelle pretended deep attachment to it. The house suggested we were among the most affluent bourgeoisie in Marseille, and she and Father clung to the deception despite our widely fluctuating finances. And somehow for them, the structure didn't seem to hold constant reminders of Mother's consumptive illness and death five years prior.

"Isabelle," Father said, looking at the floor and rubbing his head. "I must speak to you alone."

"Why her?" He turned to *me* when he was in serious trouble. And he was obviously in trouble now.

Father gave me a stern look, the one he used when my words were too sharp, or shrewish, as Isabelle would say.

I walked into the sitting room just off the entryway, and Isabelle's troubled gaze followed me, relaying her deep concern that he might not have brought her a present after all. I hoped that was all it was.

To my disappointment, Father ushered Isabelle into the formal dining room, too far for me to eavesdrop. He knew me well. I stared out the window, listening hard anyway as I watched a few carriages pass. Marseille was a busy town, certainly. There was much opportunity for Father here if he wouldn't squander it. I looked down toward the harbor. Isabelle thought it was a beautiful, romantic place, almost for the same reason I thought it was horrible—men; countless numbers of men, most of them setting off on merchant or naval ships. And many of those men would never return home. Our uncle and cousins hadn't, but Isabelle hardly noticed the casualties and never even glanced at the lists of the dead. She always had a steady stream of admirers, even with so many ships now leaving to fight with the American revolutionaries against the British. How I wanted to leave this place with all its ghosts and travel far away from my sister's shadow.

Before I could think of it further, the screaming started. Father should have taken Isabelle down the street if he didn't want me to hear what they were talking about.

"I won't go!" she shrieked. "You can't make me, Papa!"

Father raised his voice, but I still couldn't make out his words.

"I'll run away first! My friends would take me in."

I snorted. They'd take her for three days before they realized what a selfish little tyrant she was. Isabelle was expert at hiding her true nature. In public, she was all that was charming and polite, but she'd never be able to keep that up for any length of time. And where did Father want to send her? I thought from Isabelle's reaction, it must be a convent.

Their voices dropped again, though Isabelle's shrill protests were occasionally audible. I hoped no one on the street heard her. The servants had been dismissed, again, a few weeks ago, so there was no one inside to hear but me. Father paid our servants well when we could afford to hire them, and that was often enough to ensure their return despite his fluctuating pattern of prosperity and financial embarrassments.

I sighed. It was almost dinner time. I wasn't the best cook, but we didn't starve when Nicole was let go. She taught me

3

enough to get by and came to check on me from time to time. When I expressed concern over her employment, she always shrugged and said it was time she started collecting suitors. I selfishly hoped Father would come into money again soon, so she could come back. Not only would it be a tremendous load of work off me, but Nicole was my friend. As often as she complained about not having time for a man in her life, I knew she needed the work. And she could have stayed if Father hadn't bought Isabelle the last gown. It was an extravagant pink brocade with innumerable pleats and a full skirt. It cost 150 livre, enough to pay Nicole for a year. Isabelle had thought it a worthwhile sacrifice, but I'd wanted to cut it to pieces.

I gave up trying to listen to Father and Isabelle and made my way to the kitchen. Since I refused to spend all day cooking in the summer, I simply sliced some bread and set out some cheese. A cold chicken and some summer vegetables rounded out the meal. I set plates at the kitchen table. I never served Father and Isabelle in the dining room. It was bad enough that Isabelle treated me as a servant, complaining if things weren't done perfectly but never lifting a finger to help when she could possibly avoid it. When Father was gone, I made her prepare her own food, partly so she would know how, and partly because I wanted time alone and knew she'd rather visit friends at meal-times than fend for herself. But when Father was home, and I made meals for him, he insisted Isabelle join us.

As I set the last dish on the table, Isabelle burst into the room, Father trailing behind her. Her blue eyes were reddened from crying, but she had a very determined set to her mouth.

"Father owes Monsieur Durant 8,000 livres, and he wants to sell me to him to pay the debt. Me. In the home of that monstrous-looking beast of a man."

"You've never seen him before, Isabelle." I corrected her out of habit, but my mind was whirling. Isabelle would be sent away?

"*Sell* you to him? What on earth do you mean?" I couldn't let that happen. She was horrid, yes, but she was my little sister, and I loved her. And 8,000 livres was enough for three of us to live well on for a year, though with Father and Isabelle copying the queen's spending habits, we could never do it. Father had gambled larger sums several times, but not when he was so close to financial ruin.

"He wants *me* to come, but that's because he doesn't know *you* exist. You can go instead," Isabelle said fiercely. "I can't manage a household. I'm only seventeen, and that's not old enough."

"You thought you were old enough to leave home last year when the Allertons invited you to Paris." I didn't bother reminding her I was only two years older. "*Why* does he want you to come?"

"He wants me to be his...his..." She paused to glance at Father then back at me. "*Housekeeper.*" She said the last word in a rush.

"Monsieur Durant wants one of us to be his *housekeeper?* But it would take half a lifetime to pay the debt that way."

Isabelle paced the length of the kitchen, her high-heeled shoes beating out a nervous rhythm. "Not to replace the debt. No." She took a deep breath and turned to face me. "As *insurance*. To be sure he does pay. Papa *will* pay him. Won't you, Papa?" Her eyes held a manic gleam. There was something else going on.

Father, who had remained silent so far, now opened his mouth but only looked helplessly at me. He turned to Isabelle, whose scowl seemed to startle him into speech. "Of course, my jewel. You know I always do, in the end. It wouldn't take me more than a month, two at the most."

"Please do it, Celeste. I can't. I'm too frightened." She clasped her hands together.

My heart softened toward her a degree.

"And besides, there's no one more capable than you," she added, almost as a taunt.

My protective feelings for her lessened. "Is he quite honorable, Father?" I asked.

"Honorable? Yes, yes. His appearance is distressing, certainly. Nasty business, war. But he is a gentleman, even if he does sometimes work his own land."

Isabelle shuddered, as though working one's land was a heinous sin.

"His great-aunt lives at the château and would be your chaperone," Father said.

"A chaperone? For a housekeeper?"

Father looked to Isabelle, who said waspishly, "Well, it's not a *usual* situation, is it?"

I took off my glasses and polished them as I thought. Isabelle wanted me to go in her place, which meant I shouldn't go. I shouldn't let her bully me. On the other hand, my father was on the verge of ruin, and I seemed to be the only one to review the accounts often enough to realize it. If he defaulted on this payment, he could be imprisoned. Someone had to go, and if it was my little sister, the man's house would probably burn down, and we would be worse off than if we hadn't sent her.

I glanced blindly in her direction. Would she even be safe on her own? She was just as likely to come to some folly of her own making as she was to be harmed by strangers.

Housekeeper. The idea wasn't as distasteful to me as it was to Isabelle. It was basically the same role I filled now. And quite frankly, it would get me away from Marseille. I was ready for a change, to say the least.

I put my glasses back on, and Father winced. He didn't want me to wear them at all, but I preferred seeing to looking pretty. Not that you could really call me pretty, even without the glasses. I wasn't a troll. It was more that I was extremely...ordinary. My brown hair was thick and shapeless, and I kept it in an unfashionable tight knot most of the time. My curves and smile were nothing compared to Isabelle's.

"All right," I said with as much indifference as I could manage. There was no point in giving my sister a reason to gloat. "I'll go."

Isabelle gave me a look of relief and—was it guilt? As far as I knew, she'd never felt a twinge of guilt over the way she treated me. Maybe she wasn't completely hopeless after all. She shot Father a warning glare before giving me a light embrace.

"Thank you, Celeste. You are so good to me." She kissed me on the cheek as she used to years ago when I did her a favor.

It felt good to be appreciated, even though I knew she was deliberately manipulating Father and me.

Dinner was a quick and mostly silent affair. Isabelle hurried off to visit a friend after eating only a few bites. Father decided to review his accounts, but he turned at the door to look back at me. The worry lines between his brows deepened again. Normally Father was robust and handsome and could be mistaken for a man half his age, but when he worried over something, he looked his full sixty years.

"Celeste, I..." He paused to run a hand through his hair, turning on the spot as though looking for something.

"Are you sure you're all right?"

He rubbed at his temples. "My good girl, to worry about me." He called Isabelle his sunshine, his jewel, his little flower. When I wasn't being mouthy, I occasionally got, "My good girl."

He did appreciate me. It wasn't the same as love. I remembered Mother well enough to know what love felt like. But appreciation was a good thing.

"You really should go rest, Father. You've been traveling for over a week."

He gave me a troubled smile and left me to ponder the happy prospect of a new situation in which no one would compare me to my sister.

~

Henri

"Henri, quit prowling, and sit down," Aunt Inese said, pushing a stray lock of grey hair back under her cap. "She'll get here soon enough. There's no point in worrying over it."

I smoothed the front of my cravat, and Aunt Inese smirked. I knew she was trying not to laugh, but I wasn't about to change back into my everyday clothes. I'd do anything to soften the effect of my appearance when I first met Mademoiselle Lebeau. She was exquisite, and I had a face that made children cry and women cross themselves.

"How could I not worry?" I said. "I'm afraid she'll take one look at me and run screaming back into the carriage."

Aunt harrumphed. "*I'm* afraid she'll be a spoiled, empty-headed ninny."

"Why would she be?"

Aunt Inese only stared at me, her pale blue eyes incredulous.

"You're the one who suggested I improve business by marrying a pretty wife who would be good at talking to people."

She turned away, suddenly intent on her needlepoint, and I realized she'd probably only suggested it so I *would* marry. But she'd been right. With a beautiful woman about, no one would look twice at my burn and knife scars, and Mademoiselle Lebeau was probably the most beautiful woman I'd ever seen. I'd never actually met her, just seen her once at a gathering in Marseille less than a month before I sustained my injuries. It seemed a lifetime ago that I'd been a junior army officer attending parties with my friends, but I remembered her. Anyone would. Mademoiselle Lebeau was stunning with luxurious dark curls and a fine figure. And she was rumored to have the sweetest disposition imaginable.

When I'd suggested his daughter come to visit, Monsieur Lebeau had been incredulous. "You want to court my daughter?"

"Yes. And in exchange for her staying here a full two months, I will forgive half your debt, the full debt if she marries me."

He'd turned his hat over in his hands a few times. "And if she wo—" He wet his lips. "If she doesn't come?"

"Of course she'll come," I said, crossing my arms. "Eight thousand livres is a lot of money. She wouldn't want you in debtors' prison." Perhaps I should have been kinder. I was talking to the man I hoped would someday be my father-in-law, but he'd been avoiding my communications for almost a year. I never should have trusted the lavender shipment to him without demanding half-payment in advance. I hoped his daughter had inherited his power of persuasion.

Production was high. The lavender fields were doing better than ever. With Mademoiselle Lebeau charming my buyers, the farm would be secure again. My only other option was to look for buyers outside of Aix, but my father and grandfather had always sold locally, and I'd learned from Monsieur Lebeau to distrust outsiders.

People in my own town were bad enough. I'd never dreamed they would turn on me just because my face had become a little scary. Well, *very* scary. Especially if I moved my mouth too much. But my buyers had cut their purchase prices by twenty-five percent last year, and they had done it all together in a group. When Jean, my friend and bookkeeper, told me about it, he ranted that I should whip each one of them. I would never do it, but it made him feel better to think of it. I wouldn't even want to face them, knowing how affected they were by my disfigurement.

"There," Aunt Inese said as she snapped a thread from her needlepoint. "That must be her now."

I strode to the window, my stomach in knots. It was late

afternoon. I couldn't let her see me in full light the first time we met.

"You'll greet her, won't you Aunt Inese? Get her settled? I've remembered something in the fields." It was a feeble excuse, but I needed to find my courage, and *she* needed to see the beauty of the house and grounds without me there to ruin the effect.

Instead of slipping out the kitchen entrance and heading toward the fields, I ran upstairs and scaled the ladder into the attic. It was hot as the devil but had a view of the drive below. Monsieur Lebeau's carriage was stopped already, and the driver was just stepping down. He opened the door of the carriage, and a woman appeared. Her face and form were mostly obscured by her hat at this angle, but I caught my breath. She really had come. The most beautiful young woman in Marseille, and possibly all of Provence, had come to my home.

I felt a surge of pride mingled with panic. A woman that beautiful, when she saw *me*... I squared my shoulders. It wasn't as though I had nothing to offer her. My home was the nicest in all the surrounding area, my financial situation promising, especially if she joined me, and I wasn't difficult to get along with. She wouldn't fear beatings or harsh reprimands. But could she see past the burn marks?

By early evening, I'd snuck downstairs half a dozen times to eavesdrop. Mademoiselle Lebeau had a beautiful speaking voice, her tones measured and purposeful. She sounded sensible. Of course, I couldn't hear most of the words, only the tone, but it was still promising.

At last I could stand waiting no longer. It was an hour yet until dinner, but the natural light would have mostly faded from the east sitting room where she sat with my aunt. I took several deep breaths and even said a short prayer before stepping into the room.

My first impression was that she was taller than I remembered. Her back was to me, and when my aunt greeted me with an uneasy smile, Mademoiselle Lebeau kept her face turned for a small moment as she fiddled with something at her ears. Then she slipped an object into her pocket and turned around.

What?

"Who are you?" I asked, more gruffly than I intended.

"I am Mademoiselle Lebeau," said the girl before me. She didn't flinch at my appearance, so I had timed my entry perfectly with the light, but everything else was wrong.

"You are not Mademoiselle Lebeau."

"I beg your pardon, but I believe I know who I am," she said, straightening her spine and narrowing her gaze.

"Mademoiselle Lebeau is a great beauty. I find you only passably pretty." I regretted the words immediately, but I was taken so off guard that I didn't know how to soften them. This girl could never be mistaken for a beauty. She wasn't hideous, but her features lacked distinction. Her cheekbones were a little higher than was fashionable, and her nose had a bit of a hook to it. Her green-brown eyes were a little unfocused, and her hair was a neither-here-nor-there light brown pulled into a tight knot.

The slightest expression of annoyed resignation flitted across her face before she lifted her chin and said, "You're probably referring to my younger sister, Isabelle Lebeau. I am Celeste Lebeau. My sister and I talked the matter over and realized that I could fit your needs better."

Aunt's eyes widened in surprise at her words. I stared at the girl, dumbfounded. I honestly had no idea what to say.

She spoke into the shocked silence. "I hope you don't mind our decision. We would have consulted with you if it had been possible. Isabelle has almost no housekeeping experience, and has never cooked. I have been managing our household since I was twelve years old." Her voice was so measured and matter-of-fact, she could have been discussing projections for the price of barley.

I was enough of a gentleman not to speak my mind at that particular moment, but it meant I didn't say anything at all. It wouldn't do to inform the sister of my future intended that nothing could induce me to marry her and that it was barbarously unladylike to parade into *my* home without an invitation and simply assume that *I* would be amenable to courting *her*.

So I simply stood there, stunned, my mouth opening and closing idiotically as I began to say something and stopped myself several times over.

Aunt Inese came to my rescue, stepping forward to catch Mademoiselle Lebeau's attention. "May I ask what terms you are suggesting?" she asked.

"Well, just what I was told," Mademoiselle Lebeau said with a nod. "I will serve as your housekeeper as insurance against my father's debt. When my father is able to pay you, he will bring the money and collect me."

"What?" I choked out.

"Are those not the terms you discussed with my father?" she asked, an impatient snap in her voice.

"No. They are not," I exclaimed, sounding surly and angry. I *was* angry. Monsieur Lebeau had purposefully sent the wrong daughter, and if he thought I was going to forgive thousands of livre for *this* girl, it was time I found my horse to go after the man myself. Perhaps Jean's bloodlust was infectious after all.

Her brows contracted. "They're not?" She was a good actress or had been duped by her father as well.

"I was promised the younger daughter," I said, glaring. To my credit, I didn't shout at her or break things as I wanted to. I'd spent so much time and energy preparing the house for Isabelle Lebeau to come to it. How had I been stupid enough to trust Monsieur Lebeau?

"I don't know why you'd want *her*," the girl said, pink spots forming on her cheeks. "The only good thing that can be said for her is that she is beautiful. What use have you for beauty in a housekeeper?"

I didn't need a beautiful *housekeeper*, and the words were on the tip of my tongue, but she didn't give me a chance.

"I love my sister, and it pains me to say it, but she has never performed a jot of work in her life. It isn't entirely her fault. It was never expected of her. But she'd be more likely to run you to ruin than be any benefit to your household whatsoever." She said the last through clenched teeth, and in the back of my mind, I wondered if her sister could possibly have a matching temper. But that was impossible. Isabelle Lebeau was beautiful, an angel.

Aunt gave me an I-told-you-so look, but I didn't acknowledge it. Monsieur Lebeau had betrayed me. He'd kept his favored daughter and sent a shrew in her place. Mademoiselle Lebeau was obviously speaking out of jealousy and desperation. The little snip stared me down as though she had every right in the world to be in my sitting room, demanding to work as my…housekeeper.

And was that a tear forming in the corner of her eye? I cursed under my breath. I was going to throttle Monsieur Lebeau.

CHAPTER 2

Celeste

I would *not* cry in front of this horrid person. Pretending he hadn't made the *stupid* bargain with my father. Suggesting my ridiculous sister would be a better housekeeper than *I* would. If he believed a beautiful face made a good worker, he was as idiotic as he sounded. I blinked back angry tears as my mind scrambled for purchase. I had just escaped Marseille. I couldn't go back now.

Oh. I *couldn't* go back. The carriage had left hours ago. Monsieur Durant had made me wait so long that there was no hope of catching up to it now.

"Might I suggest a temporary solution to this problem?" I said, my voice deceptively calm and business-like. "My father promised you Isabelle, not me. And I can see how that could be a disappointment." *You pig.* "By now our carriage has already met up with my father in Aix and is taking him to Italy where he is conducting business over the next month. He intends to stop and check on me on his return journey."

Was Monsieur Durant actually grinding his teeth? I had no way of knowing other than what I heard. Without my glasses on, he was only a tall dark-haired blur in the dim light. All I could really make out was that one of his eyes was horribly blackened. I wondered if he was accustomed to brawling. Father said the man was honorable, but I was happy to have Madame Sauveterre in the room, even if she was his aunt.

I went on, ignoring his anger. "During that month, I will remain here as your housekeeper. If you aren't satisfied with my work by the time my father comes, I will go back with him to Marseille, and he will bring Isabelle back here."

The blur that was Monsieur Durant turned to look at the blur that was Madame Sauveterre. The silence stretched on while I looked back and forth between them, pretending I could actually see their faces.

"I could certainly use the help," Madame Sauveterre said.

He breathed out a growl. "Very well, Mademoiselle Lebeau. One month. And at the end of the month, you *will* be going back with your father."

He stomped from the room, but I was too relieved to care about his temper. I would stay. And when he saw what I could do, he'd beg my father to let me be his housekeeper forever. I smiled in the general direction of Madame Sauveterre.

She gave a wry laugh. "You'd better put your glasses back on, so I can show you around the house."

I was happy to do as she said. The parts of the house that I'd already seen were incredible. It was much older than my home in Marseille. That house was a show house, designed to look expensive and easily accommodate large numbers of people in a few rooms intended for entertaining. I'd never cared for that house, even less so after my mother had died. That's when I realized the cold, empty rooms had only felt like home because I was loved there. Once she was gone, that all changed.

This house was entirely charming, despite it being half a dozen times the size of ours. Everything in it suggested comfort and hospitality, from the lighting, to the furnishings, to the layout of the rooms. I was only more impressed when I saw the kitchen, a large cheerful room with two cook-stoves and three separate pantries, all managed by Suzanne, a red-haired cook three times my age who glared at me with the fires of hell in her eyes when Madame Sauveterre introduced me as her temporary assistant and companion. Obviously she didn't welcome a change in household authority.

"Is that risotto?" I asked with interest. Nicole was a wonderful cook, but she was resistant to trying new dishes, and I'd wanted to learn to make it for some time.

Suzanne's furrowed eyebrows relaxed. "Just started it," she grunted.

"Would you teach me as you go?" I asked, not bothering to hide my interest.

She regarded me through a narrowed gaze.

"The cook I usually work with doesn't care for certain foods. My guess is that she simply doesn't have the experience. If I could learn a few dishes while I'm here and teach them to her when I go back, it would be a good thing for her." And for me. Suzanne didn't know I was the daughter of a one-time wealthy merchant, and I had no desire to enlighten her. That is, if the entire house didn't already know my father's shameful financial circumstances.

Suzanne's expression softened by a degree. Evidently she *didn't* know. She shrugged dismissively, but I could see the pleasure in her eyes. She must have never had anyone to teach.

"You don't mind, Madame Sauveterre?"

"Not at all, Mademoiselle Lebeau." She gave me a mysterious look, a hint of surprised interest mingled with...amusement, perhaps. "I believe I'm tired. I will rest before dinner."

The moment her back was turned, I moved toward one of the stoves. "What can I do?" I asked, clapping my hands together and practically bouncing on my toes.

Suzanne cracked a smile at that.

I hardly knew where the time went. Suzanne was nothing like Nicole. Where Nicole's deep brown eyes and almost permanent smile mirrored her own peacefulness, Suzanne's temperament matched her flaming hair. She gripped her ladle as though to strangle it, but her wry humor, mixed with an excellent culinary knowledge, endeared her to me almost immediately. By the time Madame Sauveterre returned just before dinner, I was filled with information as well as risotto.

Madame Sauveterre's eyes were troubled, immediately setting my nerves on edge. Had Monsieur Durant changed his mind? Did I have to leave?

"Perhaps for today," she suggested, her lined cheeks faintly pink, "You would care to take dinner in your room?"

Oh. That was all. The beast didn't care for me to join him. Well, that was fine with me. I gave Madame Sauveterre a warm smile. "I'm afraid I have sampled too much of Suzanne's cooking as it is," I admitted. "If it wouldn't inconvenience you, I'll retire early tonight. I'd like to survey the needs of the garden in the morning, if that is to your liking."

The tightness around her eyes relaxed into smile lines.

I quickly thanked Suzanne before following Madame Sauveterre upstairs and through the long hall of family chambers.

"This is my nephew's room," Madame Sauveterre said, waving at an open door to an enormous bedroom. "And this one," she gestured at another on the opposite side, "is mine." It was also open, and the furnishings were heavy and ornate, yet still feminine. Two doors after that, she paused and pressed her lips into a thin line. Before I could ask what was behind the closed door, she marched on. I glanced back over my shoulder. Was there something about that room that she disliked? We turned and passed down another hall before she opened a door and ushered me inside.

"It's a smaller room," she apologized. "But it's my favorite view in the house."

"It's perfect," I said. And it was true. It was the most perfect room imaginable. Her idea of small meant the room was larger than mine at home, and better furnished. The settee and the bedcovers were a pale blue, and the wall hangings were embroidered with pink and blue flowers. It was far more comfortable than a housekeeper of no relation could expect.

We moved to a window overlooking the ornamental gardens, and beyond the hundreds of summer roses was the lavender-flanked gate of the vegetable garden. The far border was the foot of the hillside, making the garden truly enormous.

Madame Sauveterre had said the man who tended the gardens had died shortly after planting this year and that Maurice, who managed the stable, had taken over the basic needs of the ornamental garden. The basic needs must have included trimming the roses. Even in the fading light, I could see they were well-tended. It was good Isabelle hadn't known about the roses. She may have been tempted to come instead of sending me. Aside from herself and her clothing, roses were the thing she loved best in the world.

I turned back to Madame Sauveterre. "Thank you for letting me stay," I said in my usual straightforward manner. "Truly, I'll do my best."

She gave me a troubled smile, as though she thought my best wouldn't be a tenth of what it would take to keep me here. "You are more than welcome to undertake any portion of my duties that interests you," she said. "As long as you're here," she added as an afterthought.

I thanked her as she left, and then I turned to look around

my room. *As long as I'm here.* I sniffed, trying to bury my anxiety. I'd show them. When Monsieur Durant saw what I could do, he'd never want to replace me with my empty-headed sister.

But what could I do to prove my competence? The house seemed to run smoothly despite them being shorthanded. Madame Sauveterre hadn't explained *why* they had difficulty with finding more staff, but I doubted it was the same reason my father had trouble hiring servants. Did Monsieur Durant scare them away? Had he been even ruder to them than he'd been to me? It couldn't simply be for his physical appearance. I'd seen him. Sort of. Other than his black eye, there was nothing particularly concerning about him. Isabelle said he was disfigured by scars and that his hair was a mass of twigs and brambles. He might have had scars, and he might not have been handsome, but even with my limited vision, I could see that he stood strong and tall, and that his dark brown hair was nothing like a bird's nest. I truly cared very little about the man's looks. What mattered was whether or not he would send me packing for *my* lack of beauty.

It was a very good thing I'd removed my glasses before turning to meet him. I'd almost been thrown out for only being passably pretty *without* them. If he'd seen me with them on... I sighed. He probably wouldn't even have allowed me to stay the night. I would have been sent back to Aix on foot.

Henri

I woke almost as angry as I'd been when I'd gone to sleep, but for a few minutes, I couldn't remember why. Had I been dreaming again? Reliving the torture I'd endured two years ago? No. I remembered. It was the Lebeau girl. Celeste. I closed my eye and leaned back into my pillow, rubbing my face and forcing myself not to grind my teeth.

The shrew. Her father intended to mock me, sending her rather than the beauty. But when he came back in a month's time, he'd pay for his prank. He'd put me in a terrible position. I couldn't tell the girl what I thought of the arrangement, couldn't even send her away. If I had any hope of her being my sister-in-law, I had to be patient. Polite, at least. And at the same time, I had to avoid leading her on. I couldn't let her think she could stay, or, heaven forbid, that I was the slightest bit interested in her. I had to make it very clear that I was *not* pleased she was here. I had been raised to treat women with respect, but it probably wouldn't be hard to be aloof and distant with her. Especially if I continued to be needed the better part of every day in the fields.

I was downstairs to the kitchen in a flash, my work clothes on and my eye patch carefully in place. I was determined to make my escape before the girl woke. I had mountains of work to get through in the next month, and only two farmhands to help, the Fontaine boys a mile to the west. I offered better wages than anyone in the surrounding area, but that wasn't enough to tempt anyone else to work for me. Jean had tried multiple neighboring towns, but without luck.

I almost tripped over the door frame when I realized who was in the kitchen with Suzanne. Mademoiselle Lebeau stood next to one of the stoves, stirring something and asking Suzanne about her herb garden. Their backs were to me, and like a common sneak thief, I edged around the corner, snatched three rolls from a tray and edged back out of sight.

What was she doing awake at this hour? And how on earth had she managed to get Suzanne to talk to her? Our cook was extremely private and tended to be surly, especially in the mornings. I paused to listen.

"And don't forget to beat the eggs well. That's part of the

problem with this dish. People forget to beat them to the right consistency, and if you stop early, you'll get a pudding."

"That might explain my failures in the past," Mademoiselle Lebeau said with a little laugh. "My family's situation has fluctuated in extremes, so sometimes I'm cooked *for* and sometimes I do the cooking."

"And sometimes you're a housekeeper?" Suzanne asked, curiosity in her voice.

As much as I wanted the girl gone, I still felt a sudden discomfort. I *didn't* want her embarrassed.

"No," she said without hesitation. "I've always been the housekeeper. I think a girl should always be able to support herself, don't you?"

"Obviously," Suzanne grunted. After a moment, both women giggled.

Suzanne? Giggling? I'd known her since I was three. I'd never heard her giggle before.

I stayed a couple minutes more, listening to Celeste Lebeau. It was no wonder I mistook her for the beauty. Her voice was cultured. Smooth. If I could put a different face with it, I could listen for hours. A different face? A different everything. She was certainly bossy and confident for someone whose eyes couldn't seem to focus.

I shook my head as I made my way to the fields. Paul and Jacques Fontaine were already there, getting water to the wheat. It had been dry this week, and the water was crucial. I rolled up my sleeves. It was already warm. The brothers greeted me by nodding their heads respectfully and getting right back to their work. Paul, a couple years my senior, was my friend, but he wasn't a man of many words. His younger brother shared his dark hair and short, strong build, and between the two of them, they did the work of four men. I still desperately needed to hire more workers, but they kept the farm going.

My eye patch was itching like mad within the hour, but I

cared too much for Paul and Jacques' comfort to take it off. The work and my itchy eye socket should have cleared Mademoiselle's laugh from my ears. It must have been too long since I'd heard women laughing. All I had to do was picture her in my mind and the sweetness of the laugh was lessened. Of all people, I had no right to think ill of someone for their lack of physical beauty, but she had been so unapologetic, so absolutely irritating.

I sent Jacques back to the house to retrieve lunch and clean water to drink. It was cowardly, but I found I didn't want to face my possible future sister-in-law. I'd likely say something I'd regret. By evening it couldn't be helped. I returned home to dinner, washing up and entering the family dining room only to find Aunt Inese surveying me with dissatisfaction.

"Well?" I said as pleasantly as I could.

"She won't be joining us for meals," she said, her lips a tight line.

That was good. "Why not?"

"Because she knows you don't want her to."

That wasn't good. I frowned, and the motion pulled at my scars. "She said that?"

Aunt Inese gave me the look. "Of course not. But she retired to her room early again, giving a very polite excuse." She allowed me to seat her at the table. "She's a well-spoken girl," she added as I lowered my tired body into the chair across from her.

I was silent a few moments before observing, "She was up very early this morning."

"And did as much work as any three people today," Aunt added with a sniff.

"But surely you told her she wasn't here to work?"

"Of course," she said, an acidic bite to her tone. "I simply told her that her father had sent her here to marry you, but that you didn't want her because she isn't as pretty as her sister."

I tried to ignore her sarcasm. "I didn't tell the girl to scrub floors, and neither did you." What would she have me do?

"And what of hiring workers for the harvest?" Aunt asked.

"It's proving more difficult than last year." I suppose I shouldn't have let them see me last year, but it wasn't in my nature to sit inside while the work was going on outside. I must have scared them, because none of them would agree to come back this year.

"Perhaps you ought to go yourself to—"

"No," I broke in. "That would only make the problem worse."

We ate in silence until I finished and began to excuse myself.

"Don't forget Suzanne is away tomorrow," Aunt Inese reminded me.

I sat back down and half-filled my plate again. Suzanne's occasional replacement had a tendency to burn things. She probably spent more time worrying she'd have to see me than she did actually watching the food.

But the next morning, when I headed down to the kitchen for a quick bite before going out to work, I was pleasantly surprised to smell sweet rolls. There was a large plate of them on the sideboard, and no one to scold me, so I scooped up the entire plate and took it with me. I was thrilled that Suzanne hadn't left, and Paul and Jacques deserved a better breakfast than they probably got at home.

They greeted me with more enthusiasm on their faces than I'd seen since we were children. In minutes we'd devoured over a dozen sweet rolls. Suzanne had outdone herself. Later I went home to fetch the mid-day meal, intending to tell her so myself. The Lebeau girl stood surveying the garden. She fumbled with something at her face, stuffing it into her pocket before she turned around.

I groaned internally and detoured to speak with her. She didn't seem at all alarmed by my approach. I'd become accustomed to people avoiding me, so her apparent lack of distress was a relief.

"Madame Sauveterre said I am free to engage a maid and a gardener," she said before I could get a word in.

"I wish you luck with it," I said, folding my arms across my chest. I was sure she knew the reason no one wanted the job.

She gave me a satisfied smile, staring in the general direction of my nose. Perhaps if her sister agreed to marry me, it would be altogether appropriate for me to suggest she visit my friend, Bertram, a promising young eye doctor, fresh out of school, but already very well respected. Perhaps there were eye exercises he could teach her.

She nodded politely and turned to walk away, stumbling against a small bush in the process.

"Mademoiselle Lebeau."

She righted herself and looked back toward me with raised eyebrows. A faint blush was the only indicator she knew she'd been clumsy. I held back a smile with effort.

"I hope you understand that you are very welcome to join my aunt and me at mealtimes. You are a guest here as much as a...housekeeper." My tone could have been better. I suppose the invitation held too much sarcasm.

"Thank you," she said with the dignity of a duchess. "I will be glad to join you for a meal when I have the time."

I almost snorted. She obviously thought she'd be doing me a favor. The harpy. I turned to go.

"And Monsieur Durant?"

"Yes?"

She hesitated a moment, then shrugged. "Your mid-day meal is waiting on the sideboard."

I nodded once, wondering what insult she'd first intended to deliver. I didn't have time to ask. There was too much work to be done that day. I was soon back in the fields with a very full pail of food which had the Fontaine brothers praising Suzanne's name. I didn't get to thank her that evening because I was so late coming home for supper. I ate alone, Aunt Inese having long since gone to bed. After a full day of work, I was grateful to have my belly full of real food, not the cold potatoes I usually had when Suzanne was gone.

Aunt Inese appeared in the doorway of her bedroom when she heard me in the hall. Her silver braid hung over one shoulder of her dressing gown as she raised her candle to peer through the hallway at me.

I moved closer, so she could see I was safe and well. She had no business worrying about me, but I knew she did anyway.

"Goodnight, Auntie. Thank you for all you do," I said, bending to kiss her wrinkled face.

"I didn't do a thing but knit today, sweet boy."

"Well, the food you and Suzanne decided on was delicious. I'm sorry I missed dinner with you."

"Suzanne left to see her sister last night, just as usual. But I had a lovely dinner with Celeste. She really is the most interesting girl I've ever met. You would never guess she'd come from such a father." She smiled at me, apparently enjoying my astonishment, and then disappeared back into her room.

I wandered back toward mine, trying to accept what she'd said and what that meant. I had to sort it out before I fell asleep. The slightest bit of agitation tended to bring on the nightmares. Another door opened down the adjacent hallway, and I leaned back against my door frame as Celeste Lebeau hurried around the corner and padded down the hall. She didn't carry a candle, and didn't seem to notice me.

When she was only inches away, I greeted her. "Mademoiselle Lebeau."

She gasped and covered her face with her hands as she leapt away in fright.

Without a thought, my arm snaked forward to keep her from crashing into the wall. In my haste, I jerked her a little too roughly, and she ended up in my arms. During the half-second that she was pressed against my side, I came to some realizations. First, having Celeste Lebeau in my arms wasn't an unpleasant sensation. Second, it was impossible not to notice in this proximity that the girl had a very feminine figure. Third, her smell was heavenly; a mix of baking bread and perfumed soap. And fourth, I was about to be slapped.

CHAPTER 3

Celeste

What on earth did the miscreant mean by jerking me around like that? My mind caught up to my reflexes just in time to avoid slapping my employer, and it was a good thing, since my heavy glasses were still clutched in my right hand. I'd snatched them off my face as I'd jumped away from him, the need to hide them apparently as strong as my need to avoid danger.

He gently righted me and stepped back, his hands held up in front of his chest, as though he expected me to attack him like a wild animal.

"I'm sorry to startle you." The smile in his voice contradicted his words.

He probably deserved a sharp reprimand for sneaking up on me like that, but my voice was still frozen. I should have waited longer to sneak down and clean up after him, but I'd been so tired that I'd dressed for bed and waited until I was half-asleep before shaking myself and padding out into the hall.

He still waited for me to speak. Isabelle would have

commented on the strength of his arms. They *had* felt very strong. Or perhaps she would have sweetly thanked him for rescuing her from harm. When I'd gulped a few times and got my voice back, all I could say was an accusatory, "You hold very still in the dark, Monsieur."

He gave a low laugh. I hadn't guessed until then that he could laugh. It was a pleasant sound and sent an odd pang of wistfulness through my chest.

He cleared his throat. "Where are you going?"

It was fortunate it was dark. He probably didn't see me roll my eyes at him. "You are short one maid," I informed him. "And a cook."

"Yes?"

"That means the things they do at night need to be done by someone else."

He didn't answer, just stood facing me in the dark. I could hardly see him, but I hadn't heard him move, so I imagined him looking at me with a dimwitted expression.

After a long pause, he said in a humorous tone, "Do you mean to tell me that you are acting as cook *and* scullery maid today?"

I changed my mind. His expression was probably impertinent and snide. It was too bad I hadn't slapped him when I had the chance. "Some people might surprise you," I said, raising my chin. I turned abruptly away and collided with the wall.

He didn't bother to hide his snort of laughter. It wasn't a mean-spirited laugh, but it was still a laugh. "Mademoiselle Lebeau," he said with exaggerated gallantry, "allow me to fetch a candle for you and escort you to your very important engagement."

I sniffed. I wanted to tell him that his head might have an engagement with the mop if he followed me around, but I managed to remember that I needed to impress him. I settled for a prim, "No, thank you," and turned away, this time keeping my hand on the wall as I walked down the hall.

He followed me anyway. I walked faster, wishing he'd go away. I couldn't clean up after him if I couldn't even see where he'd left his dishes.

"Mademoiselle Lebeau," he said impatiently, "could you tell me what it is scullery maids do when everyone else goes to bed? I saw the kitchen. It's already clean."

I rounded on him, intending to give him a piece of my mind. Unfortunately, his vision wasn't perfect in the dark either, or perhaps he had his eyes closed, because in the next moment he ploughed right into me. We went down together that time. With incredible speed, he clutched me around the waist and spun me, so that in the next instant, I landed on top of him instead of the other way around.

He gave a muffled "Oof," and a moan.

"Monsieur Durant," I exclaimed, his role as my temporary employer forgotten. I squirmed to get off him, but he was somehow laying on the hem of my dressing gown, and I was trapped. "Are you injured?" I asked anxiously.

"What on earth?" Madame Sauveterre exclaimed as she hurried toward us with a candle.

Monsieur Durant muttered a curse and boosted me up by my elbows.

There was a horrible ripping noise as the portion of my dressing gown pinned underneath him was nearly torn away.

"Goodness," Madame Sauveterre said as I tried desperately to push her nephew off my clothes.

I hadn't realized before that he was such a heavy oaf. He finally understood and rolled away from me, lumbering to his feet. Something waved in my vision, and after a moment, I realized the blur was his hand reaching down to help me up. I sighed, placed my fingers in his, and was immediately hauled upright.

Another rip. I caught back an unladylike expression. The hem of my nightdress had been under my foot. I leaned down to feel the fabric. There was a slit up to my knee. I tried to pull the fabric together and stand up at the same time. I must have looked like such an idiot.

"It's not my fault," Monsieur Durant said. "She tackled me, just because I said she shouldn't play scullery maid tonight."

Madame Sauveterre stared at us for a moment before barking a laugh. "Henri, you fiend," she said. She had that right. "You know I don't believe a word."

They both snickered. So nice they could enjoy themselves while I was in such a predicament. I wished the candlelight, *and* Monsieur Durant, would go away.

"He is a rather tidy person, my dear. We needn't fear for mice or insects," Madame Sauveterre finally said. "Now Henri, if you'll leave us alone, I'll walk Celeste to her room."

He bowed in our direction and turned away, his form melting into the darkness outside the candlelight. I was glad to see him go. Besides, I was still angry enough for my face to be an unbecoming, blotchy red. No need for him to see that too. When I was certain he'd gone, I slipped my glasses back on.

Madame Sauveterre regarded me with a kind smile. "I am quite good with a needle," she said. "If you still intend to take care of breakfast tomorrow before we go into town, I would have my time free to take care of those." She gestured toward my torn garments.

I thanked her and returned to my room as quickly as possible. I'd been humiliated enough for one night.

The next morning I woke early enough to make breakfast and leave it on the sideboard before Maurice, who tended the horses and the formal gardens, hitched up the carriage. Madame Sauveterre appeared, clutching a list, and Maurice handed us into the carriage. By the time Monsieur Durant came outside, we were in the light open carriage headed to town. He waved at us, but I turned my head and pretended not to notice because I didn't want to take off my glasses.

"How do you intend to find a maid and someone to fill in when Suzanne is gone?" Madame Sauveterre asked as she leaned back into the cushioned seat.

"I hope she will be the same person," I said. "I'll make a few friends, see what I can learn."

"Make friends? In one morning?"

"I love talking to people, and excluding young men, most people don't find me repulsive."

She sniffed. "In my experience, young men are unfortunately the worst judges of character."

The city of Aix was lovely, the church beautiful. After stopping at a public stable, we went our separate ways. I spent the first hour talking to shopkeepers and learning everything I could about the business culture of the town. Carrying the purchases I'd made at their shops, and on the advice of two separate clerks, I walked half a mile to a cloth warehouse teeming with women. I soon knew of four different women looking for work, two of whom had homes close enough to the château to make it worth their time.

"Widow Bochard might do for you," the warehouse owner told me. "A washerwoman. Has a couple young ones, but they might be old enough to leave to themselves now. She's a solitary one, but if you don't mind that, *and* that her grandfather was Protestant—" she spat on the floor— "she might just be the person. Needs work enough not to mind that Monsieur Durant hates people."

"Hates people?" I said with a laugh.

She smiled back at me with a sheepish shrug.

"Because he mostly stays home?"

She pulled her shawl a little tighter around her shoulders. "Everyone says it. I suppose that doesn't necessarily mean it's true. If you've been out there a few days, you'd know better than the rest of us. He's hardly been seen since he came home a couple years ago. He was healing up for almost a year, and after that, he mostly stayed away. The army turned him away from people. It happens sometimes."

"What was he like before?" I asked, curious.

"Well, the Durant family, they were so sociable, so many parties, you know. And he seemed to enjoy it all. He was a handsome fellow, but what I remember about him was that he liked to pull a prank." She shook her head. "He and that Vrai boy used to get into all sorts of trouble. Mischief in their eyes, you know."

I laughed with her. "I've met the type. Well, who knows? He might decide he likes people again." Her eyes turned sharp, and I hastened to add, "It would be such a waste of that pretty house not to have parties there again. I hope to help Madame Sauveterre get it running smoothly again before I go back to Marseille." I wasn't ready to go home, but I didn't want the suspicion she was forming to go any further.

Two hours later, Inese and I arrived at the widow Bochard's home, a tiny farmhouse neighbored only by scrubby trees. She came to the door as the carriage approached, a hard-looking young woman with her brown hair in a knot as tight as the lines around her dark eyes. Her somewhat worn dress was pinned neatly in front, a modest kerchief tucked into her neckline. Two small fair-haired children appeared behind her. The youngest, a little girl, couldn't have been more than five years old. My heart sank. She'd never agree to work away from them. The boy was older, probably seven.

"I'll be right back," I told Madame Sauveterre. I jumped down from the carriage.

"Good afternoon," I called. "Are you Madame Bochard?"

"Yes."

"I am Celeste Lebeau. I'm temporarily helping Madame Sauveterre care for the Durant house. I hope you don't mind the intrusion. I understand you take in wash?"

"Yes." She didn't look pleased about it.

"We're looking to hire a maid, and someone in town suggested your name."

"It won't work," she said with certainty. "I don't leave my children."

The five-year-old crept closer to me, looking with awe at my skirt. It was nothing special, but fine enough to catch her attention. The little boy eyed my glasses with distrust.

"I see. Well, it is nice to meet you." I looked at the little girl. "Hello, princess. Perhaps, as we're such close neighbors, you would like to come eat some of the peas in the garden?"

"We don't accept charity," the woman said, frowning.

It hadn't taken me long to offend her. "That isn't what I meant," I said with a smile. "You see, we don't have anyone to tend the garden, and until we can find someone, the place is overgrown. If you're free on Saturday, I wonder if you could come and help me harvest some of it. You'd take twenty-five percent as your fee for helping."

Her eyes held a hint of longing, but she turned away, ushering the children back into the house. "I don't leave my children," she explained again.

"I hadn't thought of you leaving them behind," I called.

She paused, then turned back to me, anxiety plain on her face. "And what would Monsieur Durant think of that?"

Henri

S he wore glasses. That explained it. Her unfocused eyes. Her clumsiness. I should have realized before. When she left the house that morning, I saw her with them for a short moment before she turned away. She must have snatched them off her face when she leapt away from me the previous night.

That was what she had shoved in her pocket. I laughed quietly into my glove. She'd been so funny, so indignant, then so worried she'd hurt me when I spun her on top of me. I was glad I hadn't hurt *her*. I'd never been described as a small man.

When her dressing gown and nightdress had ripped, it had taken all my effort not to grin. The expression on her face had been priceless. And I really shouldn't have glanced at her leg, but when the fabric ripped, I looked right to the tear. It was impossible not to notice the smooth calf and trim ankle exposed by the torn clothing. I'd looked away, and I don't think she'd noticed, but the image was fresh in my mind all through the next day.

I shook myself, knowing I shouldn't even think of *Isabelle* Lebeau's ankles, and there was a good chance I'd *marry her*. Oddly, it hadn't been Celeste's sister that had occupied my dreams last night. And in none of those dreams had I relived my injuries.

Suzanne was back from her sister's home, and when I came in for lunch, she verified it had indeed been Celeste Lebeau cooking for us while she was gone.

"She insisted you and Madame Sauveterre didn't need an incompetent cook. Said she could manage it all. From what I'd already seen her do, I believed her," Suzanne said. "You weren't disappointed?"

"No, no. Her sweet rolls were delicious. I was only surprised she could make them."

Suzanne responded with a severe frown, and I retreated to my work.

I came home from the fields early that day. The Fontaine boys could manage, and I desperately needed to go through my accounts. Jean had explained them to me, but the numbers hadn't made sense with him rattling through them so fast.

Aunt Inese greeted me near the entryway, and we both

turned toward the stable at the sound of Maurice's laugh. Mademoiselle Lebeau stood at the stable door, talking and gesticulating, apparently telling some sort of story. Maurice, who was nearing sixty and usually cared more for horses than he did people, threw back his head and laughed again. Did I imagine the surprised looks on the oxen watching him from the corral?

"How did she enjoy her failure today?" I asked my aunt as I frowned at Maurice. He was only encouraging her.

"Failure?" Aunt Inese said, tilting her head to the side. "I wouldn't call it that yet." And she sauntered away, if a seventy-two-year-old woman with a rheumatic hip could saunter.

I shook my head. I was only marginally certain Isabelle Lebeau could convince people to work with me. I had no hope at all that her sister could perform such magic.

I locked myself in my study for the next few hours, determined to understand the accounts. But Jean had changed the format of his bookkeeping again, and by the time dinner was on the table, I was exceptionally irritated.

Only Aunt Inese met me in the dining room.

"Mademoiselle is not joining us again?" I didn't know why I felt slighted. It shouldn't have concerned me a bit if she didn't want to join us. Me. She obviously didn't mind sitting down with Aunt Inese.

I strode from the room without another word, not stopping until I reached the kitchen.

"Mademoiselle Lebeau?"

Suzanne looked up, a few recipes in her hand. Mademoiselle Lebeau sat near her at the table but slipped something into her apron pocket before she turned around to face me.

"Can I help you, Monsieur Durant?"

"Won't you join us for dinner?" I said, my words clipped. "You haven't eaten yet?"

Her brows drew together. "Did I do something...?"

"Not at all. I'd like to hear your ideas for the house. My aunt tells me you have several."

Her shoulders dropped an inch in apparent relief. "I would be very happy to come. Thank you."

She preceded me out of the room, walking far too slowly. Suzanne gave me a warning look as I left. I was supposed to mind my manners.

When we finally arrived in the dining room, I seated Mademoiselle Lebeau, whose fingers trailed gently along her chair before she sat down.

Aunt Inese greeted her and began passing food. There *had* been a time when we had a footman to serve at mealtimes. When my aunt passed the food to our guest, she slowly, gracefully passed the dishes on to me. She didn't serve herself.

"You don't intend to eat, Mademoiselle Lebeau?" I asked.

"Oh, of course."

"Well, that would mean you have to put food on your plate," I said. I speared a few cuts of meat and leaned toward her to slide them onto her plate. Bread and vegetables followed.

She thanked me with a regal little nod, as though I'd just handed her into a carriage. Her fingers inched up over the table until they met her napkin, which she slowly unfolded and placed across her lap. Aunt Inese had begun talking again, and Celeste Lebeau looked toward her, all the while sliding her fingers across the tablecloth, around her utensils, and around the margins of her plate.

"Twelve farmhands?" she asked.

"That was before the crops changed," my aunt said.

Mademoiselle Lebeau moved her fork slowly across her plate, gently pushing the food around but not picking up anything.

"Enough," I said, more sharply than I intended. "Mademoiselle Lebeau, wouldn't you like to put your glasses on before you hurt yourself or one of us with your knife?"

SISTER TO BEAUTY

She gave me a stricken look, and I immediately regretted my words. But I had to do something. She shouldn't have to hide her glasses.

She recovered and said with barbed undertones, "When I put on my glasses I transform from *passably pretty* to truly hideous. I wouldn't want to spoil your supper."

We stared at each other for a few moments. Well, I stared at her eyes. She calmly regarded my nose.

"No one will ever forget that remark, I suppose?"

She only arched an eyebrow.

I cleared my throat. "A person such as myself should have no reason to find fault with others' appearances. I'm sorry." It wasn't a very good apology. Maybe I should have pointed out some of her good features or made a comment about how unimportant physical beauty was. But physical beauty *was* important, as I'd learned from unfortunate experience. And I wasn't about to tell her that she had the loveliest eyes and the prettiest ankle and calf I'd ever seen, no matter how true it was. So instead I added, "I do hope you will forgive my behavior and put your glasses on."

She stared toward me a moment more, and I added, "So that we all will survive you holding a knife."

The corner of her mouth twitched, but she only said, "Then I suppose I can trust you not to run away screaming when you see them on me?"

As she withdrew her glasses from a pocket, I suddenly realized that in the days she'd been here, she hadn't actually seen *me*.

I crushed the familiar urge to run. She'd see the pink scarring across the left side of my face, the ugly eye patch, and the way the scars pulled my mouth grotesquely when I spoke or smiled. I hated the way people looked at me. The revulsion was always hard to take, as was the pity.

Aunt Inese watched me, probably understanding my sudden tension.

Celeste Lebeau placed the most horrible pair of glasses I'd ever seen across her pert nose and looked right at me with a challenge in her eyes, not a hint of horror or surprise.

"Well, that's a relief," Aunt Inese said, pouring a cup of water. "Does it make a tremendous difference?"

Our guest hiccupped a little laugh. "I'm afraid so. You've both only been blurs since I walked in. The evening light makes it worse." She daintily speared a piece of meat. "And Suzanne really is an amazing cook. I would have hated to miss this."

She and Aunt Inese continued their discussion on farmhands, and I listened in stunned silence. When Mademoiselle Lebeau pushed her plate aside and offered to fetch coffee for everyone, I couldn't stand it any longer.

"Well?" I demanded. "No comments about appearances, Mademoiselle Lebeau?"

One side of her mouth rose cynically. Here it came. "I know it isn't an improvement, but aren't you glad I could safely wield my knife?" she asked.

What? "Not your glasses. My face. "

Her brows rose an inch. "Your face?"

"Everyone has something to say about my face the first time they see me. Don't tell me you don't. You seem to be the sort of girl who *always* has something to say."

I had the distinct impression she was trying not to roll her eyes. She leaned toward me and looked long into my face, her eyes traveling over every individual scar. I kept my scowl in place, feeling as vulnerable and exposed as a patient on a surgeon's table.

Finally she cocked her head to one side and said, "I think someone who loved you very much had access to a great deal of proteger leaf. No other herb could have prevented you from dying of infection or, for that matter, kept your scarring so minimal. Am I right?"

She turned to my aunt to ask the last, and Aunt Inese

clapped her hands together once, smiling as though she'd just received a gift. "You know your herbs."

"Not as well as I'd like," Mademoiselle Lebeau said. "I used to sneak out of the house to learn from my friend's mother. She was the local midwife and took care of everyone too poor or too afraid to see a physician."

"Your father never would have allowed that," I broke in, unable to believe her.

"My father was often away from home, and the chaperones he employed were much too busy with my sister's safety to notice my absences." She turned back to my aunt. "Was it you? Did you really find that much proteger leaf *and* keep it boiling all that time? It must have been a month or more."

"*Three* months. And on top of that, I had to keep the idiot physician away. He kept wanting to bleed him."

That started them off on an enthusiastic discussion on how to achieve the highest potencies of medicinal herbs. I half-listened, too dumbfounded over her confession and assessment to really participate in the discussion. Monsieur Lebeau's daughter snuck out of the home to learn about herbs? *Minimal scarring*, she'd said. *My aunt had saved my life*, she'd said. Well, I'd already suspected that, but for different reasons. Could Mademoiselle Lebeau really not care about the disfigurement brought on by fire and those cursed Englishmen? Could she not appreciate that adults kept their distance and children cried when they saw me?

And if it didn't bother *her*, would her sister overlook it as well?

CHAPTER 4

Celeste

Eventually I excused myself to fetch dessert, a beautiful berry trifle that I'd convinced Suzanne to create. It was pathetically easy. All I had to do was offer to wash the dishes after supper so she could go to bed early. I promised myself I would do it at least twice a week. Well, maybe once each week. I didn't like doing dishes either. I'd rather scrub floors, and that was saying something.

I put the trifle on a tray and stoked the fire, trying to encourage the teapot to heat again. I stared into the embers, thinking of the man in the dining room. Monsieur Durant must have experienced something terrible to give him such extensive burn scars. The trauma had been bad enough to take his eye, and I was grateful I'd never mentioned what I thought was bruising, since it turned out to be an eye patch. I can't imagine what my embarrassment would have been if I'd mocked him for his black eye.

In truth, the damage to his face hadn't been nearly as bad as I'd expected. Madame Sauveterre had warned me the first day I came that he was sensitive about his scarring, so naturally I'd envisioned something horrible. He had stripes and patches of pale pink scars stretched across half his face, more pronounced in comparison to his naturally tan coloring.

Nicole's mother had been a genius at treating infection, and she was well-known for her precision in making poultices and remedies. Inese must have been just as careful with her nephew's wounds as Nicole's mother had been with those she treated. The scars didn't disfigure his face by any means. He was actually quite handsome if you looked beyond them. And he was much younger than I'd expected, only a handful of years older than myself perhaps. Very young to be managing a farm this size on his own.

I placed the heated teapot on the tray with the trifle and turned around, only to gasp in surprise when I saw the subject of my thoughts standing not two feet away.

"Why must you sneak up on people?" I demanded.

Monsieur Durant snorted. "Your mind was elsewhere or you'd have seen me come in. Unless those glasses work as well as they look." He snapped his mouth shut, and I wondered if he hadn't meant to insult me again.

"They work *much* better than they look, thankfully." I'd once had a slightly prettier pair from a peddler, but they didn't work as well and had broken within a few weeks.

Monsieur Durant frowned at the stove a moment before offering, "Aunt Inese said I should come carry the tray and apologize for my..." He paused. "I believe she called it my 'childish outburst.'"

I raised an eyebrow, trying to suppress a smile. "And?"

He rolled his eye. It was blue, clear and expressive. "And I am sorry for my childish outburst. May I carry the tray back?"

My haughty look slipped, and I laughed aloud. His aunt had taught him to mind. I wondered if I'd be able to teach Isabelle's children to mind someday.

41

He gave me an odd look. He must have unknowingly agreed with Isabelle that my laugh was callous and unrefined.

"Of course," I said. "I wouldn't presume to interfere with Madame Sauveterre's plans for you. And thank you." I pointed to the trifle and tea.

He leaned over the tray and inhaled deeply. "Maybe we ought to just get a couple forks and eat it here."

I couldn't tell if he was joking. His expression was so serious. I pretended to consider. "It's easier to lick your own bowl than it is to lick the trifle dish."

One corner of his mouth lifted by a degree. "Then I suppose we ought to go share with Aunt Inese." He hefted the tray and motioned me to precede him.

His moment of lightheartedness was soon replaced by his usual frown, but by the end of the evening, I couldn't have been happier. Madame Sauveterre had insisted I call her Inese and promised me a tour of her herb garden first thing in the morning. And at least for now, I didn't have to go back to Marseille.

The next week flew by. I helped Suzanne in the mornings, sometimes working in the enormous vegetable garden before lunch. In the afternoons, I assisted Madame Sauveterre with the work previously done by the maid, and on most evenings, I joined her and Monsieur Durant at dinner. That was my favorite time of day. They were both well-educated, and we all argued amicably about the trade situation between Marseille and Aix, the likelihood of another invasion by the English, and the possible outcomes of the war in America. Inese loved to gossip about Monsieur Benjamin Franklin, who often visited Versailles, and the way he collected women, both French and American. Monsieur Durant liked to argue over the best ingredients for a trifle. He insisted chocolate couldn't be beaten, but I noted that Suzanne had already proven him wrong with her berry creation the previous week.

Whenever I caught him staring into my eyes, he quickly

looked away. Apparently he thought my glasses were fashioned by the devil himself. In the evenings when they'd been weighing on my nose and ears all day, I might have agreed, but the ability to see was a tremendous gift, and I wasn't about to give it up just to look a little prettier. There really was no point in trying to compete with Isabelle in that arena anyway.

I hoped he'd noticed the improvements I'd made to his home, but I decided to keep a list just in case. As I hunted in a desk drawer for ink and a pen, I heard Monsieur Durant speak. He was so close by that I nearly answered him before I realized he was talking to someone else just outside the open window.

"The wheat will be ready soon," he said.

"I'm still no closer to bringing up the price from Monsieur Farine," another voice said. "The man is completely unreasonable. A ten percent reduction from his price last year, and all over the country the price of wheat has gone up."

"I'll have to go with an outside buyer," Monsieur Durant said, an unhappy note in his voice.

"But is that wise? Consider how Monsieur Lebeau cheated you last year."

A well of shame opened up in my stomach. Father had not paid Monsieur Durant, had cheated him in his business dealings. I'd always resented my father's recklessness, but never more so than now.

The other man's voice continued, "An entire crop of—"

"Hush. His daughter is staying here."

"What?" The man sounded stunned. "Isabelle Lebeau? How did you get her here?" The excitement in his voice soured my stomach.

"Not her. Her older sister."

"Oh. The plain one. Horrible glasses?"

I hadn't met the man, and I already detested him. And once again, I tried not to detest my little sister.

Monsieur Durant didn't contradict him. And why would he?

Compared to Isabelle, I was hardly what one would call attractive.

"Jean, I need you to go over the books with me. I know I'm not good at understanding the numbers, but—"

"Henri, I've redone the calculations three times. I'm happy to go through them with you, but it's no use. We can't make the numbers change. "

I'd heard enough. Monsieur Durant was in difficult financial straits. I knew all about that. It was I who came to father's rescue every time he failed in his financial planning. I'd simply have to find a way to look at Monsieur Durant's records. Maybe something could be done. If I solved such a difficult problem for him, he'd never think of exchanging me for Isabelle.

"Celeste?" Suzanne called from the direction of the kitchen. I quietly moved from the window and hurried away, anxious not to be seen by Monsieur Durant or his nasty friend.

I arrived in the kitchen a little out of breath, but Suzanne couldn't have noticed because she hardly looked up from her work. "Someone to see you," she grunted, jerking her head to the side.

I turned and then grinned. "Madame Bochard," I exclaimed. "I'm so glad you're here."

She hadn't come the previous Saturday, and I'd worried she'd lost interest, but now here she stood in the center of the kitchen, looking around as though she wasn't sure she should be there.

"And I'm happy to see you two again." I waved at her children who smiled at me from behind their mother's skirts.

"Mademoiselle Lebeau," Madame Bochard began, glancing once toward Suzanne.

"Please call me Celeste."

"I am Carine," she said with a great deal of dignity. "And here are Martin and Marie," she said, pointing to the children in turn. "They won't be a bother," she said quickly.

"I hope you both came ready to help us," I said, bending down to look them in the eye.

They nodded solemnly.

Suzanne pressed her lips to a thin line. She had no use for Protestants. Or I suppose even the Catholic granddaughter of a Protestant.

I hurried to collect a few bowls and buckets, handing one to each of the children.

The five-year-old actually squealed with excitement.

"Marie, manners."

"Wait until they taste the blackberries," I said grinning. "There aren't enough anymore for Suzanne to use, but there are still enough for us to taste."

Carine smiled in a cautious sort of way, as though she was unaccustomed to having a good time. I wondered if such a reserved woman could work hard enough to be of use.

In fifteen minutes, I had my answer. Carine dug potatoes ten times faster than I did and had her bowl of broad beans filled almost before I'd started. By the time we finally pulled the ladder away from the mulberry tree, the sun suggested it was late afternoon.

"Suzanne will make mulberry tarts," I told Carine as we entered the kitchen and set down our burdens. "Can you stay long enough to have some?"

I washed my hands, waiting for her answer.

"Is the beast man here?" little Marie asked timidly.

Henri

I stopped in my tracks just outside the kitchen and clenched my teeth together. Celeste Lebeau should have known better than to bring children here. They'd have nightmares. I'd seen a woman working in the garden and had come to see who'd been hired when I heard the little girl ask about me.

I leaned against the stone wall of the hallway as the mother shushed her daughter. There was only a corner separating me from their view, but they'd never know I was there. I pushed off from the wall.

"What?" my housekeeper said with a laugh. "Who told you he's a *beast*? Didn't you hear the story? Here, I can chop those."

"No," said the little girl innocently.

Of course they knew the story. Everyone knew the story. I was an idiot, tried to play hero, failed miserably, and then the British sliced me up and threw me into a fire. Hardly a tale to tell to children.

I took a step away but was instantly arrested by Mademoiselle Lebeau's next words.

"It's really a secret." Her voice dropped to an exaggerated whisper. "He's actually a *prince*."

"What?" It was a young boy's voice, but the fact that there were two children didn't even register in my mind, because I was so shocked by what she'd said. What was she thinking?

"Yes, a prince."

"Truly?" the little girl asked.

Over the kitchen noise, Celeste said in a conspiratorial voice, "I didn't believe it myself until I saw his armor and his crown hanging up in a secret room in the house. And then, while I was picking beans a few days ago, I saw a tiny pixie, and she told me the entire story. She'd been right there when it happened."

I didn't even remember moving forward, but in a moment, I was peering around the corner and into the kitchen. Everyone faced Celeste as she chopped vegetables. The woman, whom I now recognized as Urie Bochard's widow, stood next to her, mirroring Celeste's motions with her own blade. Their fingers simply flew. I was certain Celeste would cut herself.

"When *what* happened?" a little blonde girl demanded, jumping up off her seat and nearly knocking over her brother.

Celeste's knife paused, and she glanced between the children and their mother with a very convincing look of concern. "I don't want to scare you with the tale. Stories of dragon fire always scared my stockings off when I was little. Perhaps we should wait until you're older."

The children squealed in protest, and she relented. "About the time you were just little things toddling around your mother's skirts, a great dragon came to lay waste to a neighboring village."

"No such thing as dragons," the boy muttered, his expression clearly pleading with Celeste to convince him otherwise.

"There aren't *anymore*," she said. "Thanks to *him*."

She had their complete attention. Even their mother's knife was still.

"Like I said, the dragon came to lay waste to the countryside. You've heard people talking about years of bad crops and financial strain?"

They nodded, eyes wide.

"They're too afraid to talk about it even now, but it wasn't just brought on by drought and the king's debts. The fields were being burned up by the creature. Dogs and sheep were carried off in the night to satiate its fearful appetite. No one was brave enough to face the dragon. His breath was hotter than the smithy's fire, and his teeth longer than that carrot." She pointed theatrically to a pile of vegetables on the counter.

The children's eyes grew larger.

"When Prince Henri heard of the villagers' plight, he rode fearlessly to the rescue. He approached the monster in its own den, and drew his sword to kill the beast. But the monster was clever, and evil throughout. He'd heard the horse approach and was waiting for the prince. When he was close, the dragon rose up and unleashed his fiery breath. The prince was engulfed in fire like you've never seen and fell to the earth in agony."

"Oh, no." The little girl took a step toward Celeste.

"The dragon thought he was dead. But you see, the prince was even cleverer than the ancient beast, and when it came in to gobble him up..." She dropped her knife and jumped toward the children with arms arched like jaws. They squealed and crowded back. "The brave prince stood and swung his sword, taking the monster's head from its shoulders. The villagers and sheep and fields were saved. But the prince had paid a terrible price," she said, her voice dropping to a whisper. "Painful dragon fire burns. A wise woman used herbs to make an ointment that helped ease the pain and stave off infection. The angels themselves came and shed a few tears into his wounds, keeping him safe from the evil that still threatened his life. But the angels' tears *also* kept the scars from healing over too much. They didn't want the people to forget how brave the prince had been. Now his scars remind everyone that service and bravery are more important than beauty."

Her knife began slicing again, and almost immediately, Widow Bochard's followed. The children stood awestruck for some time before the oldest asked, "Then why do people say he's so angry?"

Mademoiselle Lebeau's mouth curved up. "Have *you* ever seen him angry?" she asked.

"No. We've hardly seen him at all."

"Well, I'm not sure what's wrong with *those* people, but he's only ever acted like a prince that I've seen. Of course," she added frowning, her eyes distant, "I imagine princes are a little spoiled and used to getting their way. But I think deep down, he's really quite gentle and sweet."

Carine Bochard raised her brows, and Celeste rolled her eyes. "Not *that* sweet," she said under her breath to Carine.

The children didn't notice their mother giggling. They were

too busy chattering about princes, and the older one glanced around the kitchen, as though he might see evidence that I really was a prince in disguise.

I eased myself back around the corner and slowly walked away before anyone could see me. It was a ridiculous story. What a thing to say to impressionable young children. But my heart felt oddly light as I made my way down the hall.

I was glad Jean had already left. He wasn't as respectful to women as I'd like, and I didn't want him insulting Celeste. Jean was one of the few friends I had. Aside from the Fontaine brothers and my childhood friend, Bertram, he was probably my *only* friend. And I wasn't ready to kick him out of the house for arguing with my guest. We hadn't been friends before we joined the army, but his bravery and loyalty had saved my life, and I would never forget that.

I wondered idly who would come out on top in a verbal skirmish between Celeste Lebeau and Jean. I grinned. There was no one around to see, so what did it matter if I smiled? She would coolly put him in his place in a matter of seconds, I was sure. Her sister had beauty, and that made her perfect for my business, but she couldn't possibly have a sharper tongue.

I wandered toward the parlor in a pleasant daze that I couldn't exactly justify to myself. Aunt Inese sat in her usual chair, stitching away on a piece of soft white fabric. I kissed the top of her grey head before moving to the desk and pulling out the household ledger. "Did you know Celeste Lebeau engaged Carine Bochard to help?" I asked.

"Just for today," she said, snipping off a thread. "We'd like her to be a permanent addition. It's only the children holding her back, I think." She knotted her thread and started again. "Being a mother makes things more complicated, but the woman lives less than a mile from here."

"I liked Urie Bochard," I said irrelevantly. A sudden pneumonia had taken him while I was first recovering from my wounds. "He had an odd sense of humor, but still."

"There. I think I'm done," Aunt said, unfurling the soft whiteness.

"That's pretty, Aunt Inese. Is it curtains?" I asked, thinking of Urie and Carine.

She favored me with a long stare. "I'll ask Suzanne to make a chocolate trifle if you can guess."

I did like chocolate trifle. I came forward to inspect her needlework. She handed me the smooth white cloth. Too smooth for curtains. My aunt had worked a delicate spray of lavender into a few places. I turned it this way and that until I found two identical seams and unfurled the rest of the cloth. It was a white gown with a simple shape. "You did a lovely job on it, but it looks too long for you."

Aunt Inese had turned quite pink.

"Are you all right?" I asked.

She glanced over my shoulder, and a little snort escaped her before she burst into unrestrained laughter.

"Aunt Inese."

It finally dawned on me just what kind of garment I held in my hand.

At that same moment, someone behind me said, "I believe that's mine, Monsieur Durant."

CHAPTER 5

Celeste

The expression on Monsieur Durant's face when he turned around was the funniest thing I'd ever seen in my life. His jaw slackened, his eye widened, and an immediate brilliant blush spread across the right side of his face.

But I didn't dare laugh, didn't even let my mouth twitch.

Inese reclined in her seat and laughed heartily. I *really* had to leave.

I arched one eyebrow. He might not have noticed because my glasses were so big, so I also extended my hand.

He mechanically placed the silky night dress in my arms.

"Thank you for fixing this, Inese," I said. "And for the beautiful embroidery."

"You're welcome, dear," she cackled before going off in peals of laughter again.

I glanced one last time at Henri Durant. His mouth was moving now, reminiscent of a gulping, landed fish. I held my breath and turned my back on him, walking away without looking over my shoulder as I was simply dying to do.

Once I was sure I was out of earshot, I laughed my horrible laugh. Inese may have been responsible for the incident, but Monsieur Durant's expression had been worth the embarrassment of seeing my nightclothes in a man's hands.

Inese had given me back my mended dressing gown several days before but had stalled in giving me back my nightdress. I'd had enough to do around the house and hadn't even thought about it. I'd brought an extra, and my nice one was a ridiculous garment anyway. I'd made it in a fit of rebelliousness. Isabelle always had pretty things. Wardrobes full of dresses, drawers full of the softest, silkiest stockings and underthings. And I think she owned more shoes than any ten of Marseille's finest ladies put together.

I, on the other hand, tried very hard not to squander Father's money. When he could afford to give us coins, Isabelle spent every last denier on adorning herself, but I invested mine. During Father's absences, I worked with an old friend, Monsieur Descanfort, a merchant like my father, but an honorable one. He'd been a friend of my father's since before I was born, and after I'd warned him away from one of Father's worst business ventures four years ago, he'd promised to help me learn the trade. He'd been more than good on his word, allowing me to purchase and sell goods with him, building my savings. He said he did it because I could make him laugh like no one else could, but I thought it more likely he was grateful I'd saved him thousands of livre.

If Isabelle or Father found the petticoats under my floorboards and realized a small fortune was sewn into them, I'd lose it all. That money had a purpose, and I never touched it, except to buy us food on the rare occasions when we had none and to pay Nicole's mother for her tutoring. I knew I had to be careful with my future, and I bought clothes for myself only when necessary. But once, when Father brought home an outrageously expensive bolt of silk and gifted it to Isabelle, I shamelessly stole a few yards of it for myself and made the nightdress. Isabelle couldn't sew, and she never missed it. Later, when Father didn't have the money we owed the butcher, I sold the rest of the cloth so I could pay him. Neither Father nor Isabelle noticed.

My fingers traced the elegant embroidery Inese had added to the gown. My nightdress was now twice as pretty. I loved it.

Monsieur Durant worked late the next evening, so Inese joined Suzanne and me for dinner in the kitchen. But the evening after that, when I knew he would be there, I accepted Inese's invitation, insistence really, to come to dinner, not because I didn't have plenty to do, but because the imp in me wanted to enjoy seeing Monsieur Durant uncomfortable. It was horrid of me, but the scarlet blush that came and went from the unscarred side of his face all throughout dinner was extremely entertaining. Inese snickered occasionally for no apparent reason, and every time she did, her nephew's scowl dissolved, and he looked heavenward with the air of a martyr.

"It was too hot today," Inese finally said into the silence.

"Yes, but the air was so fragrant," I said. "The lavender bushes in the garden are incredible. I can hardly believe those few bushes could make such a difference."

They both stared at me.

"You haven't been to see the lavender yet?" my employer asked, clearly surprised.

"There's more?"

"You should take her to see the fields, Aunt Inese," Monsieur Durant said before taking a bite of food.

I turned toward Inese, thrilled at the prospect, but she only sniffed. "I am seventy-two years old and have no intention of getting heatstroke. Take her yourself."

Monsieur Durant gave his aunt a resentful look as he chewed his food. I was disappointed, certainly, but disappointments were not unknown to me. My pride was well intact, however, and I was not about to let him refuse to take me on a walk, which I hadn't even wanted to go on with him.

"I am sure Monsieur Durant has better things to occupy his time than giving tours. When I have some free time tomorrow, I'll walk out to see them myself, if that is all right."

"Don't be silly," he said curtly after swallowing his bite. "You can't go wandering alone in the fields."

"Are your workers untrustworthy?" I asked impatiently. Let him dare tell me a woman would get lost. He might get a real black eye.

"Of course not," he said, apparently insulted. "But vagabonds have been seen out this way before, and I'm responsible for your safety. As unhappy as I am with your father, if something happened to you while you were here..." He let his sentence hang and scooped more potato onto his fork. "I will take you," he said grudgingly before taking his next bite.

I almost refused his offer on the spot. I didn't want to be victim to his pity or his sense of duty, but I really did want to see the lavender. And I was anxious to talk him into letting me help with the household budget and the farm accounts. I had no idea how I could bring that up without offending him, but if I never talked with him, I'd never be able to do it. I also wanted to brag a little about hiring someone to help, even if it was temporary.

"Thank you," I said, probably less graciously than I should have. He closed his eye a moment, as though praying for patience, and we continued our meal in silence.

Once dinner was over, I exchanged my soft shoes for walking boots and fetched a parasol. Monsieur Durant waited for me in the entryway. He paused awkwardly at the door before ushering me through it. We walked in silence, which was fine with me, taking a path from the stables around the hillside. We rounded the bend ten minutes later, and I stopped short, staring like an idiot.

I'd seen lavender fields before, but I wasn't expecting anything like this. The sea of purple seemed to stretch into the sunset, contrasted by wheat fields on either side. It was no wonder he worked his own land. Who would want to be anywhere else?

Isabelle liked to read romantic nonsense about dashing lovers who gave girls roses and jewels under spectacular sunsets. Unrealistic idiocy. But she would probably love being fawned over at a place like this. Thankfully she was far away, leaving me to enjoy the sublime peace of the place. And instead of being fawned over, I stood next to a man who could barely tolerate my existence. But that didn't matter to me. At least, not much. He knew how to stay quiet anyway.

After several minutes, the peace was broken by footsteps behind us. Monsieur Durant turned and said, if not jovially, then at least pleasantly, "Hello, Paul. Did you get dinner?"

Drat. I whipped my glasses off and stuffed them in a pocket before turning around.

A short, stocky man with dark hair approached us from the direction of the house. "No," he said with a chuckle. "I know better than to snitch from Suzanne's kitchen."

He ducked his head at me, and Monsieur Durant said, "Mademoiselle Lebeau, this is my friend, Paul Fontaine. Paul and his brother help me with my fields in exchange for a percent of the profits." He turned to Monsieur Fontaine. "Mademoiselle Lebeau has come to visit my aunt and help her around the house for some time. Her sister will replace her later."

Oh, really?

I exchanged pleasantries with Monsieur Fontaine, then said, "You probably would like to discuss the farm. I'll just pick a handful of lavender, if that's all right."

"Of course," said Monsieur Durant, a hint of amusement in his voice. He'd probably enjoy seeing me trip and fall on my face without my glasses.

I turned and pretended to enjoy the view while I very carefully moved my feet along to the place where the path met the first clumps of lavender. I bent and picked the first few stems slowly, lifting them to my face one at a time and enjoying their fragrance. Deciding to pick a bouquet to hang in my room, I closed my hand around a larger amount and pulled. I was instantly rewarded with a sudden, horrible, stinging pain. I gasped and snatched my hand away, silently cursing my vision and stupidity.

Henri

As much as I'd imagined bringing *Isabelle* Lebeau to this spot, I was proud that her sister was not immune to its charms. When she first saw the fields, a breathy "Oh," escaped her lips, I'm sure quite unconsciously. She didn't say anything else, but the pleasure was evident in the upward tilt of her cynical mouth.

It was a good thing Paul arrived, because when he did, I realized I'd been staring at the girl instead of at my fields. Not that she was beautiful to look at. She certainly wasn't. I silently wished her father would come back early from his trip to Italy.

But there *was* something fascinating about the green glinting within her brown eyes. Then again, it was probably only her terrible glasses that kept drawing my attention. She hid them in her pocket before turning to meet Paul, and I took some steps away from her, anxious to put some distance between us. Paul smiled knowingly, and I wished I'd never drawn close to her to begin with.

When she offered to let us talk, I was happy to agree. She walked away, her steps slow and graceful, and I had to admire her skill as an actress. Most people wouldn't realize she was walking half-blind.

When her gasp of pain interrupted our discussion of plans for the harvest, we both hurried to her.

"Mademoiselle Lebeau?" Paul said worriedly.

"It is nothing," she said, a wry twist to her lips. "I was only surprised. I think I may have been stung." She held one hand fisted in the other.

While Paul bent to retrieve the lavender she'd dropped, I grasped her wrist and turned her hand to inspect it.

"Yes, I see it. One moment." Without thought, I put my free hand to her waist to turn her so I could better use the fading light. "There." I withdrew the stinger and looked at Mademoiselle Lebeau only to find her much closer than I'd realized. Her eyes were closed and her posture tense. I was an idiot. I'd drawn her close so I could see her hand, but I'd taken no thought for the lack of distance between us. No one felt comfortable this close to me.

It was impossible not to notice how good she smelled.

"Poor bee should have already gone home," Paul said, picking twice the bouquet she'd dropped. How like Paul to sympathize with the bee instead of the person who was stung.

I stepped away from Mademoiselle Lebeau as she opened her eyes and, with her good hand, accepted the lavender from Paul. I noticed she let Paul place the stems in her outstretched hand, but I doubted he thought anything of it.

"Thank you both," she said. "I should have been more careful." She had to be in pain, but her smile was calm enough.

Paul smiled back. It was a different smile than he used around his brother or around me, and I looked at him more closely. I did not altogether *like* the look in his eyes.

"Shall we go back to the house?" I said, managing not to glare at Paul.

Mademoiselle Lebeau nodded, but her footsteps were slow as she turned back to the road.

There was no help for it. I wasn't going to make her put on her glasses if she didn't want to. I gently took her hand and wrapped it through my arm. Let Paul think what he wanted.

"Thank you," she murmured.

I didn't answer. It had been a long time since any woman aside from Aunt Inese had taken my arm.

"Will you stay long, Mademoiselle Lebeau?" Paul asked.

"I'm not sure what day my father will come for me," she said vaguely. "I would like to see the lavender harvested, though. Do you think that will be soon?"

One minute later, I shook my head in disbelief. Paul Fontaine, one of the quietest men I'd ever known, was talking animatedly about lavender and his honey bees with this girl, practically a stranger to him.

She laughed at something he said, and I felt an odd jolt in my chest. Her laugh had caught me unaware once before, and I was annoyed that it still made my insides feel funny. Such a throaty, happy sound for such an unpleasant sort of girl. I eyed her in total confusion. What was going on? Paul looked sideways at me, a little smirk at his lips. If he wasn't completely infatuated with another woman, I would have thought he was flirting with her. As it was, he was obviously enjoying my discomfort.

"I hope you'll be able to stay for the dance they're holding in Aix in a few weeks," he said. "All the prominent families in Aix attend. Not the nobility, of course, but it is still quite an event."

What? I frowned at Paul, who gave me a challenging look. Every once in a while he liked to suggest I become more social again. The hypocrite.

"A dance? That does sound enjoyable," Mademoiselle Lebeau said without a hint of excitement.

"Of course, you'll want to wear your glasses so you can see who you're accepting dances from."

Celeste Lebeau stopped short. "Why, Monsieur Fontaine," she exclaimed with a laugh. "You knew the entire time."

Paul chuckled. "I saw you working with Madame Bochard earlier."

Celeste pulled the glasses from her pocket. "For your teasing, I shall punish you by wearing the horrible things," she said with a laugh.

"You have beautiful eyes," Paul said with a shrug. "You can't ruin that."

I glared at Paul, who ignored me.

She immediately put on her glasses and looked at him with arched brows.

He pressed his lips together a moment. "Well, you certainly can try, I suppose," he said hesitantly.

Celeste Lebeau laughed in earnest then, an indelicate, enthusiastic, altogether delightful and infectious laugh.

Paul chuckled with her, and I almost wanted to laugh too. But that wouldn't do. When I smiled or laughed, my scars distorted my mouth horribly.

Once she had herself under control, Mademoiselle Lebeau asked Paul, "Do you suppose Carine likes to dance?"

His laugh died. "I don't know. Perhaps."

She changed the subject, but when Paul's back was turned, the look she gave him was entirely conniving. Someone must have told her. Aunt Inese, perhaps. Paul was two years older than me, but even I remembered how much he admired Carine, and how it had broken his heart when she married Urie Bochard.

When Paul parted from us at the stables, Mademoiselle Lebeau insisted he call her by her first name and that when he next brought honey to my Aunt Inese, he should time his visit to coincide with Carine's. "You must tell us both more about the bees," she insisted.

He left with a dazed look in his eyes, and she instantly rounded on me. "How long has that been going on?"

"What do you mean?"

She arched one of those perfectly sculpted brows.

I knew exactly what she meant, of course. "How is your hand?" I asked, ignoring her question.

She raised it for my inspection. Twilight necessitated me moving closer, and, watching her cautiously to make sure I didn't irritate or disgust her, I took her hand in mine once more. Celeste's hand was truly beautiful, smooth with long, slender fingers that weren't too delicate to be capable. I retained it longer than I should have before tilting her palm to look at the reddened skin.

"I'm glad you don't have bad reactions to them," I said, my voice coming out softer than I'd intended.

"Me too," she said, her outward confidence slipping. For a small moment, her lips parted, betraying a hint of vulnerability. I looked into her beautiful eyes, noting the green rings hidden in their brown depths. In those few seconds, I forgot about her ordinary face and hideous glasses.

But that would never do. I couldn't let myself forget about those things. She was all wrong to be here, wrong for what I needed. Why on earth had Monsieur Lebeau cheated me again? Her sister was the beauty, I reminded myself. Her sister would be charming and attract buyers. Her sister would be exactly right for us. She'd have all of Celeste Lebeau's good qualities, hopefully none of the bad ones, and would attract people to her like flies to honey.

I excused myself, and she thanked me for showing her the lavender, her tone once more business-like and unshaken.

"Of course," I said, a curt note in my voice. I turned back to the stable, leaving her on the gravel walk in front of the house.

CHAPTER 6

Celeste

I'd been serving as housekeeper at the Durant home for over three weeks when the first letter from Isabelle arrived. I'd posted her a short note my first week and had wished for a response but not really expected one. She'd always had me to look after her, and I couldn't help worrying over how she was getting along without me. I stuffed the letter in my pocket, not wanting to read it until I was alone. I knew there wouldn't be much I could share that would reflect well on my sister, and I preferred not to expose her deficiencies to Inese or her nephew.

After Jacques Fontaine, a sixteen-year-old version of his older brother fetched the lunch Suzanne and I had prepared, I moved to the next item on my list for the day: learning about drainage systems. The château's system was in working order but was quite outdated. I thought if I could at least sketch out a new plan, it would show a way I could help in the more distant future. Henri Durant had given me an odd look when I'd asked him if he had any books on the subject, but quickly encouraged me to use any of the books in his study.

I found the room and stood just inside it, admiring its stately beauty. One entire wall was obscured by wooden bookshelves, and a heavy desk stood in the middle of the room, its polished surface glowing in the light streaming from the windows.

I found a stepping stool and moved it to the bookshelves, intending to investigate the highest shelves first. Only after I'd climbed up did I remember Isabelle's letter. I pulled it from my pocket and skimmed her inane missive.

She'd been to several parties, dodged her chaperone for three walks in the park (stupid girl), and bought a new parasol, two new hats, and a cape. In the heat of summer. I rolled my eyes and skipped to the end.

"Papa wrote me and does not expect to come home for another month, but I'm sure things are working out well with you and Monsieur Durant, so that shouldn't be a problem."

I dropped the letter as though it had burned me. Another month. Father had not written to me as he'd promised me he would. Worse, he had not written to Monsieur Durant, who would never want me to stay if Father tricked him again. He'd have me tossed out. I'd have to take a hired carriage home. Had I even brought enough money for that?

I thought of all that I'd accomplished over the last few weeks. The enormous vegetable garden was practically in order, I'd redone the kitchen budget and menu to please both Inese and Suzanne, and under the supervision of Inese, I'd harvested and dried enough herbs to last several months. With the sale of the extra vegetables from the garden to a grocer in Aix, I'd purchased the more expensive items Suzanne wanted so she could make some of her specialties.

Inese had been very pleased with my work and had praised me, even more than I thought I deserved. I never actually gave the list of what I accomplished to Henri Durant because his aunt updated him daily on my work. Whenever she brought it up at the dinner table, he only said in flat tones, "That is very good," or "Did she now?" He never seemed impressed, never complimented me.

There were those odd times when I caught him staring at me in a way that made me sure he didn't disapprove of me altogether. There were even times when I thought we might become friends. We argued enough for ten people, but they were grand arguments, politely waged. Usually. He was so well read, knew so much of the world for being so young himself. And sometimes I wondered if it was actually kindness that glimmered under his gruff demeanor.

He'd answered my barrage of questions about lavender with patience and even interest, teaching me about harvesting and distilling, about its uses and markets throughout Provence, northern Italy, and beyond. I'd learned a great deal about wheat too, but it seemed to be a more straightforward market.

He hadn't touched me again, not since he'd shown me the lavender fields. Having his hand at my waist when he moved me to catch the light had been the oddest experience. I hadn't been able to breathe for a moment for my surprise. But when he'd taken pity on my blindness and given me his arm a few minutes later, it had felt so...comfortable.

Now, after reading Isabelle's letter, the thought of leaving was doubly painful. I loved my work here. I enjoyed talking to Inese, Suzanne, and Carine. It was bad enough that Monsieur Durant didn't want me to stay, that Father had betrayed him by bringing me instead of Isabelle. But now to have to tell my employer that my father had no intention of taking me away, it was humiliating.

I closed my eyes tight, trying to clear my thoughts as well as the tears that threatened. I leaned my forehead against the tall bookshelf, appreciative of the cool, smooth wood against my cheek. Once I'd gained control of myself, I made a very silly mistake. Of course, I blame my vision, because if I wasn't accustomed to going about half-blind, I would have opened my eyes *before* I jumped down from the stepping stool rather than *as* I jumped down from the stepping stool. But as it was, I opened my eyes just in time to see a very startled Henri Durant, just before I collided with him.

A little shriek escaped my lips as a grunt of surprise and probably pain escaped his. He half-caught me, stumbling backward and knocking my glasses off in his attempt to keep us upright.

"Celeste," he exclaimed as he tried to free himself from the tangle of arms and legs that we'd become. It was the first time he'd used my given name, and I looked toward his face in some bewilderment. I was only an inch away from his nose, but I still couldn't read his expression.

"Must you always sneak up on me?" I demanded loftily as I stepped away from him.

"Must you tackle an innocent man who only wanted a moment of peace in his own study?" he barked back.

We stared each other down a few moments before one of us, and later I wasn't sure who, started to snicker. Moments later, we were both shaking with laughter. I wished I could see him. I'd never actually seen him smile because he tended to hide his mouth. My friend, Nicole, had the same tendency because she didn't care for the look of her teeth. But Monsieur Durant had nice teeth and lips that I found a little too interesting.

"What on earth were you doing standing there?" I finally asked.

"What were *you* doing, leaping down from heights without looking?" he countered.

"No one had been there when I climbed up," I said.

He snorted a little laugh, then said, "You dropped your letter."

His blur started to move forward, and I jumped back to block him, while at the same time, looking frantically to the floor for my letter. I froze at the sudden little crunch under my foot. I looked down in horrified shock, but I couldn't see anything. I didn't have to see anything to know what I'd done.

"Oh, I'm so sorry," he said with more concern than I'd ever heard from him.

"*You're* sorry?" I said with an attempt at lightheartedness, though my heart had sunk in my chest at the sound of my glasses shattering. "*I'm* the one that broke them, and *I'm* the one that will go around blind until I can get them repaired."

He bent to retrieve my glasses and the letter, and I put a hand to the bookshelf to prevent making a further idiot of myself by tripping as I stepped away.

"Perhaps you will have the use of one eye, at least," he said, placing the note in my hand. He moved away, and with a sharp discomfort in my chest, I listened to the tinkling cascade of small bits of glass falling into the waste bin.

He soon returned my glasses. One side remained intact. The other was bent and the glass gone. I placed them across my nose, closed one eye, and could finally see his apologetic expression.

"Now our vision will be the same," he offered hesitantly.

I hiccupped a laugh. "I hadn't thought these could look much worse." I sighed and leaned against the bookshelves. "What am I going to do? I have so many projects, so many things I still wanted to accomplish."

"In a week?" he asked kindly. "I think you've proven your capability already, don't you?"

Hope bubbled up from deep inside me. "You mean—"

"No, no," he said, stepping back. "We'll still need to have your sister come."

I took off my glasses and slipped the broken frames into my pocket. I didn't want to see the look on his face. "The letter is from my sister," I said bluntly. I didn't know how else to say it. "She says my father has written to her." I swallowed and went on in the most business-like tone I could manage. "She tells me that he will not be here next week as she doesn't expect him for another month yet." My voice almost gave out on me. He didn't respond right away, and my fingers twitched toward my glasses. Maybe I did want to read his expression.

When it seemed he was not going to say anything, I decided I'd better make things easier for him. "I apologize most sincerely for his delay. Whenever you think best, I will go to Aix and hire a carriage to take me back to Marseille. If, however, you do not mind the delay, then I will continue to serve as your house-keeper until my father comes for me."

~

Henri

I stared at Celeste Lebeau with utter amazement. The girl poured her heart into arguments over berry trifle, delivered caustic censure with haughty pride, and laughed with abandon when a joke was played on her. But when she learned that her father was even more despicable, more worthless than either of us had thought, she stood there and announced it like it was supper being prepared and she wished to know my preference of meat.

Had this been part of her plan all along? I very much doubted it. But it was hard to know for sure. I'd underestimated her so much at the beginning.

"Monsieur Durant?" she said quietly.

I shook myself from my thoughts. "I suppose I should not be surprised," I said curtly.

"I suppose not," she said in monotone.

I didn't have the slightest idea what to say to her.

"What would you like me to do?" she asked even more quietly. Her expression betrayed no concern, but it really was difficult to read someone when their eyes were so unfocused that you couldn't tell what they were looking at. Despite that, she really did have pretty eyes.

"I suppose we'd better continue on with what we've been doing."

Her answering smile was sedate but still made me want to return it. I was being such an idiot. "Well," I said with a tired sigh and looking around. "What *had* you been doing?"

"Looking for information on drainage systems."

I shook my head, not even bothering to cover my broad smile. She couldn't see it anyway. "Perhaps you can tell us what you learn at dinner tonight. By the way, I expect an old friend to visit Aix this week. Bertram Vrai. He may be joining us in the evening without notice."

"Thank you for the warning. I will be sure enough food is on hand, Monsieur."

I turned to go but paused and said over my shoulder, "I can't tell you how tired I am of hearing Monsieur. Please address me as Henri." She and Paul were on a first-name basis within an hour of meeting each other, but she'd been here close to a month with all formalities still intact between us.

"I believe Celeste would do as well."

Was it that easy? All I had to do was suggest it? I shook my head at myself and left the study, only to remember when I found myself in my room that I had gone to my study specifically to write Bertram and request he examine Mademoiselle Lebeau's eyes. Celeste's eyes. Now he was doubly needed since the horrible glasses were smashed.

I found Aunt Inese in the little parlor where she liked to work. "Bertram should visit in the next few days," I said as I penned a quick line to him at her desk.

"I'd better make sure we have enough chocolate. That boy drinks it up like some men drink their ale."

"Celeste is staying," I blurted out.

She stuck herself with the needle and gasped before whipping out a handkerchief to wrap around her finger. "What did you say?" she asked carefully.

"Celeste's father isn't coming for another month." I said moodily. "She had a letter from her sister."

Aunt Inese frowned as though disappointed in me before inspecting her finger. "I'm glad. I like the girl," she said. "And she certainly knows how to manage a home. I wonder if she would ever consider any of the men in Aix."

"Why would she?"

"That dance would be a good opportunity for her to meet them," she said, ignoring my question.

"Name one eligible man in Aix that her father would approve," I said. "We have one of the largest châteaux in the entire region. Short of the nobility, he couldn't do better, but the only reason he'd consider me for a son-in-law is that he owes me 8,000 livres."

"Oh, there are plenty of men who would do," she said, waving her hand dismissively. "I get the impression it will be *her* making the decision, not her father. The important thing is that she gets to talk to them. She's charming enough that half the single men there would be after her by the end of the evening."

"Charming?" I asked in disbelief. "Celeste Lebeau?"

She gave me the look.

Three days later, Bertram arrived. It was perfect timing because, aside from us needing his professional expertise, he could tell Aunt Inese that keeping Celeste here was a horrible idea.

Bertram clapped me on the arm when he met me in the parlor. "Aunt Inese says there is a girl staying here," he said with a grin. Bertram never flinched at looking me full in the face. Since my injuries, he was the only one who I felt never saw me as a different person. "You must tell me about her. I can't believe she is really here to help your auntie." In a quieter voice, he asked. "Henri, are you to be married?"

"No, absolutely not," I said, wishing I'd made time to have his note delivered. "And do not say such things." My aunt's tread sounded in the hall. "I'll tell you about it once we're outside. Come see the farm before dinner."

"Yes, and you must come see my new horse and tell me what you think of him."

"For heaven's sake, do not forget to wear a cravat to dinner," Aunt Inese said as she entered the room.

"Yes, Auntie," we said together. Bertram grinned saucily at her, and she rolled her eyes with a laugh.

"Have you asked him?"

"Asked me what?" Bertram said.

Aunt Inese rested her fists on her hips. "I'll talk to him about the glasses. You see if Celeste already has dinner planned."

Bertram smirked at me, but I only shrugged. "If it pleases you."

Aunt Inese immediately began asking Bertram questions about his work while I slipped out of the room. I found Celeste arranging a vase of roses, one of her eyes tightly closed as she squinted out the good side of her glasses.

"I saw a man come. Is that your friend, Bertram?" she asked.

I stared at her too long, and she took off her glasses. "I've been thinking about how you may want to manage dinner," she said as she tapped the frames against her shoulder. "You don't have a footman anymore. In such cases, it would be appropriate for a female servant to serve dinner."

Was she suggesting…

"I could manage, and it would look better to have a female server than none at all."

I turned my back to her.

"Monsieur? Henri?"

The laugh choked out before I could stop it. "Celeste, you are truly the silliest thing," I said, covering my mouth.

"I'd like to know what you find so humorous," she said huffily.

I kept my hand over my grin. "Bertram Vrai practically lived here for over ten years. He's like one of the family."

"Oh. Oh, I see," she said, still behind me. Her voice grew fainter as she began to walk away. "I'll make sure everything is on the table before you all sit down."

I spun around. "You have to come."

She glanced back at me. "What?" The angle of her neck and shoulder was mesmerizing.

"Please join us for dinner, Celeste. I think you will enjoy talking to Bertram."

Her features softened, and she blinked at me. "Oh. Thank you."

I left her there, mostly so I wouldn't keep staring at the upward tilt of her lips. Later, as I told Bertram the tale of Monsieur Lebeau's deception, I finally felt my mind clearing.

I suppose I expected Bertram to give me some sage advice, but he only laughed at me. "Henri, how foolish. Did you really think you could convince the Lebeau girl to marry you? I've heard of her. She has dozens of men at her fingertips and the disposition of a spoiled peacock. You should count yourself lucky that her father is such an idiot. It serves you right to have to live with an ugly shrew for a couple months."

"I didn't say she was ugly," I protested.

"Close enough."

I gave up. Bertram certainly didn't have the answers I was hoping for.

A few hours later, I stopped in my room to quickly arrange my cravat, and almost ran into Celeste on my way back out the door. Well, I suppose, I actually *did* run into her, but it wasn't my fault, because I was the only one who tried to avoid the impact. She kept walking right into me.

By the time I stopped snickering at her little shriek of

surprise when she collided with my chest for the second time in one day, I realized what I was looking at. Celeste Lebeau had always worn muted colors and a severe hairstyle, ever since she arrived at my home. Now...now she looked different. Her hair was formed into a loose twist, and her gown was a rich green that complimented her eyes. A stray piece of hair gently followed the contour of her graceful neck. I couldn't look away from her.

For a brief moment, my face was so close to hers that I could have just bent my head and kissed her. But that was stupid.

"I don't believe I'll fall over now, Henri," she snapped, putting on her glasses.

I'd forgotten that I'd caught her. I loosed my hold on her waist and stepped back, trying not to stare. I wished she'd kept her glasses off so that I *could* stare. As it was, I had to stop myself from sneaking glances at her.

Isabelle Lebeau's figure was well admired, and for good reason. But where Isabelle's shape was alluring, Celeste's form was tall and, well... elegant. I never would have guessed it with the simple dresses she usually wore.

"You look..." I said stupidly.

"Is it wrong?" she asked, smoothing her skirt. "Inese said I should dress for dinner, and this was the only thing I brought that—"

"It's fine," I blurted out.

She relaxed a fraction before her hands tightened again. "And I forgot to ask if Monsieur Vrai liked or disliked any foods in particular."

"He likes everything."

She smiled a little and took off her glasses, folding the bent frame and slipping them back into her pocket.

She fluttered her fingers at me and put her hand to the wall, moving slowly away.

I shook my head in defeat. "Celeste, wait."

CHAPTER 7

Celeste

I looked back over my shoulder. I don't know why. He was only a blur.

"You aren't going to wear your glasses?"

Had he really forgotten how hideous they made me look? The man wasn't stupid, so he could only be toying with me, like he probably had been the minute prior when he'd clasped me around my waist. Though I couldn't account for why, I'd really thought he might kiss me when he was that near. Stupid. And it was beyond stupid that I should feel disappointed when he didn't.

"No. I'd prefer not to embarrass you and Inese," I said.

He sighed and drew near me. Unfamiliar wings took flight in my chest, and I took a tiny step back before catching myself. To put myself at ease, I imagined what he would say and how he would look at me if I *did* kiss him. That did the trick. I couldn't remember the last time I'd wanted to act with such spontaneity, but I'd suffered enough rejection in my life to know how to avoid that sort of behavior.

"Are you planning to knock me over again?" I asked, giving my head a little toss. "It would be best to give me *some* warning."

His hand gently took mine and pulled it through his arm. His hand was warm and calloused, and I was too surprised to pull away.

"I believe it is perfectly appropriate for you to take my arm on the way into dinner," he said drily. "And it just may save the paintings on the wall."

A tiny laugh escaped my throat. "And possibly my pride," I admitted.

He turned to look at me. My appearance didn't typically bear well under scrutiny, so I averted my face.

We moved forward, and I allowed myself to enjoy the warmth of his closeness. I was no longer accustomed to friendly physical intimacy. My mother had adored me and had showered me with affection. Since she was gone, I'd grown into a tall, awkward girl, and Father had dispensed with goodnight kisses. Isabelle's affectionate attention was reserved for her friends and her many beaux, so I almost never received sisterly embraces from her. And my friends always seemed to remember I was the daughter of their employer, and there was an unspoken barrier.

I wouldn't say I was starved for attention or physical affection, but I was smart enough to recognize something I generally lacked. And I certainly recognized it in the companionable proximity of Monsieur Durant. Henri didn't seem at all repulsed by me, even if he didn't think I was pretty enough to be his housekeeper. There was something reminiscent of a brother in his demeanor. An annoyed brother, certainly, but still a hint of someone who cared, even in a small measure. But then, I might have imagined it.

I expected Henri to drop my hand once he'd navigated me close to the dining room, but he kept my arm when he introduced me to Monsieur Vrai, a blur of a man who said in tones of surprise that he was absolutely delighted to meet me. Then

73

Henri guided me gently to a chair and assisted me to my seat. I was grateful for his thoughtfulness. I didn't enjoy looking clumsy and incompetent.

"Dinner looks lovely, Aunt Inese," Monsieur Vrai said. "But not near as lovely as your guest."

I managed not to snort. I didn't have to be able to see him to know he was ridiculous.

"Celeste has been a tremendous help to me," Inese said. "I don't think I'll ever be able to do without her."

Inese and Monsieur Vrai kept up a cheerful conversation. I joined in when it seemed appropriate. Henri, who sat closest to me, served something onto my plate. I edged my fingers forward and managed to navigate my silverware without difficulty. I ate two bites, and I never reached toward my cup, knowing I would likely spill it.

When I put down my silverware with relief, Monsieur Vrai said, "Why, Mademoiselle Lebeau, you are to be congratulated."

Henri's form turned to look at his friend.

"Congratulated, Monsieur Vrai?" I said.

"Yes, of course. I've never met anyone as blind as you who could wield a knife and fork so delicately and expertly."

"Oh, Bertram, don't tease the girl," Inese said.

I immediately turned to Henri. "You told him."

Henri's shoulders moved. I think he shrugged, but he didn't say anything.

Monsieur Vrai muttered something that sounded like, "The only true thing you told me," before saying in normal tones, "Henri asked me to examine your eyes. I am an eye doctor. He tells me your glasses have been broken."

Feeling completely confused and a little embarrassed, I produced my glasses from my pocket.

"Oh, no," he said with a laugh. "A woman as lovely as you shouldn't be wearing these anyway. When was the last time you had your eyes examined?"

The heat of a blush crept across my face, but I answered with a careless lilt, "Oh, at least two years." It had been six years. The year before Mother had died, but I wasn't about to admit it. Henri thought little enough of me as it was. He didn't need to know my father thought my glasses less important than Isabelle's spring wardrobe.

"Well, there is no time like the present."

"Excuse me?"

"To examine your eyes. I think I could have new glasses to you in less than a fortnight, maybe even in time for you to wear them to the dance in Aix."

"New glasses?" I couldn't possibly afford to pay him to examine my eyes and get new glasses. I'd only brought a small fraction of my savings with me to the Durant château. As it was, the total expense would probably take too much of the money hiding under the floor in my bedroom. My mother had told me it would be wise to save my own dowry. She knew Father well. I'd given up calling it my dowry by the time I was fifteen, though it had grown to a significant sum through my business ventures with Monsieur Descanfort. A girl should be realistic, after all.

"Yes, of course, new glasses."

"But Monsieur, I couldn't possibly—"

"Go to the dance without them? I know. Can you imagine how difficult it would be to dance blindly, let alone know which dance partners you should accept and which you should send packing?"

"Monsieur Vrai, I'm afraid you've been at the wine and for shame. We've barely started dinner."

"You wouldn't deny me the honor, would you?" he asked mischievously. "I truly have never seen eyes as beautiful as yours."

I snapped my mouth shut. I wasn't used to receiving outright compliments, and I didn't know how to take it.

"Don't be silly, Celeste," said Inese. "If a handsome, young doctor wishes to look long into your eyes, it would be a waste to say no."

"I owe Henri far too many favors not to provide a free eye exam here or there," Monsieur Vrai said. "I carry samples of styles with me, and Inese already claimed the honor of helping you choose the frames."

"They are a thank you gift, my dear. For all your help this past month."

I could barely believe what they were saying. My throat tightened.

Half an hour later, when Monsieur Vrai placed yet another set of lenses before my eyes, my lips parted in surprise. I knew my old glasses weren't perfect for my eyes anymore, but I had no idea what I'd been missing. I could see all sorts of details. And Inese had been right. Monsieur Vrai was very handsome. He had thick brown hair and a devilish smile. A hint of a red-brown beard glinted at his chin, and his brown eyes met mine with curiosity. Something in my expression satisfied him, and he said, "These are better, aren't they?"

Henri

Celeste smiled angelically at Bertram, her face lit with excitement. If he complimented her eyes one more time, I would throw him from the house. He behaved as though he'd discovered something amazing. I already knew she had pretty eyes. Just because I didn't prattle on and on about them didn't mean I didn't notice. As it was, Bertram must have felt me glaring at him because he stopped staring and leaned back from her a few inches. Something inside me relaxed a fraction. I hadn't liked Bertram so close to her, looking so deeply into her eyes as he examined them. His expression hadn't been entirely professional. His parents were on the verge of announcing his engagement to a girl from a prominent family in Aix, but I still suspected him of being too interested in Celeste.

Aunt Inese paused in her embroidery to ask, "Is it a big difference?"

Celeste beamed as her gaze flitted around the room. "I can see actual veins on the leaves of these flowers," she said, indicating a vase nearby. "I'd forgotten leaves had veins." She turned farther in her chair to look directly at Aunt Inese. "I can see the lace at your collar is exquisite, that there is a visible grain in the wood of your chair." She turned toward me. "And that your nephew—"

She broke off and stared at me a moment, her lips forming a small, "Oh."

I froze. What would she say about my scars?

"Has the longest eyelashes I've ever seen," she said, blushing a little.

"Don't tell me. Your old glasses are so bad that you never noticed his eye patch before," Bertram accused with a laugh.

"No." She giggled. "But when I first met Henri, I wasn't wearing my glasses, and I simply thought he had a black eye. For some time, I wondered he was prone to brawling." She grinned at me. "I was worried as to the type of household I had come to."

Bertram leaned back in his chair and laughed openly. Aunt Inese snickered into her embroidery. I realized I was smiling, but Celeste had taken the glasses off and couldn't see me anyway. I caught Bertram eyeing me in confusion. I didn't know what his problem was.

He turned back to Celeste. "One of the many reasons you must come to the dance. You should meet more people from the region so you'll know we aren't all as gruff and abrasive as Henri."

"May I come in?" Jean stood at the parlor door. He removed his hat quickly when Aunt Inese turned toward him. "I did knock," he assured her. "But no one heard me."

My aunt's lips tightened, but she nodded curtly. Years ago, she had given Jean the scolding of his life for some act of bad manners. I forgot what. But ever since he'd brought my bleeding body home to her, they'd managed to abide by a sort of truce. She still didn't like him. It seemed saving my life wasn't enough to see him completely forgiven, but she didn't object to him visiting. For his part, he generally minded his manners in her presence.

"Did I come at a bad time?" he asked, hefting the large ledger he carried.

"Not at all," I said. "There's dinner if you're hungry."

"I won't intrude," he said, bowing to the women.

Oh, yes. "I don't believe you've met Mademoiselle Celeste Lebeau. Mademoiselle Lebeau, may I introduce Jean Mason, my friend and bookkeeper."

Her smile immediately faded. "No. I don't believe we've met."

She already didn't like him? I knew it had nothing to do with his job. She'd been quick friends with Carine and Suzanne, so station didn't dictate who she liked.

"I do, of course, know of your beautiful sister," Jean said. He could be so senseless.

"Of course," Celeste said, her eyes narrowing.

"What brings you to Aix?" he asked.

"I'm very grateful Celeste came for a visit," Aunt Inese answered before Celeste could say anything. "She's been an invaluable companion and helper. She set the house accounts to order in under an hour." She didn't mention the twenty percent decrease in the household expenditures that Celeste had managed without Aunt or me noticing a difference. I was glad I hadn't told Jean the true reason Celeste was here.

"Is that so?" Jean asked with an uninterested smile. "A woman of talent, I see."

"I'll walk you out," I said quickly. "We don't need to bore the others with the farm business."

"Yes, I'm afraid ladies are not interested in this sort of thing."

"You don't think ladies have many interests?" Celeste asked innocently. There was something about her that put me in mind of an asp ready to strike.

"Come along, Jean," I said before he could answer. "I'd like to get back to my company as soon as possible." And I didn't want them hearing any bad news Jean might have.

Jean glanced dismissively at Celeste before ducking his head in my aunt's direction and following me out of the room.

"Well?" I asked when we were out of earshot.

"No luck at all. No workers will come. No buyers will compromise on price," he said.

"I didn't know you were having trouble finding workers," Bertram said from behind me. He'd followed us into the study.

"I didn't want to bother you with it," I said shortly.

"He shouldn't have to confide his troubles to anyone he doesn't wish to," Jean said, glaring at Bertram. Didn't he remember the time Bertram broke his nose and arm in a fight? We'd all been fourteen, but Bertram was still as hot-headed as ever.

"Thank you for coming, Jean," I said irritably. "I think you ought to go now. We can talk tomorrow."

Jean took his leave without a word.

"I don't know why you keep him around, Henri."

"Be truthful," I said tiredly. "You don't like him because of what he said about your sister ten years ago."

"I don't deny it," Bertram said calmly. "And if I so much as see him within a hundred yards of her, I'll break *both* his arms. "Now, *you* be truthful."

"What?"

"About Celeste."

"What about her?"

"You said she was ugly."

"No, I didn't."

"You said she was a shrew."

"I said she could be unpleasant, and she can be."

He gave me a disbelieving look. "She's a pretty enough girl, Henri."

"Pretty enough for who?"

He shook his head at me. "She is charming, sweet, and clever. I could tell that by spending an hour with her. How could you not see it in a month?"

"I was promised her sister," I said coldly.

"So you'll waste this opportunity?"

"Opportunity for what?" I asked in astonishment. "I'm not going to take advantage of the girl."

"Well, it's good to see Jean's character hasn't *completely* rubbed off on you," Bertram said sarcastically.

"What's that supposed to mean?" I asked.

"And how are your dreams?"

"What?"

"Your dreams. Are they any better?"

I had no idea what he was getting at. My dreams had troubled me for the past two years, and I occasionally woke with my voice hoarse from yelling. I wished I'd never told Bertram about them. Perhaps it had been Aunt Inese who told him.

"A little better, perhaps." I think I'd only had one in the last two weeks. That was quite an improvement.

Bertram was about to speak, but snapped his mouth shut as Celeste suddenly joined us.

"Inese is retiring to her room," she said. "She'd like to wish Monsieur Vrai goodnight."

"You must call me Bertram, please," he said, offering Celeste his arm. She took it with a curious look over her shoulder at me. I could only stare at the angle of her neck and shoulder as I followed them.

Bertram kissed my aunt on the cheek, promised to be back to visit the next day, and then turned to Celeste. "I hope you don't mind me hanging about the place during your visit. My parents love me but don't want me constantly underfoot when I come to Aix."

"Not at all. At least, as long as you don't expect me to be idle."

"I was actually hoping you would teach me what you've learned about drainage systems."

She rewarded him with an amused laugh, and he kissed her hand before calling, "Goodnight, Henri," and disappearing.

The moment he was gone, Celeste threw her arms around Aunt Inese. "Thank you," she exclaimed. "Thank you for the glasses. I love the frames you chose. It was all too kind of you."

Aunt Inese muttered a few words like, "Of course, dear," and "Silly," before Celeste released her, gave me a little curtsey, and walked off toward her room, trailing her hand delicately along the wall to guide her as she went.

"She thinks the glasses were my idea," Aunt Inese muttered with a disapproving look.

"That's just fine." I didn't want her to feel beholden to me.

"No, it isn't. Misunderstandings are stupid, so it's better to be clear from the beginning, don't you think?" Her tone told me it was a loaded question, but I didn't see how.

CHAPTER 8

Celeste

The morning after my eye exam, Carine Bochard arrived, just as she had for the last two Saturdays, her children in tow. Suzanne rolled her eyes, but perhaps with less distaste than she had when Carine first began to come. It really was difficult to be surly around little Marie, who instantly greeted Suzanne with a little curtsey and a flurry of explanations of what they'd seen on the road that day.

"Hush, Marie," Carine said gently. "We must allow Suzanne some peace."

"I don't mind her prattle," Suzanne grunted.

I decided I had better separate all of them on that note of success. I explained to Martin and Marie about my broken glasses. "I'd like to work in the garden, but my vision is going to be dreadful. Will you help me while your mother works with Madame Sauveterre?"

We went our separate ways, and when I left the children in the garden so I could fetch lunch, Inese met me at the kitchen door. "Do you have any idea how quickly Carine works?" she whispered. "I think she's accomplished more in these two hours than our last maid did in two days. I don't even have to tell her what I want done. She just sees it and does it."

Suzanne glanced at us and then to the opposite end of the kitchen where Carine packed a sack with food for the men in the fields.

At that moment, Henri walked into the kitchen with Paul Fontaine. Paul stopped in his tracks and stared a moment at Carine before snatching off his hat. He stepped back into the shadows as Inese said, "Henri, your lunch is ready."

Henri planted a quick kiss on his aunt's wrinkled cheek and nodded at me, an amused glint in his eye as he looked at the broken glasses planted squarely on my nose. He turned to Carine, who gave him a curtsey. I was pleased to see she met his eye without hesitation.

"Carine, thank you for your help," he said calmly, though his stance was tense. I doubted he'd talked with many people beyond his own circle since he'd acquired his injuries. "My aunt tells me you do amazing work and hopes you'll consider working here more."

"I would like that, Monsieur Durant," she said without flinching. "Unfortunately, my young ones are too little to leave as yet. They are enjoying your garden as we speak."

Henri shrugged. "As long as they aren't any trouble, I don't see why they can't come with you every day, if you'd like. Your boy looks almost old enough to help Maurice in the stables, if he's interested. I hope you'll think about it."

I wanted to shout with excitement. I'd been wondering how I could plant the idea into Henri's mind, but he'd taken care of it for me. If she could bring her children, we wouldn't need to hire anyone else to help with the house. Then I could set myself to finding field workers and tidying up the farm accounts.

"I certainly will," she said with a grateful smile. She gave him the sack of food, and as he turned away, her gaze moved beyond him to where Paul stood, still half-concealed in the shadows. Carine's lips parted in surprise, and she blushed fiercely, suddenly very interested in her shoes.

"Do you have time to help me in the garden now, Carine?" I blurted out.

She moved to follow me without comment, and I tugged on Paul's sleeve as I passed him. With very little maneuvering I was soon striding along in front of both of them.

"Henri?" I called as I left the pair to catch up to him.

Paul spoke in low, shy tones to Carine behind me, and they seemed happy enough to hang back so I could talk with Henri.

"And what is that smile for?" Henri asked as I met him near the gate.

"Carine," I said, clutching his sleeve in excitement at my triumph. "That is so good of you."

Henri shrugged. "There's nothing kind about it. She's the only person interested in the position, and Aunt Inese really likes her."

I realized I'd been grasping his sleeve like a little child and loosed him quickly. I intended to leave him and go back to my work, but Martin and Marie suddenly appeared from behind the hedge, both looking in awe at Henri. I hoped they wouldn't do anything to make him change his mind.

"Monsieur Durant," I said quickly. "Have you met your fine neighbors, Monsieur Martin Bochard and his sister, Mademoiselle Marie Bochard?"

He gave me a tolerant look before bowing smartly to them.

"Children, this is Monsieur Durant."

Marie executed a perfect little curtsey before stepping closer, tugging on the corner of his shirt, and asking in the confidential whisper of a five-year-old, "Monsieur Prince, is the dragon *really* gone?"

I was horrified. It had never occurred to me when I told the children that silly story that they would actually confront *him* about it.

Henri stared at her, his eye wide in surprise. I suppose he wasn't accustomed to being addressed as Monsieur Prince. I pressed my lips together to avoid smiling. He gave me a look that assured me he knew this was entirely my fault, then bent down to say quietly, "Marie, there are certainly no more dragons to worry about." He tweaked her braid and added, "And let's not tell anyone about the prince business. Sometimes Mademoiselle Lebeau's imagination gets carried away, and we wouldn't want me to get into trouble." He had a point. Inese said the local nobility were often away at court and rarely interfered with the running of the city, but if rumor circulated that Henri was claiming nobility, he could still face severe consequences.

Marie shook her head solemnly, and Henri stood again, giving me a long look that unnerved me and made me want to laugh at the same time. "Paul, you ready?" he called without looking away from me.

A moment later, Paul strode past us with a silly grin on his face. Henri's head snapped back an inch in surprise. "Good day, Celeste," he said with an odd lilt to his voice. He turned to follow Paul, and I heard a definite chuckle escape him.

I stared after him several moments before Marie said, "Mamma. We met him."

I spun to find Carine right next to me. She spoke to her children as she eyed me with interest, her gaze flickering to Henri's retreating form and back to me. "Yes, darling. I hope you both minded your manners."

"What do you think about what he said?" I asked, hoping to distract her.

Her expression softened. "That was very kind of him. I'm not sure he understands what he's offering."

"I think we can make it work if you're interested, Carine."

"The pay is certainly better than doing wash. And more

consistent," she said, staring after Paul and Henri. "And the children enjoy glutting themselves in the garden. I just worry that we would be a nuisance."

"We could trial a few days," I suggested.

"That would be nice," Carine said vaguely. "Perhaps you would consent to walking over to my home to work out the particulars. Right now I've promised Suzanne I'll clean the kitchen top to bottom."

"Yes, and then you can tell me about Paul," I said with exaggerated innocence.

Her eyes snapped away from the men's retreating forms and to me. I bit my lip, wondering if I'd overstepped. But then her expression turned shrewd as she shrugged lightly. "And *you* can tell me about Henri Durant."

My mouth dropped open. I'm sure I looked like an idiot, but she shooed her children back to the garden, pretending not to notice.

What *could* I tell her about Henri Durant? That he believed housekeepers must be beautiful and therefore wanted me to leave as soon as possible? That he'd been kind to me, even though my father had tricked him into taking me instead of my beautiful little sister? That I didn't want to leave him or his gorgeous château? I *wasn't* going to tell her that when I first looked through Bertram's lenses, I'd seen a depth and emotion in Henri's gaze that unnerved me to my core. I groaned inwardly. I'd sounded so stupid, commenting on his lashes, which *were* actually quite long, but at least it had kept me from saying something more humiliating. I don't think I could have lived under his roof another night if I'd said what was on the tip of my tongue; that he was even more handsome than I'd thought before.

It wasn't just that I was feeling more charitable with the world once I could see it so well. He really was an attractive man, especially when he wasn't frowning. He was tall, and years of work in the fields had given him muscle that couldn't be hidden. He had a strong jaw, and his thick brown hair begged to be tamed. All in all, it was difficult to keep my eyes off him, especially when I could actually see him. And there would be snow at lavender harvest before I'd admit it to anyone.

Henri

I smiled at the way Celeste had managed Paul and Carine. She'd thrown them together and pretended to need to talk to me so they would have time alone. Not that I minded. Carine was a sweet girl, and Paul had been heartbroken when she'd fallen for Urie. He'd been too shy to chase her back then.

My arm still felt warm where Celeste's hand had been, and my steps had a new buoyancy. I think having Celeste and little Marie both unconsciously reach out to me had done something to my heart. Not many people chose to come that close to me anymore, let alone touch me at all. Of course, there had been a distinct difference in the way I'd felt when each of them reached out to me. Marie's gesture had been surprisingly comforting, and I hadn't realized that I'd needed comfort. Celeste, on the other hand...having her that close to me had made me want to gather her into my arms. Though it may have been a reaction to my nightmare-ridden sleep last night, I suspected what it really meant was that I was pathetic and very ready for a wife.

I couldn't help smiling a little over the look on Celeste's face when Marie had called me Monsieur Prince. As though she'd been caught sneaking cake.

Paul cast a sidelong glance at me, and I dropped the smile and cleared my throat. "Carine looked well," I said.

"She always looks well," Paul said, staring off toward the

fields. He didn't say another word the rest of the afternoon other than to agree the wheat was almost ready to harvest.

I wish I hadn't spoken to Bertram about my dreams the other day, because that night they were particularly bad. I relived the loss of my eye over and over, and when I finally was able to wake myself, it was to find my voice hoarse and my eye socket on fire with pain. I stomped out of my room and was startled to come face to face with a white-clad figure.

"Monsieur Durant?" Celeste said. "Are you all right?"

I choked back an angry expletive. It wasn't her fault. "Quite," I said.

"Do you need something to help you sleep?"

"I was just going to the kitchen to find the lavender oil."

"Do you require assistance?"

"No, thank you," I said curtly.

She pulled her wrap more closely about herself and turned away. "Goodnight, then, Monsieur."

"Goodnight." I was incredibly grateful she asked no questions.

The next morning, I apologized for waking her. "I don't usually make enough noise to disturb anyone."

She just blinked at me a moment before saying quietly, "I'm sorry you have troubled sleep."

I turned away, uncomfortable with the level of understanding in her eyes.

A few days later, Bertram showed up for the apparent sole purpose of entertaining Celeste, who laughed at his antics and still managed to balance the general household accounts through her broken glasses. I looked them over after she finished. She'd corrected four separate errors that I'd made, one from being unable to read Aunt Inese's handwriting correctly.

"Bravo," Bertram exclaimed when she finished. "I've never seen anyone do numbers so quickly."

She smiled wryly and took off her glasses. "I've had a lot of experience catching the problems in my father's bookkeeping."

"No wonder he's done so well for himself." I immediately regretted my sarcastic words and didn't need Bertram's glare to feel abominable. I had no call to take out my anger with her father on her.

Celeste's expression went blank, but a pink infused her cheeks. "Indeed." She gave a careless shrug, which contradicted her next words. "You'd think after I kept him out of prison so many times, he would have just handed the accounts over to me." Under her breath so that Bertram didn't hear, she added, "I suppose he didn't think me *pretty* enough to manage the numbers."

"And do you need to send home for a party dress?" Bertram asked with a brilliant smile, capturing Celeste's attention for himself again.

"I haven't decided to go to the dance yet," she reminded him.

"I'll come for you myself," he suggested as though it had suddenly occurred to him. Bertram never said a word without thinking it out first. He must have been planning it. "That would be perfectly appropriate, wouldn't it, Aunt Inese?"

She had just come into the room after fetching her needlepoint, and when it was explained, she said coldly, "You weren't planning on going without me, were you?"

Bertram popped up from his seat and kissed Aunt Inese on the cheek, grinning enthusiastically. "I'll be escorting the two most delightful women at the dance."

"Hold a moment," I said. "What about your fiancée?"

"She won't mind at all. She'll be thrilled to see them."

"And do you really think I'd let Mademoiselle Lebeau, or my aunt, go all the way to Aix at night with only you for protection?"

Celeste turned slowly to stare at me. I could almost see sparks flying from her eyes.

"I *beg* your pardon," said Bertram. Something was off about his outrage. His eyes were laughing. He was baiting me.

"You know you are mobbed by your patients any time you're in public," I pointed out. "And Mademoiselle Lebeau is an important enough woman that there are those who might trouble her." Like her father's creditors. "I am responsible for her safety, and I'll not risk it."

"Then I certainly hope you're prepared to come, Henri," Aunt Inese said. "Because I intend to go *and* take my pretty friend with me." She nodded with finality.

Bertram studied me expectantly, and Celeste watched me through narrowed lids. Her expression might have been frightening if her eyes weren't so unfocused.

"I'll take it under consideration," I heard myself say.

Bertram mouth dropped open, but he couldn't have been more shocked than I was. Had I really said those words?

"Well, I suppose I should be getting along," he said.

"Yes, why don't you."

He grinned at me, kissed my aunt's cheek, and turned to Celeste. "A pleasure," he said, a little too affectionately.

She smiled and moved to join Aunt Inese and me in walking him to the door. Bertram shared a conspiratorial look with my aunt. I clenched my teeth together and, for almost the first time, was thrilled to see my oldest friend walk away from the house and toward the stable.

"You needn't worry, Henri," Celeste said as we walked back to the parlor. "It's unlikely the new glasses will be ready, and I refuse to go without them or with this broken pair."

"I don't know why," I said. "You can dance without them."

"What? Can *you* dance with your eyes closed?" Her eyes widened. "I mean eye. I mean—"

I ignored her little blunder. "Well, perhaps not a gavotte, but certainly you could manage an allemande."

She sniffed. "I'd like to see *you* do it."

"Very well," I replied. I don't know what had gotten into me.

Her lofty attitude had pricked me, perhaps. "You take off your glasses, and I'll not look either. We'll see how we fare."

"You haven't danced in two years, Henri," my aunt reminded me.

"One doesn't forget the allemande."

A smile pulled at the corners of Celeste's mouth. "And you think Inese will still have a parlor afterward?" She really did have a pretty smile, even when she was being snide.

"You have so little faith in me."

"Very well. I call you on your bluff," she said. "I accept."

"You do?" I stared at her stupidly. It was one thing for her to catch my arm in excitement, another thing entirely for her to be so close to me for an extended time.

"My hands don't move as quickly on the harpsichord as they once did," Aunt Inese said with a little smirk. "So I don't think I can manage a fast-paced allemande, but at least you'll have less chance of injuring yourselves." She ushered us into the music room and took her seat at the instrument. I cast a startled glance at Celeste, but she'd already taken off her glasses and stood waiting for me in the center of the room.

Aunt Inese started the first measures, and Celeste gave me a curtsey and began the first steps. I hurried to join her. My aunt seemed busy with her music, so I peeked frequently, completely amused by what we were doing. Celeste was more graceful than I could have guessed, but when she moved to take my hand for a turn, her hand collided with my shoulder. She snorted a little laugh, and I quickly grasped her hand.

"You cheated," she murmured. "Quit peeking."

I allowed myself to smile, because she couldn't see it.

We made it through several turns without mishap, Celeste laughing occasionally. I couldn't stop smiling over our silliness, and each time she laughed, I forgot all about keeping my eye closed, and just watched her. I took her hands, and we turned our backs to each other, our arms raised. It was easier to dance with her than I'd expected. Of course, Celeste was taller than most of the dance partners I'd ever had. We came out of the turn, and she was in my arms again.

In my previous life, I used to dance at every opportunity, but I didn't remember enjoying it as much as I did at that moment. I decided it was simply because I'd missed dancing, and that it had nothing to do with the brightness of Celeste's beautiful eyes, the pleased upward turn of her mouth, or the way her hands fit so naturally in mine. Or even how good she smelled. I think *that* must have been what ultimately led to my – her – downfall. Literally. Her feminine, floral smell so distracted me that I made a wrong step. Celeste made the correct step and tripped right over my foot.

When I held her tight to keep her from falling, she made the oddest choking noise. I thought my grip might have pained her until she burst out laughing. Celeste's laugh wasn't a coy little giggle. It was loud and uninhibited. And it was one of the most beautiful sounds I'd ever heard. It also didn't stop.

I couldn't help laughing with her. Or maybe *at* her. Probably both. She looked so funny with her face bright red and actual tears leaking from her eyes.

"That," she wheezed between fits of laughter, "wasn't my fault."

I just laughed at her.

"And you weren't even... closing your eye."

"How do you know?"

"I can see when you're very close," she said, finally getting her laughing under control. "And your eye is so bright blue that even when you're farther away, I can still see a blur of color." She turned her head to look right at me.

Our laughter faded away, but I stared into those fascinating eyes a few more moments before it occurred to me that our mouths were only inches from each other and that I was still holding her very close.

CHAPTER 9

Celeste

My horrible laugh subsided just as I realized that I was close enough that if I simply leaned forward, I could plant a kiss on his mouth. Not that I wanted to. It was simple curiosity. Two separate boys had stolen kisses from me years before. I found out later that each was only trying to get closer to my sister by convincing me they liked me. Neither were particularly pleasant experiences, and I'm fairly sure I drew blood on one of them when I hit him immediately afterward. But it occurred to me at that moment, as Henri held me close, that kissing *him* would likely be a very different kind of experience, one that might prove infinitely more interesting.

Henri suddenly straightened, pulling me with him and then stepping away to a more proper distance. "Thank you for the dance, Celeste. It was most entertaining." His voice held a smile, but when I put on my glasses, he pulled his mouth into a frown and shook his head a little, as though trying to convince himself of something.

The music had stopped with our not-so-graceful collision, and Inese looked more pleased than she should have considering the failure of the experiment.

Henri's frown deepened when he noticed. "Does your sister enjoy dancing?" he asked abruptly.

"Isabelle?" The sudden change of topic surprised me enough that I spoke without thinking. "She loves dances. They give her license to flirt with dozens of men at the same time."

His gaze narrowed, and I realized how petty my words must have sounded. He didn't know her. I was glad I hadn't mentioned that our first dance instructor had insisted that I was a far better dancer than my sister. She soon saw to it that he was replaced.

"I'd better say goodnight," Henri said with a stiff bow in my direction. He kissed his aunt's cheek and strode from the room, leaving me feeling as though I'd missed an important opportunity.

"Don't worry, Celeste," Inese said as she rose from her post at the harpsichord. "Henri wasn't always this abrupt. And he's more his old self every day. Especially lately. Coming back to old things provokes some anxieties in him, but I'm sure he'll pull himself together."

I wondered if I could pull *myself* together. Dancing with him, even as silly as it was, had played with my emotions. Henri Durant was a ridiculous man, moody and temperamental, and more than once I'd had cause to question his intellect, especially his understanding of human nature. But there was a kindness in him and an undeniable intensity, some force that attracted me to him. And it wasn't simply his strong shoulders or long eyelashes.

"He cares about you very much," I said, shaking myself from my own thoughts.

"Yes. He takes good care of me. My niece was fortunate in her son. I wish she was here to see it."

"I think he is very lucky to have you," I said. "And so am I. You've already taught me so many things, and I've been here such a short time."

"Then we shall have to see to it that you stay longer," she said. I walked her to her room. She wasn't infirm, but I did worry about her on the staircases.

That night, Henri yelled out in his sleep again. The first time he'd done it, I'd startled into terrified wakefulness and run into the hall, ready to battle intruders. Henri hadn't been happy to see me, so this time I stayed in bed. It didn't last long. He cried out only once. Inese either slept through it again or pretended to.

I'd heard of this happening to soldiers, these dreams of the battlefield that tortured their sleep and sometimes their days. My heart hurt for him, even if he was surly and annoying.

The next morning when I came downstairs to help Suzanne with breakfast, there was a man in the kitchen. I would have swerved away, but Jean Mason had already seen me.

"Madame Lebeau," he said.

"Mademoiselle," Suzanne reminded him, beating the contents of her mixing bowl with something akin to ferocity.

"My pardon," he said with a bored little shrug. "I suppose I shall have to have coffee later."

"I brew it in time for breakfast," said Suzanne. "As I've told you before."

He walked away without responding.

Suzanne and I looked at each other, sharing our mutual dislike for the man. Then I got curious. What was the book-keeper doing here? He must know Henri would be in the field all day today.

"I'll be back in a moment," I told Suzanne before following Jean. I intended to find him and politely demand that he tell me what he was doing there. Oddly enough, I found him in the formal living room. It was a room I'd hardly entered as it was intended for high-ranking guests. I decided against approaching him and merely watched instead. I wished I had Bertram's glasses on again. My old, broken pair just couldn't compare.

Jean studied the furnishings closely. A gilt lamp, a fine painting, an intricately carved table. He traced his fingers along each at he gazed at them. I squinted my eye behind the good lens, allowing his face to swim into focus. His expression was one I knew well from the faces of Isabelle's constant parade of men. Desire mingled with smug expectation.

Isabelle had a refined talent for making men think they had a chance for her hand. Now, at the young age of seventeen, she managed to dangle up to ten men at a time. It might have been impressive if I hadn't had to witness the disgusting display over and over. Her constant flirtations had provided me with endless opportunity to observe human nature.

If I wasn't mistaken, and I knew I wasn't, Jean wanted Henri's possessions as much as Isabelle's beaux wanted her. There was something decidedly unpleasant about watching men desire something out of their reach.

I turned and slipped away, my feet silent on the hall carpet. I didn't want him to see me, not only because it seemed as though I'd witnessed something indecent, but also because I was dying to ask him what he planned to steal first. I doubted that would go over well.

When Henri came in that night, weary and dusty from his work and rubbing at the irritated skin around his eye patch, I was hesitant to approach him about his friend's odd behavior. I waited for him to eat first. My friend, Nicole, thought it best never to interrupt a hungry man at his meal, and watching him, I had to agree. So I talked to Inese about plans for the housework and about Carine coming the next day.

"I went through the empty rooms to see which needed the most cleaning," I said distractedly to Inese. How could I possibly ask what I wanted to about Jean Mason? "One of the bedrooms was locked. Did you not want that one cleaned? Two doors down from yours?"

Inese blushed. Truly. On her pale, gently wrinkled cheeks. I was instantly confused and looked to Henri. He regarded me over his plate. "We keep that door locked," he said tonelessly.

I suddenly recalled the way Inese had paused outside that door when she'd first taken me to my room. "Very well. I shall tell her to skip it," I said, as though it didn't worry me at all. But it did worry me. There was obviously a mystery there. Had one of his parents died in that room? Inese told me they were taken by a fever when Henri was only ten years old. I never wanted to go into Mother's old room. I busied myself with my meal, but was even more distressed when Jean's drawl was heard from the door.

"Pardon the interruption," he said.

I very much resented the interruption. Henri, on the other hand, seemed glad of it. He jumped up to shake hands, insisting that he was finished already.

"Did you bring all the ledgers?" he asked.

"I took the liberty of putting them in your study." He bowed to Inese, who only gave him a cool glance, and then jerked his head begrudgingly in my direction. Henri frowned at that but took his leave more graciously.

My suspicion wouldn't be silent, and I spoke quickly. "Might I come? I've always wanted to understand *real* bookkeeping." I kept my expression blank, but Henri watched me suspiciously.

Jean rolled his eyes, clearly annoyed, but waited for Henri to respond.

"I fear it will bore you, but you are welcome to join us."

There was anything but welcome on Jean's face, but I hurried to follow them anyway. I left my glasses on, in spite of, and perhaps because of, Jean's obvious disdain for them.

The men were silent until we reached Henri's study, probably because of my presence, but they forgot me as soon as the books were open in front of them. I watched carefully, attempting one of Isabelle's most meaningless expressions. Jean thought me stupid. Let him think it. Henri sent me a few confused glances.

Within fifteen minutes, I had learned enough. "So that column there is what was set aside for taxes?" I asked innocently.

"Yes," Jean said shortly, moving to point something out to Henri.

"And do I understand correctly that you keep the books in your apartment in Aix?" I asked, my tone insipid enough to annoy *me*. At his curt nod, I continued. "You must be so faithful to your work to keep the records with you when other bookkeepers leave them at their place of employment."

Jean's eyes narrowed, and Henri's widened. Before either could say anything, I prattled on. "I've always loved reading ledgers. They are so soothing, don't you think? Why, I could fall asleep to my father's ledger on any day." I added an empty-headed smile for good measure. "I do wish you'd leave the books here, Monsieur Mason, at least while I'm visiting. It is such an inconvenience to you to keep them in your home, and I would so much enjoy them."

He stared at me openmouthed. Henri made a choking sound, then turned away to cough.

~

Henri

Why Celeste was trying to irritate Jean, I couldn't imagine. That is, other than the fact that they mutually disliked each other. But she wanted the books, and I didn't see any harm in letting her go through them. She would see how poorly the farm did last year, but she already understood about that from her conversations with Aunt Inese and me. It was her own father who'd done most of the damage.

Regardless, she deserved to win this little round between them, considering his rude behavior in the dining room. For a man who had acted with such bravery and conviction, Jean unfortunately lacked skill in talking pleasantly with others.

"I can deny you no pleasure," I said with a bow to Celeste. I was fairly sure she turned away just to hide a smug smile.

"Really? Henri, a woman? Looking at accounts?"

Celeste turned to him with a murderous glare, but before she could sharpen her claws on him, I said, "Of course, Jean, of course. What harm could she do them?"

"A great deal," he insisted.

"Oh, Monsieur Mason," Celeste said. "You surely do not think I mean to *write* in them. Why, they belong to Monsieur Durant. I wouldn't consider defacing them with my practice figures." I didn't understand the hard gleam in her eye when she said *belong*, but she quickly gave a false little laugh. "Why would you need to work at them at this time of year anyway? I thought the wheat harvest was weeks away, and the lavender harvest well after that."

"It's true, Jean. I've never understood why you want to lug them back and forth all that way. Just leave them here until it's time to sell the wheat. You're all caught up, aren't you?"

"All right. I warned you." And without saying goodnight to either of us, he left in a huff.

"Why do you want to look at the ledgers, Celeste?" I asked once I heard the front door shut behind Jean.

"Mostly because he doesn't want me to."

Celeste was so funny, so ready to do battle, that I couldn't seem to help provoking her. "Celeste, I think you're very clever, to be sure," I said in as patronizing of a tone as I could manage. "But—"

"If you let me read the legers, I'm sure I'll find thirty mistakes," she cut in. Her fists were tight balls. I wasn't altogether sure she wouldn't strike me.

"If you find so many as five mistakes, I'll personally gather buckets full of lavender for you."

"Agreed."

"And if you can't find that many, then—"

"Oh, I will," she said before spinning on her heel and stomping away.

I waited until she was out of earshot before I chuckled quietly. She was absolutely entertaining. The expressiveness of her eyes. Her haughty confidence. I thought over what I would do when she was unable to find a single mistake. Jean was an arrogant idiot, it was true, but he was an excellent bookkeeper. Even he couldn't work the magic it would take to make the farm accounts healthy and robust again. That would take a different sort of magic, the type of magic a beautiful woman could perform just by charming people into forgetting about my hideous exterior.

The next morning when I came down to breakfast, I found food waiting on the sideboard. It was Suzanne's day off, and I was once again thrilled that Celeste had taken over the kitchen rather than trying to find someone else to fill in.

The bread might not have been as good as Suzanne's, but it still had a nice flavor and wasn't too dry. There were also pastries and a dish of fruit. A linen sack sat at the end of the table, and I found it full of food to take to the field with me. There was enough for Paul and Jacques, but I stuffed a few more pastries inside, just in case.

I couldn't help a peek into the kitchen. Celeste sat at the kitchen table, her back to me, and her bare feet swinging beneath her as she studied one of the ledgers. The summer heat must have overridden her sense of modesty.

I shook my head and hurried away, trying to clear my mind of the image of her pretty ankles. I was a gentleman. I had no business lingering over those thoughts. To occupy my mind, I instead tried to think of what I should ask for as my prize when she wasn't able to follow through with her boast.

Paul and Jacques were delighted with the food, especially the pastries. They each tasted one before we parted to our separate tasks. For much of the day, I thought about Celeste and wondered how she was managing. Paul caught me smiling half a dozen times, but each time he only gave me a knowing look and went back to his work.

By late afternoon, I couldn't stand the curiosity. I made an excuse to go back to the house and cautiously made my way to the kitchen entrance. I peeked through the window only to find Celeste pouring over a recipe and looking absolutely capable in Suzanne's apron. She set down the paper to place loaves of bread dough into the oven.

I shook my head. For being the daughter of one of the most well-known merchants in Provence, Celeste Lebeau seemed very at home in the kitchen. Before she could look up and see me, I turned away to dust off my clothes and wash my hands at the pump.

When I walked into the kitchen a minute later, Celeste was moving a decadent-looking trifle to the table. She turned when I entered, the trifle still in her hands.

"Paul and Jacques send their thanks and compliments on your cooking," I said, stepping forward.

"I'm glad they enjoyed it," she said, her eyes wide and trusting.

My mouth watered. It must have been the dessert in her hands that pulled me forward.

"Have you convinced Carine to work here full-time?" I

asked, changing the subject. "We have enough work for her, and my aunt already adores her children."

"She may come around to it yet," she said with a small smile. She turned and set the trifle on the table.

I drew nearer, unable to stop myself.

CHAPTER 10

Celeste

Why did I feel so flustered around him? The man was maddening. I hoped I wasn't blushing.

Had he somehow known what a terrible day it had been? Scrubbing, cleaning, and cooking non-stop, all while refiguring Jean's numbers in my head. And the idiot bookkeeper did things the oddest, most roundabout way.

"Is that for me?" Henri asked, making his way to the trifle.

"Don't you dare touch it," I said, snatching at his coat. "It was almost impossible to make." I succeeded in jerking him off-balance and away from the trifle just as he made to snitch a bit of it. I hadn't anticipated the force would spin him back into me. His head cracked into mine.

I laughed ruefully, rubbing my forehead while he chuckled, massaging his jaw. He forgot to turn away this time when he laughed, and I realized why he hid his smile. His scarring pulled at his lips, making his smile uneven. It was hardly disfiguring, but to a man as obsessed with physical beauty as Henri was, it must have been uncomfortable not to have a perfect smile.

"It's *my* trifle, isn't it?"

"Most certainly not. It is for your aunt."

"Oh, is that why you attacked me? You needn't have worried." He pressed his lips into a hard line, and for a moment, I thought I was in trouble. "She hates trifle," he added boyishly before making another lunge for the cake.

I launched myself between him and the dessert. He feinted right and left, and I blocked him over and over, laughing helplessly at his antics. "It's. For. After. Dinner." I barely managed to get the words out through my laughter.

He finally stopped and folded his arms across his broad chest.

I was instantly conscious of my unladylike behavior. "I'm sorry," I said.

"For what?"

"For my terrible laugh. I've probably impaired your hearing for life."

"I love your laugh," he said. "What's wrong with it? Everyone should laugh like that."

Including you? "I've been told rather sharply that my laugh is vulgar and an embarrassment to the family."

He was kind enough to look horrified.

"But it's all right," I said with a grin. "I very rarely want to laugh around my family. They haven't much of a sense of humor."

He looked disappointed, though I couldn't guess why.

He leaned against the wall and studied me a moment. It took all my self-control not to check my hair or smooth my dress.

I decided I might as well get the worst over with. "I'm afraid you will not have to escort me to the lavender field and pick a haystack-sized bunch for me."

"No mistakes?" he asked with a little smirk that made me want to pinch him.

"Only one, and it was a few pennies overpayment of taxes last year," I admitted reluctantly.

"You made it through the tax accounts too? I'm impressed."

I shrugged. It hadn't accomplished anything.

He tapped his chin. "As I recall, you were in too much of a hurry last night to hear my side of the bet."

I cringed inwardly. I'd hoped he'd forgotten.

"I already promised my aunt I'd take you both to the dance, so I can't get out of that," he said on a sigh. "Instead I'll have to request...information."

"Excuse me?"

"About your family. I want to learn more about your sister." My heart plummeted. "And you. Your father too, though you don't have to tell me anything condemning, of course."

"Of course," I said, trying to keep my tone pleasant. I just wanted to be free of my sister for a while, not have to hear about her, or talk about her. I didn't want to console the men she rejected, or try to be understanding to those pining after her. I'd had enough of that for a lifetime. I just wanted to pretend the only interest people took in me was for me. But I'd not been able to follow through on my boast after all, so I could hardly reject such a little request.

I'd been so certain Jean's accounting would be faulty. And I'd worked so hard to get the books away from him. I decided to go through them again the following day, just to be sure.

Henri rubbed the skin around his eye patch, something I'd seen him do before. The area was red and irritated as it sometimes was at the end of a day in the fields. I suspected dust and sweat didn't go well with the worn leather. My heart softened toward him another fraction. For having the sort of money he was accustomed to having, he really worked hard.

Henri rolled up his sleeves to help me in the kitchen, over-riding my protests.

"Auntie would be disappointed in me if I let our guest do

more cleaning up. And you can tell me about your family while we wash dishes."

Ugh. "What would you like to know?"

"Everything. You aren't at all what I'd expect in your father's daughter. You make me curious. Tell me about you and your sister," he suggested.

"Isabelle? She is beautiful," I said with a shrug. It was generally best to leave it at that.

But he didn't want to leave it at that. "I mean, is she like you? In her personality? In her likes and dislikes? In her plans for the future?"

He seemed almost embarrassed to ask, and yet, anxious to hear my answer. I paused in disappointment. Was he really just another pathetic, lovesick man willing to be strung along by my little sister?

I tried not to clash pans together as I started into the same monologue I'd recited for dozens of men before Henri. "Isabelle is seventeen, and has been out in society for two years. My father wants her to wait until she's at least eighteen to get married." He never had to make such rules for me. I'd turned nineteen six months ago. "She loves to surround herself with beautiful things, loves to read, and has a talent for being involved in multiple conversations at once." I didn't call it eavesdropping, but that's what it was.

"Is she like you?"

"We are almost nothing alike," I said, working hard to keep the disdain out of my voice.

He raised a questioning eyebrow as he dried plates.

"She is a famed beauty, and I am not, but that's not what I mean," I said. "We're different in almost every way. I think the only thing we share is a love for our father." She loved him for what he gave her, and I loved him because he was my father. "Where she has opinions, she is utterly decided and will not discuss other possibilities." Such as when she saw a hat she must have lest the world stop in its rotation. "She likes things of beauty." Especially when they enhanced *her* beauty. "And she strongly dislikes being told what to do. I suppose in that last way, we are similar."

"You're only a couple years older?"

"Yes. My parents were thrilled another child came so quickly after me, and within only a few years, they realized what a beauty she would be. She liked to impress them, and they never tired of adoring her. Father still hasn't."

"And what about you? What were you doing while Isabelle was busy being adored?"

I stared at him. No one ever asked questions about me when Isabelle was under discussion.

∾

Henri

For a moment, Celeste stared wide-eyed at me. Then she smiled and tossed a strand of hair off her face. "I was busy experimenting with drainage systems."

I laughed outright. "No. Seriously."

"Well, there was some experimentation with chemicals in the basement," she said. Her tone was serious, but her eyes held a secret.

"You have my complete attention."

She grinned. "Father went through a phase when he bought and sold quite a great deal of oils and perfumes. I liked to sneak some of it to create my own mixes."

"I imagine that didn't go over well."

"No. Father discovered the notes I was taking on the mixtures and went into a rage over it. Mother was the one to find my secret stash. She smelled each of them and chose one for herself to keep."

I shook my head, thinking of how much that might have cost her father.

She read my mind. "I only took the smallest amount from the bottles. Enough to never be missed, even when they were weighed. The scale I used was quite accurate. It was the one Father used for gold."

"You belong at the university," I said with a laugh. "Not in your father's parlor or even, I regret to say, as my housekeeper."

She gave me a wry smile. "Somehow Mother convinced me that if I ran away to the university, they would eventually discover I was a girl and expel me."

"She was very practical."

"Yes. She was the one to convince me that piracy was also not an appropriate option for a young lady."

I shook my head, smiling. "Your first choices taken away so early."

She snickered but immediately stopped when I asked, "And what of your sister's plans for the future?"

She looked away. "I suppose she intends to marry well and live a life of luxury."

Well, that fit in my plans. "And you do not?"

One corner of her mouth twitched. "I have other plans."

"You've already given up on piracy. What else is there?"

She grinned fully, and I found myself wanting to make her do it again. I shook myself mentally, reminding myself that Celeste would be the best sort of sister to the man lucky enough to get Isabelle.

"Well, there was the year I wanted to be a gypsy."

I snorted.

"And the year I wanted to become a merchant."

"What made you change your mind?"

"Father."

I didn't press her, but after a few moments of silence, I asked, "And now?"

She smiled. "Now I'm considering running away from home and opening a shop."

"What? A shopkeeper?"

"Not just a shopkeeper. That will only be the start." She spoke more quickly as she explained her dream. "I'll start a line of dispensaries with all the best oils and medications, invent new formulations for perfumes, open new markets. And whichever city I choose to live in will benefit from my patronage of the arts and schools, especially schools for girls."

I watched her closely. "You mean it?"

"Of course. Imagine all the possibilities."

She did not dream small. "But Celeste, you're an unmarried woman." The only successful businesswomen I'd ever heard of, and there weren't many, were older, married women, and their husbands owned their property. By law, women could almost never own property.

"I have a plan for getting around that."

I waited a moment before blurting out, "No one will ever believe you're a man."

She closed her eyes a moment, as though praying for patience. "I have a friend who will be owner in name only."

"Who is he?" I asked quickly, not at all willing to examine the sudden tension in my chest.

"An established businessman with an impeccable reputation."

"How could you ever trust he wouldn't take it all away?"

A flash of disappointment dimmed her eyes a moment, but she asked with a flippant wave of her hand, "Are you telling me I ought to consider piracy after all?"

I laughed again. "Tell me more," I said as I began to dry the stack of dishes she'd already washed. I stood near enough to her that I could tell she'd been cleaning and dusting today. My nose itched with a suppressed sneeze. Household dust always irritated me, though outside dirt didn't seem to bother me at all.

The scent of the household cleaner Suzanne favored still lingered on Celeste's clothes. It wasn't a nice smell, but it didn't make me want to move away from her either.

She sighed. "Isabelle has always had many friends. She adores everyone who acknowledges her beauty, and of course, that includes most of the population of Marseille."

"I know, but I meant you."

She looked at me blankly.

"I meant, tell me more about you. Your sister likes pretty things and likes to read. Do you?"

Was she blushing? "I like pretty things," she said lightly as she took hold of a broom and began sweeping. "I simply like useful things more. And I love to read. I just read very different things than Isabelle does. She spends entire days reading novels and books of fairy tales. I never had much time for that sort of reading."

"Come now. You must have had as much time as your sister did. And you can't tell me you don't like fairy tales."

She gave me a pitying look, one I was familiar with by now. She doubted my intellect. "I ran the household," she said. "I read books that helped me in that capacity and in preparing for the future."

I didn't get a chance to ask what she meant by that.

"And I've always *hated* fairy tales," she added, striking the broom against the stone floor with more force than was necessary.

I'd never seen such fierce anger in her eyes. It faded quickly when she met my gaze. "Really? You can't guess why?" she said in disbelief.

I shook my head.

She stopped sweeping around the table and put one fist on her hip. "Youngest daughters are always more beautiful and good-hearted than their older, selfish sisters. Older sisters are never clever or beautiful. They never save anyone or get rescued themselves. They merely exist to put the heroine or princess in a better light. As a point of contrast. They are overlooked and underestimated."

I stared at her. No wonder she didn't spend much time praising her sister.

She picked at something on the broom handle, apparently self-conscious. "It's not that I wish to complain for myself. I don't desire to be the center of attention," she muttered. "And I never would have learned to mix perfumes if my father hadn't so easily overlooked me." She shrugged her shoulder and smiled as she resumed her work. "And just you wait, Monsieur Durant. Some day you will be standing in line to sell your lavender oil to me."

"I don't doubt it," I said, grinning.

We soon finished and retired our separate ways. I strode toward my study, hating the idea of her going home to her father when he brought Isabelle. I wondered if things would be better for Celeste without her sister at home, or perhaps if she decided to stay in Aix. The second idea appealed to me. I'd grown fond of Celeste, despite her sharp tongue. She made me laugh.

I suddenly stopped in my tracks and leaned against the wall outside my study door. She *did* make me laugh. I'd smiled and laughed around her, and I'd not once thought to cover the hideous distortion of my face. I thought frantically back over the day, trying to pinpoint a time when she'd looked at me with revulsion, but I couldn't think of a single instance.

That night, I didn't have any bad dreams.

A few days later on my way to breakfast, I found Celeste pouring over the ledgers in one of the sitting rooms. She was stretched out on a sofa, her bare feet swinging in the air and exposing all of her shapely lower legs. She wasn't even wearing stockings, not that I could blame her. It was hot as the devil, and the sun was barely up. "You really want those armfuls of lavender, don't you?" I asked, glad that when her head whipped around, I wasn't still looking at her legs.

She jumped up to one side of the couch, pulling her feet underneath her and blushing fiercely. "Just something nagging at me," she said, her voice perfectly calm.

I tried not to laugh at the way her feet twitched, but I couldn't help my smile. My hand moved to cover my lips before I remembered I'd accidentally dispensed with that around her. Perhaps Aunt Inese was right. Perhaps I did make too much of it.

"Anything I can help with?"

"No," she said, shaking her head. She hadn't pulled up her hair for the day yet, and the wavy lengths spilled over her shoulders. How could I have ever thought her hair anything but beautiful?

"Well, maybe. It's just…" She hesitated. "Do you *know* you can trust Jean? I mean, *really* trust him?"

If her eyes hadn't been so wide and worried behind her silly glasses, I may have been angry at the question. As it was, I couldn't help chuckling. "See my poor bookkeeper as the source of all my problems, do you?"

"Why not?" she flared.

"I trust him completely," I said, the humor of her questions fading quickly.

Her gaze narrowed and she jumped to her feet. "Just like that? 'We've been friends for a long time, so even though he's a complete pig, I'll just trust him?' Is that it?"

"I would appreciate it if you would speak civilly of him, and to him," I said through gritted teeth.

"Because *he's* so civil himself?" she scoffed.

Jean had visited twice in the last few days, and hadn't even tried to be courteous to Celeste. She'd been just as stubborn.

I wasn't sure later who had moved, but within seconds we were nose to nose, glaring daggers at each other. Inside me, anger battled with the strangest compulsion to draw her into my arms. I had obviously been too long out of society. The idea never would have come to me otherwise.

"He. Is. Trustworthy."

The concentric circles of green around her pupils dilated as she clenched her jaw and asked, "How do you *know*?"

"How do *you* know he's *not*? Does he remind you of your father?"

Her eyes widened, and she stepped back a pace. I instantly felt the loss of her proximity and wanted to follow so I could watch her eyes some more. Instead I stayed rooted to the spot, regretting my harsh words and tone.

"Excuse me, Monsieur Durant. I was trying to be helpful," she said coolly. "I will attempt to keep my nose out of your affairs."

A moment later, she was gone.

CHAPTER 11

Celeste

I blinked back angry tears as I stalked through the château. The horrid man. I'd hardly been able to speak a coherent word with him so close. The muscles of his shoulders spoke as clearly as his voice. He probably knew it too, the monster. Maybe I'd deserved the bit about my father, or at least Father had deserved it, but it had still been a low trick. Just because Father didn't have the most ethical business principles, didn't mean I couldn't recognize a snake when I saw one.

I reached the door to the back gardens before I realized I was barefoot. I blushed all over again, thinking of how I'd been caught by the grumpy master of the house with half my leg showing. I wasn't five years old.

I turned back into the house just as I heard a man calling my name. For a split second, I thought my father had come. The strange mixture of excitement and disappointment instantly faded when I realized it was Bertram Vrai calling me. I found him in the family parlor just as Inese and Monsieur Durant joined him. Henri looked pointedly at my feet.

Evidently it was fine for him to see my legs but not for Bertram to see my feet.

"What's going on, Bertram?" Inese demanded.

Henri's friend practically bounced with excitement.

"Celeste," he exclaimed when he saw me.

"Monsieur Vrai?"

He didn't even glance at my bare feet. "Bertram," he reminded me, before pushing a package into my hand. His boyish excitement had me smiling before I even realized what it was.

"My glasses?"

"I just received them this morning and thought I might win favor with Auntie if I brought them right over. Maybe I could win myself an invitation to stay for the day."

"Silly boy. It isn't *my* favor you're trying to win." She winked at him as she and I sat down on the sofa. I hardly paid attention to their banter or to the glare Henri shot at his friend. I had new glasses.

I unwrapped them carefully, my lips parting in surprise when I saw them. The silver frames were dainty, pretty even. I took off my broken pair, then hesitated.

"Well, put them on," said Inese.

I slipped the frames on my face, my eyes closed a moment to enjoy the comfort of the better construction. The first person I saw when I opened my eyes was Henri. My gaze automatically found him, but his face was unreadable.

"Inese, you were absolutely right. This pair does emphasize her eyes rather than distract."

"Don't be sly, Bertram. You know you suggested them first."

He grinned at me. "And how did I do?" He turned to point at Henri. "Can you count his individual eye lashes?" Bertram laughed, and Inese and I joined him. Henri's expression was stony.

"Well, Henri, what do you think?" Inese asked.

"They are certainly an improvement." He turned his back and sat in a chair without further comment, and I tried to not feel deflated.

Inese passed me a hand mirror. I looked into it and instantly noted the glasses looked so much prettier than my old ones, but what really held my attention was myself. I'd never actually seen myself so clearly, not since I was a child. The mirror was clear, as clear as my vision. I'd never known how many freckles I actually had. The scar on my jaw from when I'd fallen when I was ten hadn't actually faded away. It was still there. And my eyes had rings of green through the brown. They didn't used to, did they?

That was me. It was such an odd feeling to see myself plainly. I set the mirror aside and looked again around the room. "Thank you, Bertram," I said quietly. "I've never been able to see so well. It's…it's a wonderful thing."

The look he gave me was radiant.

I turned to Inese, her smug smile making me laugh. Without another thought, I threw my arms around her neck. "Thank you. I love them." In a whisper, I added, "Can you help me get out of here? I think I might cry."

"What? *I* had them made. I think that should warrant a similar thank you for me," Bertram suggested flirtatiously.

Henri stood and took a threatening step forward.

"Don't be impertinent, Bertram. We have work to do," Inese said, hurrying me out of the room.

I allowed myself one small glance at Henri. I was supposed to be ignoring him after that barb about my father. But I so wanted to see his reaction to my appearance. He looked…worried?

Inese allowed me one minute to wipe the moisture from my eyes as she hurried me along and up the stairs. "We have three days," she whispered, ushering me into her bedroom.

"Three days?"

"Until the dance." Her eyes were bright as she slowly revolved on the spot, looking around her spacious apartment as if searching for inspiration. "We don't have time for a new dress, but your green one was lovely the other night. That will do."

I probably should have been afraid of the manic frenzy in her voice, but at that point, it was only funny.

"What did you have in mind, Inese?" I couldn't help laughing. "I'm going to be the princess of the ball because my glasses aren't hideous. They're still glasses."

"Oh, my dear," she said. "You don't have to be the *most* beautiful girl in the room. You are *new*. You are *interesting. And you'll be arriving with my nephew.* With these things in your favor, there will be no girl at the dance more sought after than you. The people of Aix haven't seen one of their wealthiest landholders for almost two years."

The ensuing torture of the next two days made me wonder if perhaps I hadn't actually been quite lucky to be plain. I'd avoided through my life much of the pinching and pulling and sitting still that Isabelle happily endured to attain her version of perfection. Inese displayed an incredible amount of energy for a woman who supposedly was too tired to run the household.

I saw very little of Bertram and Henri over those two days, though I heard their voices in the house occasionally. If I hadn't felt the most profound respect and affection for Inese, I would have hunted them down and begged them to let me go work in the field or let me help make glasses or *something.* I longed for activity, but Inese demanded all my time for her experimentation.

When she finally took a nap on the second afternoon, I shed the variety of ornaments she had been trying out on me and hurried away toward the garden. Halfway to the door, I remembered Henri and Paul were harvesting wheat that day. Bertram had come earlier but had been sent away by Inese. That meant the ledgers would be available for perusal without anyone to interrupt me.

Henri had hidden them, I realized, but not well enough. I found them tucked under a blanket in his study. I tossed my hair, which lay thick over my shoulders since plucking out the combs Inese had crammed against my scalp, and settled comfortably into Henri's chair at his desk. I wouldn't have taken that liberty if he'd been in the room, even if he'd invited me.

I worked through the books again, knowing that I already had them half-memorized. The ledgers seemed to mock me, withholding the secret to the change in the economic success of the farm. The crop yields had not decreased. The taxes had altered very little. The additions and subtractions had all been accounted for correctly.

I spent an hour pouring over the pages before groaning and slamming the book I was working on closed. I leaned down to rest my head on the book.

"Did you need help with something?" Henri asked quietly from a few feet away.

I jumped horribly. I'd been so focused on the ledger that I hadn't noticed him come in.

"Your chair," I said calmly as my heart hammered and my face blushed brilliant red.

He arched his good eyebrow.

"As temporary assistant housekeeper, it's imperative I test out the chairs."

His lips formed a tight line. He was trying not to smile. I was sure of it. "And?"

"I believe it's satisfactory, though it has a squeak if you lean too far to the left."

"For someone as large as me, it squeaks on the right side also."

I pretended to consider this, leaning my weight around until

I could produce a right-sided squeak. I gave him a triumphant look.

He did smile at that but then shook his head. "The numbers aren't going to change."

I shrugged. "I really did want you to pick armfuls of lavender for me."

He stared at me a long moment. "You still think Jean cheated with the numbers."

I didn't answer right away.

"I know he isn't the most charming individual, but I won't have you speaking ill of him."

I must have looked mutinous as I stood, intending to stride to the door, because Henri shook his head and sent his gaze heavenward. "Please sit."

I almost left anyway, but his next words arrested me.

"I want you to know what happened to me and why I trust Jean."

~

Henri

I don't know what made me say it. I didn't really want to tell her about it. I didn't want to tell anyone. Bertram, Paul, and Aunt Inese knew only the bare minimum, and none of them would have told Celeste all of what they knew. Everyone else only knew that I'd gone away to be a soldier and came back looking like this.

I paced back and forth a few times before leaning against a bookshelf several feet away from where Celeste stood. I ran my fingers through my hair, avoiding her gaze. "You know already that I received my scars while in the army."

I glanced at her, and she nodded.

"If I'd listened to Jean, I wouldn't have gotten into trouble.

My regiment fought British raiders who frequently came ashore around Nice. We weren't formally at war that year, but they came anyway. Jean and I were searching out places they might come ashore. I saw a fire in the distance and wanted to be sure it was put out. Jean said we had to return to camp for help, but I couldn't wait. So when I ran ahead to see what was needed, he went back for help.

"I hadn't really guessed how bad it would be. There were too many soldiers for me to fight. The home they were burning wasn't salvageable, but I thought I could still help the family. The soldiers were busy beating the father, so they didn't see me."

I paused in my telling, not quite able to describe the horror of the burning home, the screaming of the children, the jeering shouts of the Englishmen who mercilessly beat the young father. Celeste was a smart girl. She didn't need all the details to put it together.

"I took a handful of their men before they realized I was there. When they drew a sword to run the father through, I shouted, and the rest turned on me. I was able to get the man a sword, but there were ten of them, and two of us. He yelled at his wife to run, but she wasn't very fast with the babies she held. I got the man chasing her, but when I turned back, her husband was dead and eight English soldiers were rushing at me."

I didn't mention that I killed three more of them before I went down from a club to my head.

"They weren't happy with me for the loss of their friends, so they took their time with me. A few of them pinned me down while they sliced up my chest and arms."

"I thought it was just your—" She broke off and bit her lip.

I smiled without humor and untucked my shirt, pulling it over my head in one motion.

Celeste took a step back. I don't think she even realized it. Her eyes bulged a little as she looked over the scars up and down my chest and across my arms. She'd never seemed squeamish over my scars before, but I suppose no one had ever warned her that my disfigurement extended far beyond my face. She didn't look disgusted, though I couldn't really understand her expression. Perhaps it was simply shock.

"They were careful not to go too deep. They didn't want me to die before I'd had a chance to suffer. I'm not sure exactly what they yelled at me, because my English isn't very good."

That, and I blacked out a few times, especially when they took my eye. They went slowly with that, making sure I knew what they were doing. I'd never known such pain and hadn't been able to breathe for it. The resultant episodes of unconsciousness were short-lived, the pain waking me as soon as I could breathe again.

I met Celeste's gaze. Her wide eyes were fixed on me, and I felt she was hearing the parts I left out.

"When they saw Jean bringing our soldiers in the distance, they threw me into the fire and left." That brought me back to consciousness. "They didn't look back to see that I immediately rolled out of the flames."

"What about the woman and her children?" Celeste asked in a whisper as she drew nearer to me, eyeing the scars on my chest and arms. I'd forgotten she was interested in herbal remedies. She was probably trying to understand what Aunt Inese had done to them.

"I never saw them again, but the British rode off in the direction they'd run. I think it likely they were overtaken and killed. So I might have accomplished nothing at all." My voice cracked, but I didn't have a chance to berate myself because Celeste reached out her hand to trace a thick scar down my arm. "Do they still hurt?" she breathed.

"Sometimes. Nothing like they used to." I didn't tell her that right at that moment, my skin felt amazing. Her touch was light, and her hand was cool, but a very pleasant warmth travelled down my arm along the trail of her fingers.

"Jean found you," she said quietly.

I nodded. "By that time, I was half-dead but coherent enough to beg them to kill me, to put me out of my misery."

She looked up at me, her eyes betraying only sadness.

I wondered what her eyes would express if she'd seen me that night, patches of horrific burns across my face and shoulder, my eye a mangled socket, and my chest and arms in ribbons of open flesh. I keenly remembered the looks of horror and revulsion on my friends' faces.

"I think most of the men agreed with me. Killing me would have been merciful. Our captain was my close friend. I was only a sergeant, but we'd taken turns saving each other's lives. Hans Robineau was his name."

I paused, finding my throat had closed too tightly for me to speak.

Celeste filled in the gap while looking avidly at my chest. "My aunt married a man named Robineau," she said a little shrilly. "But he was never in the army. He was never in anything but wine."

I almost smiled at her anxious admission. Captain Robineau never snuck wine like so many of the men did. I'd practically hero-worshipped Hans. He was amazing and level-headed in a fight, a deep contrast to the gentle person he was off the battlefield.

"And Hans is not a French name," Celeste said, still glancing frequently at my chest. So little miss know-it-all was nervous seeing so much skin. I'd have to remember that.

My voice came back enough that I could finish. "Norwegian mother."

She nodded, not pushing me but obviously waiting.

There was no point in delaying the story. "He drew his sword. I'd never seen him so angry. I realized I was going to die, and that made me think that perhaps I *did* want to try living, but then I blacked out. I'd been holding my breath because of the pain, or maybe it was all the blood I'd lost. I woke up a bit later, just for a minute, enough to see there was a man standing over me. He was yelling that he'd kill the lot of them before he let them put me down. Said I was going to live."

"That was Jean?"

"I didn't think so at the time because it was such a foolish thing to do. Jean always acts rationally. And I have memories, just flashes really, of Hans' face inches away from mine, saying something urgent." His red-streaked blond hair made him unmistakable, even to the half-crazed, one-eyed demon I'd been. It still hurt that Hans had been willing to put me down. I don't know why, since it truly would have been an act of mercy.

I resumed my story. "But then I woke up in a hired carriage with Jean trying to give me more laudanum. He was the only one who'd thought I had a chance at being saved. He'd convinced Captain Robineau to let him take me home to Aunt Inese. The medic had given him enough laudanum to keep me near sedated the entire journey home." I pulled a book from the shelf at random and stared at it. "Nasty stuff," I said. "It took a good three months before I could stop using it altogether.

"All through that trip, when I was in and out of conscious-ness, Jean encouraged me, told me I was going to see Aix again, that we would make it back home to Aunt Inese, that she deserved to see me. He says he always knew I'd live. I'm not sure he really did. Even now, *I* can't believe I made it. I'd lost so much blood. And it's a miracle infection didn't take me, even with all that Aunt Inese did. Jean came often to help. He took over the farm bookkeeping, became my liaison in my business dealings since I could hardly go myself."

Celeste's hand found its way into mine. I started at her touch and looked down into her beautiful eyes. Her expression wasn't coy. She didn't bat her lashes at me like girls in my past life had occasionally done when they'd found an excuse to touch me. Not that she was giving me a sisterly look, but it was clear her intention was only to comfort me.

"I'm sorry about distrusting Jean," she said simply. "It seems he was a true friend to you. Thank you for telling me." She paused and looked up at my good eye, as though trying to see me more clearly. "But Henri, you were a hero. Why don't people know?"

I stared down at the book I'd chosen. It was difficult to think with her so close to me, but I finally found my voice again. "Jean was the hero. And he was smarter about it."

She opened her mouth, likely to disagree, but caught herself and instead said, "And after all that happened to you, I've never heard you curse the English or act violently. In Marseille, it seems I never hear a negative phrase that doesn't slander England."

I was glad I hadn't told her any more about killing the nine men. It still haunted me that I'd had to do it. And I didn't want her withdrawing her hand. Her gentle grip kept me in the present, pulling me away from those hellish memories. "I've known some good Englishmen," I said. "Merchants and gentlemen I'd met before all this. I was unlucky enough to come across a group of the worst sort. I wish I could say no Frenchmen ever behaved as they did."

She smiled sadly. "I think you did the right thing that night, Henri." She stood on her toes and kissed me gently on my scarred cheek. Aunt Inese had kissed me the same way hundreds of times, but I didn't feel anything like I did when my aunt bade me goodnight.

Her hand squeezed mine once before she released me and moved away. She paused to look over her shoulder at me. I wanted to reach out and feel if her hair was as soft as it looked, but my mind still clung to some semblance of sense.

"And I think you were very brave," she whispered before slipping out of the room.

I stood frozen for a long time. I don't know what reaction I expected out of Celeste, but it had not been that. Almost no one purposefully touched me. And she had more than once reached out to me in the last month. I stood staring at the book in my hand a long time before realizing it was a collection of fairy tales.

I shook my head. I'd thought for so long that I needed a heroine out of a story book to fix my problems. I wasn't able to form it into words exactly, but as I stood thinking about Celeste, I began to wonder if I didn't care about her more than I cared about my problems. And it had nothing to do with how pretty she looked in her new glasses.

"What are you doing in here half-naked?" Aunt Inese demanded from the doorway.

I snatched my shirt from the chair where I'd thrown it and quickly put it on. "I was looking at my scars," I said, shrugging my shoulders and wishing she wouldn't say anything else. I'd spent the better part of four months without a shirt on when I'd first been healing, and she hadn't criticized me over it then.

"Alone?"

I didn't say anything, and Aunt Inese smiled a little too knowingly. "Well, I'm looking for Celeste. You don't know where she's gone, do you?"

I shook my head, but when my aunt spun on her heel, I waited a moment and then followed her at a distance. She went directly to the kitchen. I stood in the dining room and eavesdropped shamelessly.

CHAPTER 12

Celeste

"Celeste. You're supposed to be preparing yourself," Inese scolded when she found me in the kitchen. "And instead you're working your fingers to the bone."

I laughed with good humor. "Suzanne wouldn't even let me touch the wash water," I assured Inese. "You two are in league with each other." It was a good thing Suzanne hadn't asked me to do anything near the oven. I was still a little dazed from my encounter with Henri, and it would have been dangerous.

Inese folded her arms across her chest and gave me a stern look. I couldn't help grinning. She was so sweet. "She's only teaching me to make meringue. Come taste this with me."

"*Celeste.* You must fit into your corset tomorrow. There will be scores of men wanting to meet you. You can eat as much meringue as you want after we get back. Come, let's finish deciding on your hair. Won't you help us, Suzanne? We can have bread and cheese for dinner."

"I'd enjoy that, Madame," Suzanne said. It sounded as though she meant it.

"I'll be right along," I said. "We need time for the curling rods anyway."

Aunt Inese gasped and swept out of the kitchen, calling back over her shoulder, "I still have to find them. I haven't used them in years."

I shook my head at her determination to transform me into her version of my best self. I turned happily back to the plate of meringues.

"She told you not to eat those," Suzanne warned.

I hurriedly popped one in my mouth before she could stop me. "Are you serious?" I asked in outrage around a bite of heaven. "I'm not about to give these up simply because my friends want to dress me up like a doll. As sweet of her as it is, *I'm* not delusional. *I've* been to at least a hundred dances. Men don't look twice at girls like me, Suzanne. And I intend to thoroughly enjoy myself regardless." I laughed, but Suzanne gave me a sharp look, so I must not have been successful at keeping the edge out of it.

A new voice cut in. "She doesn't understand about the magic, Suzanne."

I spun to see Carine standing in the door to the kitchen garden. Her children stood at her side, looking up at her in confusion a moment before their eyes were drawn to the plates of meringues on the table. The desire and longing on their faces was so raw that I had to keep from laughing.

"I don't think she actually believes in magic," Suzanne said stiffly. "That's heretical." She turned to the children, her expression softening. "Would you two help me see if I baked these long enough?"

Marie and Martin actually jumped forward at the invitation.

"If the cinders girl can get a pair of glass slippers from a fairy godmother," Carine said, her fists on her waist, "how can you not see the magic in a pair of eye glasses from your fairy eye doctor?"

I snorted, and Suzanne actually laughed.

"I'm sure Monsieur Vrai would enjoy the comparison," I said, pressing a meringue into Carine's hand. It must have been ages since she'd had something sweet, and I was certain Suzanne took note of the sheer pleasure on her face as she popped it in her mouth.

"You'd better come with us," Suzanne told Carine grudgingly. "Madame wishes to have help bullying Celeste into looking her best."

Carine agreed quickly, overly anxious to enjoy my pain, and instructed her children to play in the yard. My friends completely ignored my protests and hurried me away from the kitchen and those incredible meringues. We passed Henri in the hallway. He sent a guilty glance in our direction. He was probably headed to the kitchen to sneak meringues, although it may have been equally likely that he'd finally realized that he had stripped off his clothing in front of me not half an hour before.

I turned to say something to Carine as we passed him, just so that I could hide my blush. It had been highly inappropriate of him, though he hadn't seemed to realize it at the time. He'd expected me to be horrified by his scars, I'm sure, but who could take note of scars when there was so much musculature demanding attention? My gawking had been inexcusable. I'd probably had the same look on my face as Marie and Martin had when they saw the plates of goodies Suzanne had made.

In all fairness, I don't think it was *completely* my fault. I'd never seen anything like his chest and arms. Isabelle was decidedly wrong. It was a *very* good thing for a man to work outside sometimes. I hoped he thought I was only staring at his scars. They had been impressive, of course, and they'd made me want to cry, thinking of what he'd gone through. But they certainly couldn't keep my attention when compared to what was underneath them.

There'd been so many things I wanted to say to him about

128

what he'd shared, but I couldn't keep my eyes, *or my hands for that matter*, where they belonged. I hoped he hadn't mistaken the meaning of the little kiss I'd given him. My lips had tingled after they'd brushed his skin, and I'd had to practically run to the kitchen to make an excuse for my fierce blush and racing heart.

I spent the next few hours in Inese's room having my hair pulled and heated, but my friends didn't seem to require my opinion, so I hardly paid attention to their conversation over the latest hairstyles in Paris and Marseille. I thought instead about how wrongly I'd judged Jean and about the nightmare Henri Durant had lived. I wondered how he even survived what he'd been through, even with his obvious strength.

But mostly I thought about the way my mind and body reacted to Henri's physical presence. I finally allowed myself to really think about my feelings for my temporary employer. They were not what they should have been, especially considering his aversion to me. I should have only considered him in light of my duty to improve his household, to repay as much of my father's debt to him as possible. When I'd first met him in his parlor, I'd found him hostile and annoying, but now... things were... different.

Henri was utterly ridiculous sometimes, but something had changed, and I don't think it was him. I couldn't help being attracted to him. He was interesting, of course. A mystery unfolding. But it was more than that. I'd met plenty of mysterious people through some of Father's more questionable business dealings.

Henri was kind and attractive. But that couldn't really explain it either. Bertram was kind and attractive, but he didn't make my knees go weak just by standing next to me. And his smile didn't affect me the way Henri's uneven grin did.

I couldn't even pinpoint the time when my understanding and viewpoint of him had changed. It had happened too gradually. I thought back over everything he'd ever said to me, every gesture, and every inflection of his voice. There was nothing there to suggest I was anything but a nuisance to him. He was polite. Usually. When he wasn't knocking me down or disparaging my appearance. But he'd made it very plain he didn't want me here, that I was only saving a place for my sister.

"Celeste?"

"Yes?" I shook myself, realizing Suzanne must have said my name a few times before I heard her.

"What do you think?"

I prepared to feign enthusiasm and turned toward the mirror. "It looks very nice," I said.

Suzanne and Carine broke into unrestrained laughter, and Inese said drily, "That is Madame Bochard, not the mirror. Why don't you try with your glasses on?"

"Oh. Yes, of course."

I patted my pocket and peered around me a moment before Carine said, "Here."

"Put them on," Suzanne insisted.

I was pleased my friends were getting along well, even if it was over my hair. Once my glasses were on, I could see they wore identical excited smiles, unusual for each of them. I couldn't help smiling back at them until Inese firmly took my shoulders and turned me to the mirror.

A girl stared back at me with startled eyes. Out of habit formed of near blindness, I leaned closer, even though I could see myself perfectly well. Inese had adjusted my corset and hip pads so that I barely recognized the green polonaise. While hardly comfortable, the effect on my figure was striking. She'd also changed the overskirts to give them more lift, and I wondered if she'd been studying the fashion plates as closely as Isabelle did. It was now a gown my sister would have been happy to wear, though she certainly would have arranged to show more décolletage. As it was, I almost blushed at the amount of skin showing without the modest neckerchief I usually wore. My hair was almost unrecognizable, pulled up to a modest height, with glossy, luxurious curls cascading to one side. I'd never had it fashioned so beautifully.

"Suzanne," I breathed. "You were right about heresy. We'd better send for the priest."

"What?" said Inese. "Why?"

"Because Monsieur Vrai and Madame Sauveterre need to go to confession. He *is* a fairy eye doctor, and *she* has a magic mirror."

∾

Henri

T he entire evening was punctuated by half-hysterical laughter coming from the direction of Aunt Inese's room. I recognized Aunt's chuckle and Celeste's hearty laugh, but worried over what strangers had been brought to the house. I finally decided one of them might be Suzanne, and then Paul arrived and cleared up the rest of my concern by asking, red-faced, if Carine was still there. Another outbreak of laughter was heard overhead, and Paul smiled. "She is. Would it be all right if I waited for her to come down?"

I indicated a chair and offered him a drink, which he refused.

"Jacques and I have decided to carry our muskets with us when we walk to your fields," Paul announced unexpectedly.

I gave him a long look. "Bandits?"

"I've only seen one man. At a distance. He was too well-dressed to be a bandit."

"There are more?"

"We don't know. We've seen one set of horse prints and one set of footprints, but we can't be sure there aren't more. He seems to be watching the house."

"A more sophisticated thief, perhaps. He may know we're leaving tomorrow."

Paul nodded. "That is my guess. I worry for Carine as well. She carries a knife, but that will do her little good against a man such as that."

"I wonder if we could convince her to move here and work full-time. With a little work, we could make the empty rooms in the servants' wing almost as comfortable as her house. She could let out that property."

"You might be able to convince her."

"Me? Not Aunt Inese?"

"Carine worries the children would be a bother to you."

I grunted. They would be a bother, but that didn't mean they weren't welcome.

"Could I ask you to watch the house for me tomorrow while we're gone? It would be better for it to look inhabited. I wouldn't like Suzanne to be here alone." On a stroke of inspiration, I added, "As a matter of fact, I think I'll invite Carine too. She would be good company for Suzanne, and it would be better for appearances to have another woman here if you and Jacques will be here."

Paul nodded, but he couldn't mask the healthy dose of anticipation in his eyes. "I will keep Jacques out of your brandy. I'm afraid he's just discovered there are other things to drink aside from water and beer."

"Thank you."

"Enjoy yourself tomorrow," Paul said, his eyes now fixed on the window. "It has been too long since you joined society."

"Thank you," I said, much less graciously than before. The reality of what I'd agreed to do was already pressing on me. I hadn't been in society for two years, and I dreaded the likely revulsion on the faces of the people I'd once known.

He smirked, obviously unworried by my irritation. I didn't get a chance to tell him where he could put his concerns over my welfare, because Carine appeared on the stairs a moment later, her children in tow. Her smile widened when she saw Paul.

"Good evening, Carine," he said, his tone gentler than usual. "I found evidence of a stranger camping near here. I've come to see if I can walk you and the children back home when you're ready."

Carine blushed. "Thank you, Paul. That is very kind of you."

I quickly extended my own invitation and explained, "I would like Suzanne to have company, and it would give you and the children a chance to see if you like the rooms we have available for you."

Carine fixed her gaze on me. "Are you certain, Monsieur Durant?"

"Don't be silly, Carine," I said awkwardly. "We can't do without your help anymore. Your children are very welcome. And when we were little, you always called me Henri, remember?"

"I will be sure to come escort you back here tomorrow," Paul offered. "And Jacques and I plan to guard the house while Henri is gone."

"I'm sure that would make Suzanne and I feel safe," she said quietly.

Little Marie studied Paul a moment, her head tilted to the side and her golden curls spilling onto her shoulder. "Are you a prince too, Monsieur Fontaine?"

Paul grinned. "Why would you ask such a question, my fifille?"

Marie ignored her mother's shushing and pointed at me. "*He's* one," she said simply.

Carine's eyes widened.

"A common misconception," I said drily.

Paul chortled. "I think someone has been sneaking peeks at Monsieur Durant's sword, hmm?"

Martin's eyes suddenly shone with excitement.

"Thanks," I said under my breath to Paul.

I settled onto one knee in front of Marie. "If I show you and your brother my sword, will you promise to tell no one where it is?" It was actually quite valuable, with rubies on the hilt and a blade of the finest steel. It *was* something a prince would be proud to carry.

They both nodded solemnly.

"And will you believe me when I tell you that I have *never* been a prince? I wasn't even an important officer, only a sergeant, but I did use my father's sword in battle, and it is an impressive weapon."

Marie frowned, evidently disappointed not to know a royal, but Martin nodded excitedly. "Do you mind staying a few more minutes, Carine?" I asked.

"Not at all, Monsieur Durant. And thank you." Not Henri. Not everyone was like Celeste. No one was like Celeste.

It took thirty minutes before I could make myself tear Paul and Martin away from my sword. I had to show Martin how to hold it and keep him from accidentally hurting himself or Paul, who had bravely offered to be his opponent with a broomstick.

Carine's eyes hardly left Paul, and when she said it was time they should leave, Paul offered his arm to her and his free hand to Marie. "If we're attacked by bandits, Martin can protect us," he said.

I waved them off, feeling oddly lighthearted until I made my way to the kitchen. It was deserted with no sign of dinner preparations. My stomach growled loudly. A plateful of meringues sat on the counter. I liked Suzanne's meringues, but I really wanted supper. My wishing must have made a difference, because Suzanne appeared at the door.

"Eat your supper before dessert, Monsieur," she said distractedly as she opened the pantry door. She put a chicken leg on a plate, placed it on the table with a small loaf of bread, and then nodded at me before turning away.

"Suzanne," I protested. "This isn't dinner?"

"She's too busy for dinner, Henri," Aunt Inese said, entering the room and helping assemble three more plates onto trays.

"Am I dining alone?"

My aunt smiled at me fondly. "It won't hurt you this once, and we're far too busy with Celeste."

"What does our housekeeper have to do with this?" I asked, a smile tugging at my lips.

Aunt Inese made a face at me. "Now Henri. I've never had a daughter. You are my only family. I couldn't ask for better. But I never get to dress up a girl."

I imagined Celeste dressed as a seventy-year-old woman. Poor girl. She already hadn't had good experiences at dances. I shouldn't know that, of course, since I was eavesdropping when I heard her say it. I think I understood what she'd meant. By herself, Celeste wasn't ill-looking, but if she had to go every-where in the shadow of her beautiful sister, it could dampen her ability to attract dance partners. She was sure to have a better time at the dance without her sister there, and she'd certainly enjoy it more than I would. I'd be lucky not to be thrown from the building.

Suzanne left with one tray, but my aunt paused at the door. "I like Celeste. Very much. And since you are sending her away soon, I want to enjoy the time I have with her." She gave me a meaningful look and spun away.

I thought of Celeste, as I know Auntie intended me to. Would her father really come soon? The second month was half-finished, and while I knew I should be looking forward to the arrival of her sister, I was no longer anxious for Celeste to leave. Beyond that, my feelings were so muddled, I could hardly understand them. I could acknowledge that I'd been mistaken about her in several ways. She was sweet, capable, compassionate, and pretty. She saw things about people that others missed. She'd brought nothing but improvement to my home. And to me. And I was happy when I was with her.

It was this last thought that sent me to my study to brood over what was to be done. I forgot my supper until hours later when Suzanne brought it to me, wondering if there was something wrong with it.

"No, Suzanne, I'm sorry. I became distracted."

I ate, hardly tasting my food. I heard Celeste's tread in the hallway, but I couldn't bring myself to face her. I was such a coward.

The next day I woke resolved. Monsieur Lebeau thought he had tricked me, but he had really tricked his own daughter. He would see where that would get him.

CHAPTER 13

Celeste

T he next morning after breakfast I returned to my room to pack the small traveling case I'd brought with me from Marseille. The drive to town took an hour, so Inese planned for us to stay the night at an inn on the outskirts of Aix after the dance. I think her insistence had more to do with her wanting to spend time in town and less to do with how exhausted she'd be in early morning when the dance ended. But she'd also said a strange man had been spotted near the château, so I was pleased we wouldn't be traveling in the dark. I turned the corner into my own hallway, but stopped short.

Standing outside my door were two large buckets, both overflowing with lavender. I stared a full minute before accepting that they truly had been placed there for me, and that the only person who would have done it was Henri. A silly grin spread across my face, and my heart seemed to raise up a few inches in my chest.

A small piece of paper was tucked between some stems. In blocky print were the words, "*For finding the errors and balancing everything in the other accounts."* He must have forgiven me for accusing his friend of dishonesty.

I pulled the buckets into my room and, embarrassingly enough, twirled a few circles in sheer delight. Someone had given *me* flowers. Armloads of them.

I snuck back to my room to look at them three times during the course of the day. In between I did a little accounting and helped Suzanne plan the menu for the next month. Inese wouldn't let me near the gardens, certain I'd spoil my nails.

"Celeste?" Inese called.

"Coming." I'd been admiring my flowers again. I snatched up some hairpins and found my needle and thread. On my way back out of my room, I pulled a handful of lavender stems to take with me. I had to find a way to wear them.

"Good idea," she said approvingly when I found her. "That will complement the brooch I want you to wear."

I did not find it necessary to explain how I'd come by the lavender. I also didn't find it necessary to begin dressing three hours before we were to leave, but Inese had other ideas.

She was very particular about helping me dress my hair. "I know your eyes are much complimented, dear," she said. "But your hair is perfection. Soft and wavy, responds well to the curling rods, and so thick. I would've never known when you first came. You kept it pulled back so tightly."

"It's easier to work without your hair in your face," I said as I fixed lavender to my hairpins.

"Yes. That's the problem. You've been working too hard."

I shrugged. "You've been short-staffed, so there's been a lot of work to do."

"And you know I appreciate it. But today is not for working. Today is for enjoyment. And we, my dear, are going to enjoy ourselves." She smiled so happily that I simply couldn't point out that even with the transformation she'd accomplished, I'd still be an average sort of pretty compared to the handful of beauties that were sure to be there. Still, that was a far better comparison than could usually be said of me, so I only smiled back and handed pins to her.

When I finished helping her with her own hair (a popular style Isabelle made me learn so she wouldn't suffer when we didn't have the money to pay a hairdresser), she said, "Now get your wrap, Celeste, and we'll go down together."

Suzanne and Carine arrived at that moment to exclaim over my appearance, and I smiled widely at them. They were worse than my friend, Nicole, telling me I was beautiful. The silly things. I knew what beautiful was. I'd had to stare at it most of my life. But today, I did feel *attractive*. Truly.

I hugged them lightly. If I'd squeezed them and spun them around as I wanted to, Inese would have had a fit about my hair.

I hurried to my room but took time to inhale the scent of lavender. I stopped in front of the mirror to check my earrings, but it was really just an excuse to see once more that I, Celeste Lebeau, could, in fact, be pretty. My eyes were bright, certainly. And the curls flowing from my coiffure felt silky against my neck. The green polonaise was now even more elegant with the brooch Inese had practically forced me to borrow. I sighed happily and wandered back out and around the corner. Inese stood close by, her nephew at her shoulder. They both faced away from me, talking to Maurice, who already wore his blue livery.

"Don't you look lovely, Mademoiselle Lebeau," Maurice said pleasantly.

"Thank you, Maurice," I said. And I meant it. No man had ever actually spoken those words in sincerity to me, and I found them very pleasing, even if Maurice was old enough to be my grandfather. No wonder Isabelle was so vain. She heard those words several times each day from several different men.

"I'll have the carriage ready in a few minutes," he promised Inese.

Henri had stood very still, his back to me, but he nodded to Maurice as he passed by him. Finally Henri turned to speak to his aunt. "I took out the bags already, Aunt Inese. Are you—" He stopped short when he saw me. His lips actually parted in surprise. "Celeste." His gaze took in my hair, my face, and my neck before snapping back to my eyes. I couldn't be sure, but I thought he blushed a little. "You look—"

"Ravishing," Bertram announced as he walked up behind Henri. "I've never seen you look prettier. I see your new glasses will allow your admirers to be even more charmed by your beautiful eyes."

"Don't be silly, Bertram," I said. "But you can be sure I will tell anyone who notices my glasses what a wonderful job you did."

He grinned at me and made a little bow. Henri glared at Bertram and turned purposefully away. The bubble of excitement in my chest popped, causing my heart and stomach to sink several inches.

"Are you joining us in the carriage?" I asked Bertram, furious with myself for letting Henri's rudeness affect me. Had I expected him to fall at my feet in adoration?

"No. I'm afraid carriages make me quite ill. My only fault, I assure you. I shall ride along the side. I just came to make sure you actually—"

"Where are your gloves, Celeste?" Inese broke in.

Henri stopped studying the wall and turned back to me again. I couldn't break eye contact with him for some exceptionally stupid reason. He watched me, waiting.

"Oh. I decided I didn't want to wear any," I finally managed.

"What? Don't be silly, Celeste. You can't go without gloves."

I finally tore my gaze away from Henri and answered Inese. "I hope that is not the case, because I simply didn't bring any gloves with me from Marseille aside from the pair that match my traveling gown. I had no idea I would want them."

Inese turned on the spot, searching the air as though gloves would materialize. "You can't wear my extras. They won't fit."

She did have very small hands.

She turned to glare at Henri. "Well?" she demanded.

Henri folded his arms across his chest and returned her stare a moment before muttering, "Very well." He produced a ring of keys from inside his vest and walked away from us. For a moment, I thought he was leaving, but he stopped at the door two down from Inese's room. The locked door. The one he didn't want to have cleaned. He disappeared inside for three minutes while Bertram made idle conversation.

I was too curious to pay much attention to Bertram. Inese tapped her foot impatiently. I even thought I heard her swear under her breath, but I must have been mistaken. She was too refined to slip as I occasionally did.

When Henri appeared again, Inese flew at him, snatching something out of his hands and hurrying to me with them. Henri followed, looking troubled.

"Borrow these," she insisted.

I accepted the white fabric from her outstretched hands and instantly saw they were gloves, the prettiest, softest gloves I'd ever seen. Not even Isabelle had any this nice. I slipped them over my hands and looked more closely. Tiny sprigs of lavender were stitched in a line from the outside of the wrist up to the elbow.

"Oh," I breathed. "Thank you for letting me use these, Henri."

Henri mumbled something indiscernible, and Bertram shook his head and sent Henri a fierce glare.

I didn't understand their behavior, but I was too distracted by the pretty gloves to care. I finally took them off, folded them carefully, and placed them in my handbag. I did wonder why Henri had such fine ladies' accessories. He'd never been married. Inese had told me that. And they couldn't have been his mother's. They were too new. But I was too caught up in feeling like a princess to think too long about where another bit of magic had come from.

"Come along. We'll be late," Inese said, shooing us all through the hall, down the stairs, and out into the courtyard where Maurice waited with the carriage.

Bertram moved to hand Inese and me in, but Henri waved him off. "Go get that devil of a horse before he hurts himself."

Bertram's roan stallion was rearing and pulling at his tether. Bertram gave me a jaunty grin and ran off to wrestle his horse.

Henri handed Inese in, but instead of taking the forward-facing seat, she settled herself on the front seat and spread out her ample skirts. "You don't mind, my dears? This fabric wrinkles dreadfully, and I hoped to nap all the way there."

Henri still hadn't said a word to me since I'd come out of my room this afternoon, and I chanced a look at him, wondering if he'd be angry that he had to sit next to me the entire drive. His frown spoke volumes, but he offered me his hand to help me into the carriage. I took his hand but hesitated, suddenly anxious. What would I do at a dance without my sister's shadow to hide behind?

Henri

When I took Celeste's hand to help her into the carriage, she froze. I almost jerked my hand away, thinking that I had repulsed her. But Celeste had never been disgusted by my defects before, and besides, she didn't look disgusted. She seemed almost...nervous? Celeste was never nervous. Irritated, yes. Angry or defensive, yes. Never nervous. But there it was.

Without thinking, I put my hand to the back of her waist and nudged her gently toward the carriage. "Did I mention you look beautiful?" I murmured quietly enough that Aunt Inese wouldn't hear.

Her gaze snapped to me. She really did have the most incredible eyes. They widened a fraction, and her lips parted. I had the most irrational desire to pull her toward me and kiss her. It had been over two years since the last real kiss I'd had. I would have blamed the feeling on that, but I couldn't. Celeste was fascinating. And irresistible. My hand tightened around her waist.

She was immediately saved by Bertram, who called out something inane. I didn't even hear the words, but it was enough to break the connection that pulled us closer together. Bertram had the most ill-favored sense of timing.

I handed Celeste in while Bertram watched us in confusion. He must have asked a question. I glared at him before jumping into the carriage.

Aunt Inese had already arranged her skirts across the front seat, and Celeste sat very properly on her side of the other. I threw myself onto the bench as far away from her as possible. She was doing strange things to my self-control. To my reason and logic. I told myself that it had simply been too long since I had spent time around young women. But I knew that wasn't it. I almost wished my aunt wasn't already falling asleep against her cushion.

We sat in silence for the first mile while Celeste gazed out the window and I snuck glances at her. I don't know why I'd ever thought she wasn't pretty. Granted, her old glasses had been ugly, and the way she used to pull her hair back so tightly kept its beauty from showing, but I still shouldn't have ever considered her plain, much less told her she was. I remembered my behavior with a sharp pang of embarrassment, wondering if she still thought ill of me for it.

Another thing I'd noticed about Celeste immediately after she joined Aunt Inese and me only minutes before was that she had a startlingly feminine figure. I knew she was a woman. I wasn't a complete idiot. But she appeared far more curvaceous than I'd ever realized. It had taken all my effort not to rake her over with my gaze when I'd seen her. And *I* was responsible for keeping her safe.

"Are you sure that neckline is altogether appropriate?" I asked without thinking. It came out waspish and accusatory. I almost clamped my hand over my mouth.

She turned toward me with a look of outraged disgust. "Why, of all the horrid, barbaric things to say," she whispered, snatching up her wrap and holding it to her neck. "*You'd* have an inappropriate neckline too if Inese had cinched *you* into this corset so tightly that you could hardly breathe."

Her eyes immediately widened, and she snapped her mouth shut. I would have thought she'd regretted her words if she hadn't then raised her chin and immediately turned away again. "As a matter of fact, I'd like to see you try it on for size," she muttered.

Oh. Pretty and proper Celeste was new, but mouthy and sarcastic Celeste I thought I understood better. "Are you offering to take it off?" I immediately countered.

She spun to face me again. "I ought to slap you," she cried in a whisper.

I couldn't help laughing at her then. She tilted her chin up, but her mouth trembled and then she laughed too. She put her hand over her mouth to muffle the sound. "You are horrible, Monsieur Durant," she said once she'd gotten it under control. "How dare you make me laugh like that when Inese is sleeping?"

"She wouldn't wake up unless the carriage overturned," I said, still smiling. It was so easy to smile around Celeste. "She once slept through a slightly drunken quartet sung by Bertram, Maurice, Paul, and Jacques. It was louder than an avalanche."

"I don't believe you."

"You should. Look, I'll show you." I opened my mouth wide,

intending to break into a very loud ballad, but Celeste flung herself at me, pressing her hand firmly over my mouth before I'd gotten out the first note.

"She deserves her sleep, Henri," she whispered.

Several pieces of information assaulted my mind simultaneously. First, and most difficult to ignore, Celeste was flush against my side, and her warmth was already seeping through my jacket. Aside from our occasional awkward collisions, she had never been this close to me, and certainly not on purpose. Second, her hand smelled of soap and lavender. Third, I could feel each one of her slender fingers pressing against my lips and face. They were the same fingers that moments before had been pressed against her own lips. And lastly, when I turned to look at her, our noses were only inches apart.

The sauciness faded from her eyes, and her fingers slackened their pressure and fell away from my mouth to rest gently at my collar. I almost thought her eyes flickered to my lips, but I wasn't sure, mostly because I was too busy noticing the way her lips were slightly parted. Heaven help me, but I wanted to kiss her so badly that it was overwhelming my logic and common sense.

We leaned a little toward each other just as Aunt Inese startled in her sleep. I immediately spun toward the front of the carriage as Celeste spun away to look out the window. Once I was sure Aunt Inese was sleeping again, I snuck a glance at Celeste. I admired the way her expression didn't bear the slightest hint about what we'd been doing...had almost done. Only her faster breathing gave her away.

The next hour was torturous. We spoke occasionally, and I loved hearing her voice. But mostly, I watched her. I watched the way her hands moved when she adjusted her handbag. I watched the line of her eyelashes against the light from the window. I especially watched the curve of her neck when she turned to look out at the passing countryside. No matter how frequently I reminded myself about what her father had done or what an idiot I was, I still couldn't keep my gaze away from her for long. I don't think she ever noticed, but as we neared Aix, I quickly looked away from her for the hundredth time only to find Aunt Inese's smug eyes on me.

Unless she spoke, I didn't let myself look at Celeste again until we reached the dance. I didn't want to disappoint my aunt, and I knew she loved Celeste. I just didn't see how it could possibly work.

Celeste pulled out her little handbag and gently unfolded the gloves she'd placed there. I think her eyes actually sparkled when she pulled them on. They were nice gloves, I suppose, but I resented them covering up her elegant hands. And I cursed the room they came from. How was I to ever put that problem right?

It was still light out when we arrived. I wished for the anonymity of darkness, but I was going to have to face my former friends and acquaintances with the light of the early summer evening still streaming through the windows. My jaw began to hurt, and I stopped clenching it.

I helped both women out of the carriage. It was difficult to not pull Celeste into my arms once her hand was in mine. It might have been easier if she hadn't been so radiant. Whatever anxieties she'd felt before had somehow faded during the carriage ride, and now she turned in a full circle, excitement in her eyes. She was thrilled to be there, exactly opposite of how I felt.

Celeste and my aunt admired the stately building and the fountain in the square. When they turned back to me, Aunt Inese put her hands on her hips. "Henri, my dear, if you look so threatening and angry, you will offend all our friends."

An open carriage stopped just behind ours, and a steel-haired woman called out to Inese, who dropped her glare and returned the greeting. "Behave yourself," she whispered to me before hurrying to her friend.

Celeste watched me with an odd expression, one that made me think she could see right through my bristly demeanor. "She's right," Celeste finally said with a lofty toss of her head. "You're going to have to adjust that cravat. What *will* Inese's friends say?" she said with a completely quelling expression. "Perfectly hoydenish."

I grunted a laugh and immediately fixed my face into a stern stare.

She took a step nearer and looked me over blatantly. "The length of your breeches is far too daring for tonight, you know," she whispered, shaking her head. "All the little debutantes are sure to make much of that. I suppose you don't care, but think of your aunt."

"Celeste," I warned.

She didn't look the least bit repentant. "And look. Your aunt has already gone in, and you haven't even offered me your arm."

Startled, I turned toward the entry. Aunt Inese disappeared into the building with her friend, purposefully leaving me to escort Celeste inside.

"I suppose you're waiting for *me* to offer you *my* arm?" Celeste asked, her eyebrows arched.

I automatically raised my arm, which she took daintily.

"And don't you dare look like a hostile uncle, or no one will ask me to dance."

"I suppose you plan on flirting with every man in the room?" I grumbled as we walked forward.

"At least half of them," she murmured back. "I need the practice. I don't think I've ever done any flirting before."

"Aunt Inese should have warned *you* to behave," I said.

"Oh, I fully intend to behave myself with the utmost care."

"No doubt."

We reached the door, and servants took my coat and

Celeste's wrap and ushered us into the ballroom. They gave me curious glances but otherwise were too professional to gawk. The rest of the company certainly wouldn't think it necessary to give me the same courtesy. I tensed as we moved forward again.

I managed a terse, "Good evening," to our hosts before turning to face the crowd. Celeste's grip on my arm was almost painful, but it was obviously excitement, not nerves, that had her nails digging into my flesh. Neither her happiness, nor the pain of my practically bleeding arm could distract me from noticing the sea of faces that turned to stare in surprise, and probably a little horror, at me.

They should have noticed the extraordinary girl next to me, but they weren't looking at her. If she had been her sister, that may have been different. Why had I ever thought it was necessary to come here?

"I think they're all looking at your shamefully inappropriate waistcoat," Celeste whispered with a brilliant smile that contradicted her words. "I told you not to cinch yourself up so tight."

CHAPTER 14

Celeste

Henri coughed twice. Either he was choking or trying not to laugh. I thought them equally likely. He didn't like to be stared at. No one did, except maybe Isabelle. Henri needed to be distracted, and Bertram was stabling his horse at home, only a few minutes' walk away.

I pushed some smugness into my smile. "Can you imagine what horrible manners they have? It's an *outrage*. There's nothing for it except..."

"Except what?" he muttered.

"You're going to have to ask me to dance."

"What?" His annoyed tone was belied by a deep note of amusement.

"I suppose you want *me* to ask *you*?" I said. "Well, I won't. I don't care *that* much about keeping your hoydenish appearance from being the talk of the entire night. You're just going to have to own up to your choice of dress. The sooner everyone gets a good look at it, the sooner they'll all get over it and start gossiping about someone else." I might have been a little obvious, but he'd looked ready to bolt a moment ago. "And I would appreciate it if you would position us in the line so I can see as many of the young men as possible."

"You are the most irritating little minx I've ever met. You know that, don't you?" he said in a low voice.

"Why, I'd be delighted, Monsieur Durant," I said loudly with the sweetest smile I could manage. "I do love a gavotte."

He muttered under his breath as he led me to join the other couples lining up for the dance. Wide skirts shifted as women turned to gaze at us and whisper to each other, their tall hair arrangements threatening to topple over as they bent their heads. I idly wondered if some were actually of the nobility, considering quality of the silks and brocades they wore. Inese had claimed there would be only prominent citizens, local leaders, and businessmen. At Henri's side, I could hardly care who they were.

I chatted animatedly at him and treated his gloomy looks as though he was in the best of humor. He may have guessed my attitude was an attempt to cast him in a better light among his peers, and I *would* have been cheerful for that reason alone. I was desperate for people to understand his goodness. But mostly, at that particular moment, I just wanted to dance with him, be with him, have an excuse to look at him. I didn't have to fake my happy mood.

There was no question that Henri was an attractive man. I very much suspected that only about half the looks he was getting had something to do with his scarring. There would certainly be a good handful of girls who were smart enough to see beyond them to his broad shoulders, strong build, and handsome features. And, of course, there would be others who wouldn't care about his looks at all simply because he was a successful landholder whose family held a prominent place in the economic history of the area. Those were the people I'd need to share him with tonight. Toward them I felt mild jealousy, even though I knew I shouldn't covet what wasn't mine.

But the others... I glanced around at the crowd. Several people watched him with open disgust and haughty disdain, and I'd seen a couple women cross themselves when we first arrived. Toward them I felt an almost overwhelming desire to do physical harm. The nasty bunch of suspicious, uneducated swine. They were only scars, for pity sakes, and he earned them honorably.

I caught back my glare as the music started. Shamefully enough, when we began the dance, I forgot all about that and everything else and simply enjoyed being close to Henri. His good eye was so blue, and the half-smile he gave me when I harped at him was one of the most breathtaking sights in the world. When he looked at me like that, I could almost believe he *had* been about to kiss me in the carriage.

I suppose I'd known for a few weeks already, but on this night, dancing among the curious and hostile crowd around us, I could finally admit to myself what was really going on. His touch made my heart feel funny, and when he laughed, I wanted to shout with happiness. I craved his attention, my thoughts were never far from him, and I was never so content as when I was in his company. There was no other explanation. I was completely and pathetically in love with Henri Durant.

And I was one of the biggest fools in the world. Henri might have finally accepted me as his friend, but to expect reciprocation of my feelings... He'd made it only too clear that I was an unwelcome guest and an inconvenient little pest.

And yet I had hope. I could make him laugh. And Inese had told me multiple times that was almost impossible to do.

"You know, they seem to be looking less at your cravat."

He raised an eyebrow in my direction.

"But I think it is only because so many of them are now noticing that your trousers are too tight."

Henri snorted under his breath, as close to a laugh as I could expect in public, though I didn't intend to stop trying. He had a marvelous laugh.

"Haven't I already apologized for my behavior?"

"No, you haven't."

"Well, in that case, I'm sorry."

"For what you said or for taking so long to apologize?"

"Celeste," Henri protested quietly.

I smiled and gave a friendly wave to Madeleine, a pleasant, raven-haired girl I'd briefly met in a shop in town weeks before. She smiled uncertainly back from her position in the dance, apparently intimidated by my dance partner.

It was such little encouragement, from either of them, Madeleine's smile and his willingness to dance with me. Still, I felt my resolve grow. If Henri Durant didn't care for me by the time my father came, it wouldn't be for lack of an attempt to win him. And if he wasn't at least marginally popular in the town of Aix by then, it wouldn't be because I hadn't put enthusiasm into the task.

When the dance ended, I regretfully allowed Henri to drop my hand so we could applaud the musicians. Inese swooped in on us with one of her friends before I could decide what to do next.

"Celeste, dear, there are so many young men I must introduce you to. And Henri, you remember my friend, Andine?"

"Madame Colbert." Henri bowed politely to the woman Inese had met outside. She was steel-haired and dripping in jewels, her brown satin sack-back gown fanning out behind her.

The music began again.

"I haven't been invited to dance in years," Madame Colbert said, a stern frown at her lips as she looked him over. "What with my Matthieu's health problems. But Inese assures me that you are as fine a dancer as ever."

I almost laughed aloud.

"Come, Celeste," Inese said, leading me away. "Henri can dance with Andine while the young men vie for your attention. And don't worry, I've already assured some of them that you are not spoken for. Word will spread quickly."

I looked back over my shoulder at Henri as I followed Inese. He had taken Madame Colbert's hand for the next dance, but over her head, he gave me a glance of mingled outrage and panic. I grinned at him, but when I turned back to Inese, my hands shook a little. "Do you think he'll be all right?"

"Andine is one of the town's most influential women. Probably *the* most influential. It is good for him to be seen with her."

I didn't doubt her words, but I was envious of Andine.

The next hour was spent in the most extraordinary fashion. Usually when I went to a dance, I came with Isabelle and was largely ignored except by the men who hoped to use me to get nearer to my sister. Now there wasn't a word spoken about Isabelle. The men I spoke to asked about Henri, or about *me*. I was even suspicious that some of them were trying to impress me.

I danced with Bertram, who'd changed into satin breeches with a matching jacket. His cravat was tied in the latest style, but he didn't preen the way many young men did. Instead he grinned occasionally in Henri's direction. "He is doing splendidly. This night is already an enormous success."

"You're the one who got him here," I said with a laugh.

His smile faded. "No, Celeste. He wouldn't have come for me. I was in my apprenticeship when he was hurt. I hurried back as soon as I could, but nothing I could do would rouse him from his idiotic melancholy. *You* did this."

I should have disputed it, but Bertram's mouth was set in an uncharacteristically firm line, so I only laughed at him. "Silly," I said. "But where is your fiancée? Is she here?"

"Almost fiancée," he said, smiling once more. "She wasn't

feeling well and didn't come. But you will like her, I think. She is a sweet girl."

I looked up to see Henri watching us from across the room. He was surrounded by a few of Inese's friends and even a couple younger women. I looked away so I didn't have to watch them flirting with him.

Not much later in the powder room, I overheard several young women discussing Henri. They hadn't noticed me come in and were clustered tightly around a girl with very tall hair who'd been visiting with Henri only a few minutes before.

"He was very polite," she said in a whisper. "But intimidating with his frowns. When I got close to him, I had to crane my neck to see him. He's as tall as a tree."

"I'm surprised that you dared get so close to that face," another girl said, her lip curled. Her hoops were so large that her dress kept her from getting close to the others. "He's scarred like a demon, and my mother says it's the work of the devil himself."

I shook out my hands, which had somehow become tight fists.

"Don't be stupid," said the first. "Do you have any idea how much money he has?"

One of the other girls turned and saw me. She nudged those next to her. "You must be Mademoiselle Lebeau," she said with a smile. "Madeleine told me you are staying with Madame Sauveterre?"

"Yes." I smiled too, though I wanted to turn and punch the haughty one in the face. "She is a dear, isn't she?"

"Yes, of course," broke in the nasty one. "But how do you find Monsieur Durant?"

A few of the other girls tried to hush her.

"Henri?" I asked. "Isn't he *amazing*? I'd always wanted to meet a real army hero, but I'd never dreamed one would be as sweet and gentlemanly as he is. And so humble," I gushed. "Do you know he has his own copy of the Bible? He reads it all the time."

The girls stared at me, some with open mouths.

"It makes a girl wish she could visit his aunt a little longer, if you know what I mean," I added with a giggle. I looked into the glass and pretended to adjust my hair. I wouldn't actually change a thing about my hair. It had never been so pretty. Plus Inese would have a fit if I ruined it.

I smiled once more at everyone and left the room, feeling only mildly guilty about the lies I'd told. Henri could be gentlemanly when he wanted to, I reminded myself. And he *might* read the Bible that Inese had in one of the sitting rooms. He'd obviously gone to school.

Back in the ballroom, Bertram found me. "Truly, Celeste. I don't know that I like the looks these men are giving you."

"Don't tease," I said, letting my eyes rest on Henri, who watched us from a few yards away.

"Me?" Bertram asked. "How could you accuse me of such a thing?"

Henri bowed to the women next to him and strode toward me. My breath caught. His gaze was intense and his stride purposeful.

"Now for that unkind remark," Bertram said, "you're going to have to—"

"Dance with me?" Henri asked from behind Bertram, reaching past him to take my hand.

~

Henri

I told myself I wouldn't be too near her tonight. She made me smile and laugh all the time, and I couldn't do that here. Enough people were afraid of me as it was. But when I saw

Bertram corner her, obviously about to ask for another dance, I couldn't help myself. Something unpleasant twisted in my stomach, and before I knew it, I was holding her hand.

She seemed willing enough to be led away, and Bertram's annoyance was priceless. We sailed onto the dance floor at the beginning of an allemande.

"Don't close your eye this time," she instructed.

"I wouldn't dream of it." And I wouldn't. She was too pretty for me to want to look at anything else.

Something made her blush. She adjusted her glasses with her free hand.

We didn't talk much over the next few minutes, though the allemande was a slow one and we could have. Instead I just watched her. Her every move. She was graceful before, when she could hardly see, but with Bertram's glasses giving her confidence, her movement was exquisite. Our hands met and released over and over. Our feet followed the music, but there was something about that particular dance that was other worldly. My nose no longer recognized the nauseating combination of fifty different perfumes competing for dominance among the hundreds of bodies. Instead I only smelled the faint odor of lavender on Celeste's dress and skin. The noise in the room was almost deafening. Two hundred people talking, the musicians playing. But during that dance, all I heard was the whisper of her breath and her occasional snide little comment. And while the swirling colors of the dancers begged my eye to follow them, all I could see were Celeste's enchanting green-brown eyes and her soft brown hair, especially one particular wisp that curled against her neck. I wanted to touch it, to see if it was as silken as it looked.

She suddenly stopped moving, and I stared at her, lost in her gaze. It took me several seconds to realize the dance was over.

Bertram clapped me on the shoulder. "Henri, my friend," he

said, confusion in his eyes. "I've never seen you enjoy a dance so much. Celeste, you dance like an angel."

She tore her gaze away from me to grin at him. "Yes, yes, Bertram. Thank you *again* for making my glasses."

"Mademoiselle Colbert," he said, looking to the dark-haired girl with him. "Mademoiselle Lebeau does not understand when she is being complimented."

The girl watched me uncertainly. She must have been dancing with Bertram.

"Madeleine," Celeste said with a pleased smile. "Do you already know Monsieur Durant?"

How could the two already be friends?

I didn't release Celeste's hand when I bowed to Mademoiselle Colbert. "You are Madame Andine Colbert's niece?"

Mademoiselle Colbert nodded, her eyes downcast. She was a pretty girl with thick eyelashes and a blush to match her gown of pink silk. Celeste squeezed my hand and nodded in her direction.

"Would you allow me the pleasure of the next dance?" I asked. I would have done anything for Celeste at that moment, even embarrass myself by being rejected in front of her. But surprisingly, I wasn't rejected.

"Of course, Monsieur Durant," the girl said quietly.

"Perfect," Bertram said with a grin. "Celeste owes me a dance."

He and Celeste were gone a moment later, and I felt the loss of her hand in mine. Mademoiselle Colbert was a pleasant enough girl, though quiet, and I only caught her looking at my scars once. Aunt Inese and Madame Colbert watched us carefully, and knowing I was the target of a friendly conspiracy provoked my gratitude as well as my anger.

As I danced with Madeleine Colbert, the spell Celeste had cast on me faded away. The sights, smells, and noise came back. I tried to ignore the stares and whispers of the dozens of people we passed in the dance. Celeste watched me from her place beside Bertram, but I couldn't read the look in her eyes. Was it worry?

Once the dance was over, I was quickly surrounded by a set of matrons, each of whom had an unmarried daughter in tow. It was frightening, but not the kind of frightening I'd anticipated for the evening. Madeleine and her aunt kept the most exuberant in check, but as it was, I had to dance with five different girls, two of whom wouldn't even look up at my face. Not that I really looked at them either. I mostly watched Celeste. I thought the group around me had been ridiculously large, but hers was ten times that. Sons and mothers clustered around her like bees around an over-ripe plum. It was disgusting.

She danced with more men than I could count, and with each one, my anxiety grew. Many were from prominent families in Aix, and several seemed to hold her too close in the dances.

One boy I might have ripped away from her and thrown out the window if she hadn't been so quick to avoid his hands. As it was, he made an excuse to leave her when he noticed me glaring at him. Celeste gave me a grateful little smile before turning to the next admirer.

When I mentioned my concern to Aunt Inese, she only sniffed. "Don't be a hypocrite. None of them held her as closely as you did."

Aunt Inese used to be so sweet to me. Perhaps Celeste was a bad influence on her. And I didn't believe her words anyway. I had purposefully kept some distance from Celeste as we danced.

Bertram appeared at my shoulder. "You still think a beautiful sister could be better than that?" he asked quietly, nodding toward Celeste.

I sipped my punch before I answered. "She has been a good friend to my aunt, but her father will come soon."

Bertram made a disgusted sound, deep in his throat. "You are the biggest fool I've ever met."

How could I defend myself without sounding like a bigger idiot?

I glanced toward Celeste, only to realize that the woman greeting her as a friend was Madame Farine. And even worse, Madame Farine was introducing her son to her.

I clenched my fists. That they had the nerve to even come near my guest was outrageous. Monsieur Farine had cut his price to me by over twenty percent in the past two years simply because I wasn't pretty to look at. I had to remind myself that his wife didn't likely control his business dealings and that the boy could only be seventeen and wasn't responsible for his father's actions. The latter was difficult to remember when the dolt turned his adoring puppy dog eyes on Celeste and led her to the dance floor.

For her part, Celeste seemed completely absorbed in the boy's conversation. She spoke with him more than she had with any of her other dance partners, and she actually seemed anxious to hear what he had to say. She couldn't be interested in that scrawny, clueless…

"Henri, stop grinding your teeth. You're scaring people," Aunt Inese scolded me from nearby. "Just go steal her away if you don't want her with him, but for heaven's sakes, don't make a scene."

For once, I decided to follow someone's advice without the slightest hesitation. But when I turned back to where Celeste had been, she was gone. I felt the beginnings of panic. It wasn't real panic. I knew what that felt like. But I was very concerned. Anything could happen to her. And it wasn't as though I could trust the Farines. I immediately hurried to the place I'd seen her last. The dance had barely ended.

I heard Celeste's laugh and followed it to a library just off the ballroom. I stood in the doorway, shocked to see her standing with Madame and Monsieur Farine. Their son stood a little apart from them, watching Celeste with evident awe.

"That is very kind of you, Madame Farine, and I'd be delighted to accept." She met my eye for a fraction of a second before her smile faded and she looked away.

It took me a moment to realize the anger must have shown on my face.

"I believe it's time to bid you good night," Celeste said, her voice calm and gracious.

Madame Farine glanced toward me, her eyes worried. I couldn't even make myself meet her husband's gaze, I loathed him that much. I turned my back on them while they exchanged pleasantries with Celeste. She soon brushed past me.

I hurried to join her. "Do you have any idea who you were talking to?" I asked.

"Yes," she said, turning to me with a smile that didn't match her voice. "And if you don't want to undo everything you've accomplished tonight, I suggest you shed the evil glare, offer me your arm, and take me back to Inese."

I snapped my mouth shut, suddenly conscious of a dozen people watching.

"I'm ready to leave as soon as you are," Celeste told Aunt Inese as soon as we reached her. "Do you think Madame Colbert would be best for his last dance? Or possibly Madeleine?"

"He'd better ask Andine," she said, as though I wasn't standing right there.

CHAPTER 15

Celeste

Henri's lips tightened in a thin line. "Celeste," he said from between clenched teeth. "I'd really like to talk to you about—"

I was saved by a young man asking me for a dance. "Excuse me, please," I said.

Henri actually ended up dancing with his aunt. Inese had said she wouldn't dance, but he must have convinced her. He was careful with her, adjusting his steps to be sure she could keep pace with him. I had difficulty focusing on my partner. He was a pleasant enough boy, but nothing like the man with the eye patch who so unknowingly held my heart in his hand.

When we were finally back in the carriage on our way to the inn, Inese leaned back against her seat. "That was a tremendous success."

"You mean because I wasn't thrown out for my hideous appearance?"

"Don't be so self-centered, Henri," she scolded. She turned to me. "Celeste, you were magnificent. The most sought after girl there. I told you that's how it would be."

I knew Inese had to be inwardly dancing, as I was, over Henri's acceptance and the way he carried himself his first time back in public. There was no need to tell him that, of course.

"I've never had such a good time at a dance," I said, and it was true. Not even the night that Isabelle tripped in her new high heels and fell into the dessert table could compare. After tasting life without my sister, I was convinced I would never go back to Marseille. When my father came for me, even if Henri didn't want me to stay, I knew I would never live at home again. I had to be free from my family. Free from Marseille and who I was there.

"How did you find the Farine boy?" Henri asked shortly.

Inese gave him a sharp look.

"He was very sweet, just like his mother," I said. I knew where this was going, but even though Henri knew I'd read through his ledgers, he shouldn't have suspected that I knew what Monsieur Farine and the other buyers had done to him. Most of that I'd learned by eavesdropping.

"I'd like you to stay away from that family, Celeste. We don't associate with them."

"I associate with whomever *I* choose to associate," I said. I desperately craved Henri's good opinion, but I was not about to behave as foolishly as he did in this matter.

Inese intervened. "Celeste, dear, no one is trying to curb your social sphere. It is just that Monsieur Farine has treated us very badly."

"So we should treat his family badly?"

"Celeste," Henri said in exasperation.

"Have you ever even talked with him about it?"

"What? Who?"

"Monsieur Farine. Have you ever talked to him about whatever it is that made you unhappy with him?"

"There is nothing to talk about. I will not speak to them. And I'm asking you not to speak to them either."

"Well, you're much nicer than my father used to be about it."

"What are you talking about?"

"He used to try to tell me who I was allowed to be friends with. It didn't work for him, no matter how impassioned he grew. He and Isabelle were very firm about it. I think I even went without a few meals. Of course, they eventually gave up." I peered at him curiously in the dark. "Were *you* planning on starving me?"

"Don't be absurd."

"Because even if you were, I think Inese would still feed me. Or Suzanne would. And it wouldn't work anyway because I've been helping in the kitchen so much. It's hard to withhold food from someone who's cooking half the day."

An indelicate choking sound came from Inese's direction. I think she was trying not to laugh.

"Besides, I really do think the way to resolve conflict is to discuss it rationally, don't you? I think France would be at war half as much if we were better at convincing people of things rather than trying to hit them over the head."

"Are you telling me that you plan to associate with that family?"

"Are you telling me that you actually plan to try to stop me? It won't work. You'll only make me angry, and that's not a pretty thing."

"Really?"

"Worse than my old glasses," I promised.

Inese quickly changed the subject, asking Henri about some old friends he'd seen for the first time in years. I only half-listened as I worked through my plans in my mind. I kept getting distracted by the bump of Henri's leg against mine when we hit ruts on the road. I don't know why he was sitting so close to me, but I wasn't going to complain. All too soon we reached the inn and separated to our own rooms.

The next morning, I woke very early and readied myself, hating every little rustle that might give me away. I adjusted my petticoats and my brown- and pink-striped skirt over my conservative hip pads, then tied my matching pink jacket over my stomacher with nervous fingers. A few of my new friends had invited me to go to the market with them, and I was so anxious to get away unnoticed that I almost forgot to leave a note for Inese. I hastily scrawled a promise that I'd be back before it was time to leave. She planned to have a late breakfast at the inn with Madame Colbert, so I had plenty of time. I nearly ran into Henri by the stables where he was talking with Maurice and Bertram. I was lucky enough to slip around them unnoticed, thanks to the racket caused by Bertram's silly horse, but I felt the usual sense of loss when I walked away from Henri.

Madeleine Colbert and three other women were waiting for me at a bakery they had chosen for breakfast. Madame Farine soon joined us, her dark brown hair swept up into a beautiful chignon and her hat a tasteful blending of feathers and dark blue ribbon. Isabelle would have thought it too subtle, but I thought it was beautiful on her. She greeted her friends, then took my hand in hers. "My dear Mademoiselle Lebeau. You do not know what you have done to my poor Claude. The boy is completely infatuated, but from your expression, I can see you already have a young man."

I blushed, and she laughed.

"It is not what you think," I said theatrically. "The man I care for is only interested in my sister. That shows you what poor judgment I have."

"That is hardly believable, but I'm glad I can give an excuse to Claude. He is terribly young, and my sweet husband plans to send him away to school this year."

"Your husband is a distributor? Do you help him in his work?"

Madame Farine gave me a searching look, her light brown eyes moving back and forth between mine.

"I only ask because I do not have a strong hope for marriage. One day I would like to be a shopkeeper and sell medicinal oils and perfumes. I haven't quite decided."

Her face relaxed into a smile. "Who do you think runs my husband's store? He certainly doesn't have time." She patted my hand. "And I think you're a little young to give up on any particular plan."

The next hour was spent in pleasant chatter with good-natured women who seemed as happy to have me there as I was to be with them. It quickly became clear that, whatever her husband's faults may have been, Madame Farine was one of the sweetest women I'd ever met.

The only time the Durant household was mentioned was when Madame Farine asked after Inese. "We do miss her in town. She used to come so often," she said.

"Now that her nephew's health has improved so much, I hope she will be able to come more," I ventured.

Madeleine's sighs over a beautiful wrap displayed in a window ended the conversation, but as I was parting from the group to head back to the inn, Madame Farine took me aside. "Celeste, you know you are welcome at our home at any time. I hope you will visit when you are next in town. I'd love for you to talk business with my husband and me."

I gave her an impulsive hug and we quickly made plans before I hurried away. My steps felt so buoyant that I wasn't surprised I made it back before Inese left to meet her friend, Andine, for their late breakfast.

"Celeste, dear, you've made Henri practically frantic," Inese said as she pinned up her soft grey hair, frowning at a wisp that wouldn't stay put.

"Didn't you get my note?" I took a pin from her little case and fixed the errant lock. I helped her settle her hat over the top and pin it in place.

"Yes, but he obviously doesn't understand you are a competent woman who knows better than to stray into questionable parts of town. He's gone to the stable to get a horse ready to go and search for you."

What an interesting idea. I couldn't remember having anyone that concerned about me. Ever.

∿

Henri

Of all the foolish, idiotic things to do. And all this time, I'd taken her to be a sensible person. The stable hand eyed me nervously as he saddled one of my horses. I must have been a sight. My hand strayed to my eye patch to be sure it was in place. The boy would probably have nightmares if he saw the mess underneath it. It gave *me* nightmares, though happily, they hadn't woken me until early this morning.

When he nodded respectfully to someone behind me, I knew it was her before I even turned. My anxiety immediately disappeared, but my anger didn't.

She stood in the entryway, her back to the morning light so I couldn't see her expression.

"I won't be needing the horse after all," I said quietly to the stable hand.

I walked slowly toward Celeste. "I was worried about you."

She stepped forward out of the doorway, and I quickly looked her over for any sign of distress. She seemed her brisk, energetic self, but there was something tender in her expression.

"Were you really going to go look for me?" she asked, tilting her head to one side as she studied me.

"What would you expect me to do?" I demanded. "We had no idea where you went. I'm responsible for your safety. What would I tell your father if something happened to you?"

The tenderness disappeared from her eyes, and she straightened her spine. "I left a note with Inese. I was just at the market with friends. I'm even back earlier than I told her to expect me."

I'd reached her by then.

"Has anyone ever told you that you are most annoyingly independent?"

She considered a moment, a small smile forming again on her lips. "I don't think anyone ever said it so nicely as that."

She made it so difficult for me to stay angry. I sighed and reached for her hand, pulling it through my arm. It felt right to be close to her while we strolled back toward the inn. Perhaps I just wanted to be sure that she wouldn't slip away again and make me actually hunt her down. Whatever she thought of my motives, she didn't seem to mind it.

Once we were finally all in the carriage and headed back home, Aunt Inese promptly fell asleep, though I had my doubts that she was actually as unconscious as she appeared. I waited for her breathing to deepen before turning to Celeste.

"So you had a nice time at the dance? Truly?" It was silly to ask, of course. Her pleasure had been obvious. I just wanted an excuse to look into her eyes and to hear her speak to me.

"Of course. Did you?"

"It could have been much worse."

"Yes." She reached out and very purposefully took my hand in hers. "They are not so bad, are they?" she asked. "Your old friends. Please don't shut everyone out, Henri."

Sitting there in that carriage seat, so close to her, with her hand in mine, her optimism was almost catching. I began to wonder if perhaps the level of isolation I'd chosen hadn't actually been necessary. A girl who breathed life into me couldn't be wrong about something like that, could she?

I looked down at our hands. Her fingers were so smooth, fit so well in mine. She blushed and moved to pull her hand away, but I clasped it tighter. "Do you mind?" I asked, drawing her hand near my face so I could study it.

She shook her head, watching me with an unfathomable expression.

I traced a small scar on her first finger, then slid my thumb across the sprinkling of freckles on the back of her hand.

Finally I gave into the temptation and pressed her hand to my lips. "Thank you, Celeste. I know what you and Aunt Inese were doing for me last night. I don't know that it will make much of a difference, but I truly do appreciate it."

"I don't know what you're talking about," she said, though her faint smile gave her away.

Aunt Inese moved in her sleep, and we simultaneously released each other's hand. Celeste grinned, but to my disappointment, she didn't move to take my hand again. I was too cowardly to take hers. I was responsible for her, thanks to her father, and that put me in a very uncomfortable situation. I couldn't pursue her honorably, as she was under my roof and had no idea why she was actually there. I didn't really know either, except that her father had been unwilling to part with his favorite. So not only did I *not* have permission to court her, I suspected that if she thought she was sent here to be courted, she never would have agreed to come.

I clenched my teeth. Her father was completely dishonorable. That didn't mean I had to be.

I thought the ride home would be complete torture, but soon Celeste had me laughing over her latest and very extensive plans for my drainage systems. I was fairly sure she was making most of it up, especially her ideas for turning one of the main floor guest bedrooms into a washroom, complete with systems for bringing in and draining water.

Later, when I helped her down from the carriage, she allowed her hand to linger in mine, but Aunt Inese was watching, so I didn't press my luck. Instead I helped Maurice with the bags.

I was anxious to learn how the household had fared while I was away, but soon Suzanne greeted us and told me what a pleasant time she'd had working with Carine and that I was going to have to make the woman rest sometimes or she'd completely wear herself out.

Celeste, who had been present for the announcement, smiled broadly.

Suzanne noticed. "That's enough of that," she said, a tart twist to her lips. "It's not as though you're the only person who can recognize a good worker. The amount of wash that girl completed in less than a day is almost inhuman."

We all knew Celeste's smile had more to do with Suzanne letting go of her prejudice than it did with Carine's skill, but Suzanne didn't let her have a chance to gloat. Instead she announced that she had already fed lunch to the Fontaine brothers, who were out in the fields, but that if we were hungry, she'd just baked bread.

I opted to join Paul and Jacques and was soon working as though the very devil was at my heels. Paul smirked at me occasionally until I asked him how Carine was. Then he left me alone. Jacques obviously longed to taunt his brother but didn't dare. I thought his decision wise. Paul was built like a very short ox.

I insisted the brothers come home for Suzanne's supper, and it didn't take much convincing for them to agree. When we entered the kitchen, however, I realized I should have warned Suzanne. Not only was supper not served, it was still bubbling on the stove while Celeste, Aunt Inese, and Suzanne sat at the kitchen table, asking Carine questions.

None of them noticed our arrival.

"He was as tall as a house, with blond hair," Carine said, obviously shaken. "He seemed... dangerous."

"Carine," Paul exclaimed. "What happened?"

The women all jumped, and Carine stood as Paul strode toward her.

"Are you all right?" he demanded as he neared her.

She stumbled forward a couple of feet and right into his arms where he clasped her tight. It appeared very comfortable. I couldn't help looking toward Celeste, but she didn't seem so inclined.

"She just arrived," Celeste explained. "A man came to her home this afternoon after she went back."

CHAPTER 16

Celeste

It was some time before we could get more information from Carine. Paul babied her absurdly and wouldn't let any of us ask her questions until she emerged from his embrace and insisted she was all right. Considering how long she'd waited to *be* in his embrace, I'm surprised she let go of him at all. He still kept an arm around her shoulders and alternated between looking elated and sending warning glares around the room. The silly thing.

"I really am all right," Carine said for the third time. "It was just very frightening to have such a person appear out of nowhere after I'd heard of him skulking about. And the children and I were alone at the house."

"You'd better start from the beginning again," Inese suggested.

"Martin and I were working in our little garden during Marie's nap this afternoon," Carine said. "I don't know where he came from. We never saw him approach. He just stood at the gate, waiting for me to notice him. I was so surprised, I almost screamed, but of course, no one would have heard, so I kept it back. I didn't want to frighten Martin."

Paul winced. "Please don't stay there alone anymore."

"You and the children should stay here tonight," Henri suggested. "Paul, Jacques, and I can help you move your things in the morning."

Jacques nodded in agreement. "With our wagon, it wouldn't take long at all."

She gave Henri and Jacques grateful looks and snuggled closer into Paul's side. "He asked about you," she said to Henri. "He seemed to think you were supposed to be dead. I didn't know what to tell him, but I didn't think it would be safe to lie to him, so I told him the truth. I hope you don't mind."

Henri gave her a reassuring smile. I felt a twinge of jealousy. He'd almost never given me such a gentle look. Perhaps because he never thought I needed it.

"I thought maybe you'd known him in the army, but when I told him you were alive and still lived here, he looked really angry. Angry like some people did when my grandfather escaped a mob all those years ago, like he was ready to kill someone."

Suzanne found sudden interest in her shoes, and I wondered how many of her family members had been in that mob.

"He asked about your family and friends. He asked who you associated with and where you live."

"Why would he want to know who his friends are?" I asked, hoping it wasn't my father's fault the man was here. It didn't seem likely, but Father did owe a lot of people money right now.

"He wouldn't say. I told him I didn't generally talk to strangers about my neighbors. I told him I was expected at your house soon and could give you a message."

Inese sucked in a breath through her teeth. "Carine, were you trying to get yourself killed?"

"I had my knife. Not that it would stop him fully, but I

thought I might as well get it over with if he was going to murder us," she said with a little shrug. "He stared at me a long time, and then he just touched his hat and walked away."

Henri swept his hand through his hair. "Can you describe him again?"

"Fair-haired. The light was behind him, and I couldn't tell if it was grey or blond because it was so light. And he was really tall, as tall as you, but huge, built like Paul."

Paul grinned, and she fidgeted a little under his gaze but didn't try to pull away from him.

"And he had a strange accent."

"British?" Henri asked.

"Maybe," she said. "I don't know. I've never known anyone from England."

Henri considered a long time while the rest of us watched him.

"You think it was one of the men who you fought?" Paul finally asked.

"It's possible. They had cause enough to hate me, and could want to finish the job. On the other hand, I can't imagine an Englishman getting this far inland."

"But he hasn't been taking the main roads," I said.

Jean walked into the room at that moment and strode directly to Henri. "Why didn't you tell me you were going into Aix?" he demanded, his face flushed. "The scum there might have turned on you." I felt a small glow of affection for Jean. He wasn't very likable, but he really cared about Henri.

"Relax, Jean," Henri said, holding up a hand. "It isn't the people of Aix we have to worry about right now."

Carine had to repeat her story all over again.

Jean's blush faded to a pale green by the time she was finished. "The English raiders, Henri? How could they have tracked you down?"

"We can't know that," he said. "Why would they go to the

173

trouble?" But men had gone to less trouble to avenge a friend, let alone several friends.

"You've got to stay inside," Jean choked out. "You should send for the magistrate."

"I'm not going to stay in with so much work to be done," Henri said with a dismissive shrug.

Jean's shoulders slumped, and he shook his head wordlessly. He really did care.

"He has a point, Henri," I said. "You may not be able to stop working, but you really should take some precautions."

Jean's eyes grew hopeful. Perhaps he started to see me as an ally at that point.

Henri nodded distractedly before lifting his nose and sniffing. "Suzanne?"

"Oh, no." She flew to the stove and began to stir frantically. "Not scorched," she said a few moments later. "But you should all eat now."

"Let's all eat together in here," Inese suggested. "I'll call the children. They've probably had their fill of staring at Henri's sword."

Carine's worried eyes flashed to Henri, who shrugged and gave her an understanding smile. I could have kissed him right there.

I fetched bowls, and within a few minutes, we were all seated around the kitchen table. Jean had gone, insistent that he had to find the magistrate before nightfall. Even without him, the table had never seemed so small. The men made plans to fetch Carine's belongings, and we all discussed safety precautions in vague enough terms that the children wouldn't feel frightened. Martin was thrilled when he learned they would be staying and begged to help Maurice with the horses.

When I left the kitchen an hour later, Paul and Carine were arguing good-naturedly over the need for her to learn to fire his musket. I spent what was left of the daylight sewing in front of the window in my room. I hated sewing, but I was highly motivated over the new project I'd started.

When I finally had to light a candle, I put my work aside to unpack the little case I'd taken with me to Aix. At the top were the gloves Henri had found for me to wear. I'd never returned them. I snatched them up and hurried to his study, but he wasn't there. I decided he must have gone to bed, and that it would be better for me to leave the gloves on his desk. I took up his quill and began to scratch out a little thank you note when the room grew brighter.

I spun around to find Henri watching me from the study door, a candle in his hand. "I thought you'd be asleep," he said quietly.

"I am tired, but I came to return the gloves I borrowed."

He gave me a wary look, so I swallowed my questions about where he got them.

"I don't dare pick them up now. I think I have ink on my fingers," I said.

"I'll get them later," he said, looking away.

I walked toward him, as he obviously expected me to leave his study, but when I was only a pace away, he reached out and gently gripped my arm. "Celeste, I'm sorry. This stranger, whatever danger I may be in, I don't want any of it to fall on you."

"I am not afraid, Henri," I said, a smile pulling at my lips.

"I am. I'm afraid for you, for Carine and the children, for Paul and Jacques. For everyone. People do terrible things for revenge."

"But not you."

"What?"

"I've never heard you talk about getting revenge on the men who did this to you." I reached out and traced the scarred side of his face with my fingertips. I half expected him to jerk away from my hand, to order me out of his study. "I don't think it's in your nature," I whispered.

"No?" he said, closing his eye and leaning his face into my hand. "What is my nature, little miss know-it-all?"

He smiled as he spoke. He wasn't angry with me.

I inched forward to close the distance between us. "Well," I said quietly. "I think you are very kind. And honorable. And brave." I left out attractive and desirable.

He gave a low chuckle, and the scarred skin under my hand pulled a little when he smiled. "Don't make the mistake of thinking too much of me, Celeste. I'm afraid I can only disappoint you."

His words held a cynical note, but I hardly paid it any mind, because at that moment, he leaned his head down toward mine, and his fingers gently tilted my chin upward. I was about to be kissed by Henri Durant. My heart jumped, and I held my breath.

I watched his face, an unfamiliar hunger burning deep in my chest. He was only a few inches away when he winced. He eased backward, a determined set to his mouth. Before I could allow myself to feel hurt, my own determination took over.

Henri

Three minutes prior -
    I set down my candle on the shelf next to me when I came in the room and saw her at my desk. It occurred to me that I liked seeing her there. It was rare that anyone came into my study, but she seemed to naturally belong in my space. I'd let her pretty smile and her tender touch carry me away. I needed to get a grip on myself, but she was so kissable.

And then she spoke of the gloves. I was lucky she hadn't tried to return them to the room they came from. I'd forgotten to lock it. All the more reason that I was a complete fool. Pretending the room wouldn't matter to her. Pretending I had any right to kiss her. Pretending I had any right to even be this close to her. She was innocent, I knew by now, in her father's plot against me, but that didn't make it right.

I wanted to kiss her more than I'd thought possible, but I couldn't when things were so muddled between us. I began to move away, intending to take up my candle again and walk her to her room, but then the oddest thing happened.

Celeste's hand stayed my face, and her other hand was suddenly fisted in my hair. She pulled me down as she reached up on her toes, and before I knew it, her mouth gently pressed mine with a kiss that sent my senses reeling. I could barely return it at first because I was so surprised. She ended the kiss, her fingers softly caressing my neck as she pulled away. My senses came back to me. Or perhaps they left me altogether.

I wrapped one arm around her waist while my other hand moved up her back and to her neck. Her hair was still pinned up, but only loosely, and its softness was maddening, almost as maddening as the little surprised gasp she gave when my lips found hers. I wasn't as gentle as she had been, and she froze for the tiniest moment, long enough for me to wonder if I'd misunderstood her. But then she returned my kiss, just as strong, just as passionately. Her lips moved against mine in ways that later made me suspect she had long experience in the activity. I couldn't pull her close enough, even though I must have been crushing her.

Her hands moved up and down my arms, held my jaw, felt my shoulders. I spun her against the wall, letting my lips travel away from her mouth long enough to explore her jaw and throat.

"Henri?" she said in a breathy whisper.

I loosed my hold of her. "I know. I shouldn't—"

She kissed me firmly, stopping my words. "Thank you for letting me use the gloves." She kissed me again. "I think I'd better go back to my room."

"You will if you know what's good for you," I said, too much gruffness in my voice.

She laughed, not at all affected by my threat. She kissed me again, just once, very softly, before slipping out of my arms and through the door. I leaned my forehead against the wall, my breathing erratic. How had I let myself get to this point?

The next morning at breakfast, Celeste sat down at the table with a smile as bright and carefree as Marie's. Didn't she remember that she had kissed me last night? Didn't she remember that a massive goliath of an Englishman was stalking the countryside? And didn't she worry at all about what might happen when her father got around to coming for her?

I worried about all these enough for twenty people, and it was a little irritating that she didn't seem to be affected.

"I think Suzanne is trying to impress someone," she said with a wink at Martin, who was probably on his fifth sausage.

I gave her a hard look, but she only favored me with an annoyingly blank little smile before turning to talk to Aunt Inese about a sewing project. Did Celeste even sew?

I spent much of the morning helping Paul and Jacques move Carine to the château. The servants' wing was plenty big, and Suzanne appeared pleased to have them come. She'd been alone there since the last maid left almost a year ago. Maurice slept in the gatehouse. Unpacking was a light-hearted task, and when we were in the house, I often heard the children playing and the women laughing as they talked and worked.

My home had completely been transformed since Celeste came, not just the living arrangement or the way the accounts were done, but the way it felt inside. It was a happy place, no longer the lair of an outcast. There was Aunt Inese, smiling more than I ever remembered. There was Suzanne, who now laughed regularly. There were the children, brightening up the place. But mostly, there was Celeste. I constantly watched for her, listened for her, thought of excuses to seek her out.

When Paul and I had placed the last piece of furniture just where Carine wanted it, Maurice called to us from the kitchen. We found him there, gripping his hat with white knuckles, his eyes troubled.

"Were you expecting company?" he asked. "There are some men out front."

I shook my head, taking a fortifying breath. Violent mobs didn't usually show up in the middle of the day. Did they?

Paul followed me out to the courtyard where five men in work clothes waited.

"Yes?" I wished I'd brought a weapon with me.

Paul flexed his muscles.

"Monsieur Durant," the foremost said with a respectful nod. "We heard you might be looking for workers to help with harvest. Wondered if you could use any of us."

Oh. I repressed a relieved smile. I didn't want to scare them off. "Could you tell me your names, and more about what kind of work you do?"

They stepped forward, one by one. They were rough-looking, unshaven men, but each of them spoke respectfully and dipped their heads toward Aunt Inese and Celeste when they appeared in the entryway.

Paul and I agreed with them on a time for them to come back to work. When they were gone, Paul chuckled low in his throat. "What do you think of that?"

Aunt Inese and Celeste watched me with identical, smug little smiles.

"I think it was probably a good thing I went to that idiot dance."

Paul laughed again and then left to tell Jacques the good news.

"You did this," I said to Aunt Inese and Celeste.

"*You* finally showed up in town to prove you're not a devil or heathenish hermit," Aunt Inese said.

"Well, I don't know. He still may be a bit heathenish," Celeste said.

I wanted to kiss her, but I shook my head at her instead. "I *do* own a Bible."

She pressed her lips together, as though trying not to laugh. I hadn't said anything funny, so there was some hidden joke she wasn't telling me.

"Besides," I said, glancing toward my aunt, "*I'm* not the one who threw the priest out of this house *three* different times."

Celeste's jaw dropped, and Aunt Inese glared at me without malice. "What was I supposed to do? He kept trying to do Henri's last rites."

Celeste tilted her head back and laughed loudly, showing her pretty neck. Aunt Inese started at the sudden noise before giving Celeste a fond look. "You would have done the same."

"I might have done him violence," she said between laughs.

I chuckled, and Aunt Inese turned startled eyes on me, her smile widening.

"May I come out to the lavender fields today?" Celeste asked, changing the subject. "I want to see them a few more times before it's harvested."

"Of course. I have time to take you after dinner."

She considered. Didn't she just ask to go? Didn't she *want* to spend time with me?

"Or tomorrow before the men come to help with the wheat harvest."

"It had better be this evening," she said. "Tomorrow I plan to go to town to visit friends, if you don't mind me borrowing a horse."

"Maurice can take you," I said automatically while wondering how in the world she'd made friends so quickly. "And you just saw them the other day."

"I cannot possibly visit with *all* my friends in one day," she said with a little lift to her chin. "Besides, I don't know when my father is coming, and I don't want to miss spending time with them." She watched me steadily, as though trying to measure my reaction.

"Very well," I said, completely at a loss. The same reason she wanted to go visiting was the same reason I wanted her to stay home. I coveted the time with her.

That evening after dinner, Suzanne insisted she didn't need Celeste's help cleaning up. I shot Suzanne a grateful look, and she winked at me before shooing us out of the kitchen. Once we were outside, I immediately took Celeste's hand and threaded it through my arm. She smiled in what looked like contentment.

We walked in silence, and she remained quiet as we watched the sunset over the lavender fields. It appeared we were alone, and I so badly wanted to kiss her, but I couldn't. When her father came, I would make him tell her. Until then, any possible course of action I considered seemed wrong. It wasn't right to court her, but not behaving the way I felt toward her was also living a lie.

She walked forward to pick a few stalks of lavender. I followed her, bending down to cut some stalks with my knife.

"Thank you for all the lavender you put outside my door the other day," she said, still looking down at the purple blossoms.

"I noticed you wore some the other night," I said toward the top of her silky brown hair. "It suited you."

We stood and stared at each other a few moments. I hesitantly reached forward and settled a few stalks of lavender into the side of her loose knot of hair. She seemed to be waiting for something. If I had been handsome and whole, I might have thought she wanted me to embrace her.

Then again, she *had* kissed me last night. I looked around to be sure no one else was there.

CHAPTER 17

Celeste

I realized he really wasn't going to kiss me. It was almost physically painful. After the way we'd kissed last night, he was keeping his distance from me. He must have thought me so inappropriately forward, and I *had* been. I'd never initiated a kiss before. Isabelle had received hundreds of kisses from dozens of men, though she wouldn't admit to any of them. She wanted to keep her illusion of innocence intact. She'd never had to worry about men changing their minds and not wanting to kiss her after all.

And it wasn't that I'd never been kissed, though if I was being honest with myself, I'd have to admit the kisses I'd had before could hardly be called kisses at all compared with last night.

I couldn't stand the thought of Henri thinking ill of me, but that kiss had been the most *real* thing I'd ever experienced. I wouldn't have given it up for anything. I'd been absolutely giddy all day thinking of it. But I shouldn't have expected Henri to want to repeat the experience.

He gazed over my shoulder, studying the horizon.

"Did you see someone?" I asked, thinking of the blond Englishman.

"No." His voice cracked and he frowned, but at the same time, he reached forward to take my hand. He brought it up to his face and inhaled. "You smell wonderful."

"It's the lavender." My voice cracked too. I wanted to sink through the ground with embarrassment. Isabelle would have said something coy and charming.

His lips twisted into a half-smile. "It's not just the lavender," he said. He turned my hand up and kissed my palm. I went from disappointed to hopeful in a heartbeat. He pressed my fingers against his cheek, his scarred side, and leaned his face into my hand. With my thumb, I stroked the uneven stubble on his face, realizing with detached interest that his beard didn't grow on the worst of his scars.

His hand cupped my jaw, and I finally met his gaze. It was uncertain, vulnerable even. I turned my face an inch and pressed a kiss to his hand.

Disbelief warred with something else I couldn't identify in his expression. "Celeste," he finally said in a strangled whisper before pulling me to him. I didn't hesitate to lift my mouth to his. My heart soared higher in my chest. This was exactly where I wanted to be. His evening whiskers were rough, but I didn't care. He held me in his arms, practically lifting me from the ground. It was beginning to be just as interesting as the previous night, when someone called "Henri," in a low, urgent voice.

We broke apart, and Henri flung himself away from me, turning toward the fields as Jean rounded the hillside behind us.

The light had faded enough that if the stubble on Henri's chin had scratched me, I didn't think it would be noticeable.

"Henri, I've been worried." Jean approached us, completely oblivious to what he'd interrupted. "You shouldn't be out here."

I smiled in Jean's direction. Knowing about his service to Henri helped me see past the things I didn't like about him, such as the way he'd just ruined a very fine experience.

When he finally noticed me, I gave him a polite nod, which he returned distractedly, most of his attention on Henri.

"Don't be silly, Jean," Henri said. "I can take care of myself. And as you see, I have Mademoiselle Lebeau here to protect me."

I smiled at his sarcasm. If he only knew the lengths I really *would* go to protect him.

Jean frowned between the two of us before giving his head a little shake, obviously satisfied about something. "The magistrate should be out here protecting you, but the coward said he wouldn't shoot a man for wandering the countryside."

"Jean," Henri began, but Jean cut him off.

"You need to at least start carrying your pistol." He patted his side, and I saw for the first time the bulge of a gun. I'd never seen a pistol except on officers in parades in Marseille.

"We ought to all go in if Jean is going to talk to me about pistols," Henri said with a mock sigh. "Last time he tried to prove something with his gun, he almost shot me."

"I did not," Jean protested as we all turned back toward the house.

Jean spent much of the evening jumping at sudden noises and peering out windows. Only when I mentioned that my sister would eventually be coming did he remember my existence and talk excitedly with me. Isabelle had a way of stealing people's attention, even when she wasn't physically present. If Henri heard my comment, he pretended not to.

Jean stayed so long that I finally gave up on having any more time alone with Henri and retired to my room. In the morning, I learned Jean had stayed over in one of the guest bedrooms downstairs rather than travel at night. I thought that was a wise decision considering the man stalking the area.

When I left for Aix an hour after breakfast, he chose to ride with me, his horse tethered to the back of the carriage.

"Henri told me about what you did for him," I said bluntly once Henri's house had disappeared from view. It was difficult to leave him. It. Even for the day.

"He'd already saved my life twice by then," he mumbled, his ears turning pink. "It wasn't as though I didn't owe him."

That didn't surprise me at all. "It was still wonderful, what you did."

He studied me a moment before asking, "I don't suppose you told your sister about it?"

I wanted to roll my eyes. I should have known that was coming. "I just learned about it all and haven't written my next letter to her yet, but of course I plan to tell her about it."

He sat up a little straighter.

I held back a sigh of relief when Maurice stopped at Jean's home to let him out. His conversation was tedious, but mostly I didn't want him to know where I was going next.

I left Maurice at the town livery and wandered through town until I was certain he hadn't followed me. I wouldn't put it past Henri to send him after me.

I met Madame Farine at the little café as we had planned. She wore a fawn Brunswick gown that complemented the rich brown of her hair and was as delightful as ever. She insisted I call her Charlotte. We sipped our tea, talking and enjoying the view of the square and the fountain shaped of dolphins just outside. Later, as we walked to the short distance to her husband's shop, she was greeted by so many people that it was clear she was well-liked. Their son, Claude, almost tripped in his haste to meet us at the door. He took my hand, blushing and smiling. I'd seen over a hundred boys act like that around Isabelle. I knew what it meant. It was just completely shocking that someone would act like that around me. I was flattered, certainly. He was a cheerful boy, perhaps a year or two younger than I, with a ruddy complexion and curly brown hair a few shades lighter than his mother's. It would have been very convenient if I felt anything for him. But he wasn't what I wanted. He wasn't Henri.

Monsieur Farine sat at his books behind a long counter and did not look up when we first came in. "I'll be with you in a moment, my quail," he called as his pen scratched carefully in a book of figures.

"My husband never likes to stop in the middle of a task," Charlotte said with a fond smile in his direction. "He is very single-minded."

I didn't snort, but it was a close thing. If I was to learn about this man, I shouldn't judge him too quickly or openly.

"Your shop is very well laid out," I complimented quietly. "Do you have much competition here in Aix for your perfumes?"

"Oh, of course, but I keep my prices comparable, and my customers keep coming back for all the lavender we sell. Most of it is shipped away to different parts of Provence and northern Italy, though we also have buyers in Spain and Germany."

"This shop mostly falls under *your* care," I said.

"Yes. I confess I could let someone else do it. My husband does well with the other part of the business, the more lucrative part," she said, her smile dimming.

"But not the most fun," I reminded her.

"Certainly not. This shop is where we started, and I love it."

I saw the truth of it in her eyes as she looked around us. Light filtered in from several windows, and plants were spaced throughout, making the room feel more like a conservatory than a shop. The air was perfumed with lavender. A few customers entered, and Madame Farine and her son went to help them. It was then that Monsieur Farine put down his pen and joined me near the counter.

"You must be Charlotte's friend, Mademoiselle Lebeau," he said, bowing over my hand so that I could see the small bald patch at the top of his head. "My wife tells me you intend to open a shop someday."

Monsieur Farine was difficult to read. His manners were stiff, but his eyes were kind.

"Yes, though far from here, I'm afraid." No reason to make him think I'd infringe on his clientele. "Charlotte says I must buy through you if I'm to get the best products at the best price."

"I pride myself on being fair," he said quietly. "Though perhaps that is not enough for some people." He studied me with troubled eyes.

"You mean Monsieur Durant," I said boldly.

"I understand you are visiting his household," he said with a note of melancholy. "I used to buy from his father and grandfather."

"And you buy lavender from him too."

"Lavender, wheat. As much as he'll let me buy, though I understand he does not care to do business with me. Last year, he sold most of his lavender crop to an outside merchant."

I thought it better not to mention that merchant was my father, who still hadn't paid him.

"I understand Henri has become very bitter toward me." His voice held only sadness, and I began to wonder if perhaps Henri did not really understand the lavender market. Monsieur Farine seemed only sincere. Of course, a lot of people made the mistake of believing the same about my father. But my father wasn't a vindictive or a cruel person. He simply made poor and often selfish choices over his business commitments. Perhaps Monsieur Farine was the same.

"I think he endured much pain," I said quietly as Charlotte bustled by with her arms full of cloth. "But he seems more and more willing to join the human race again. Perhaps you will find it easier to work with him in the future."

"He was always a good boy," he said, brightening a little. "Though a bit mischievous. Perhaps he will come around." He shook himself a little. "But there. I promised my wife I would tell you about the products I sell. Shall we discuss business?"

I followed him to a table behind the counter where he began to tell me about taxes and profit margins for local products. I knew much of it already from observing and helping my father, but I didn't want to seem too knowledgeable. Being too smart had caused trouble for me in the past, and I really did want to learn from him. Charlotte and Claude joined us when they were not seeing to customers, and by the time I left, I had half a dozen pages of notes folded in my handbag.

~

Henri

I thought of Celeste all day. I couldn't get her out of my mind as I worked with Paul and Jacques and half a dozen other men who had come to work for me. I worried over her safety. I worried over what people would tell her about me. Paul had to remind me to dismiss everyone at the appropriate time because my mind had wandered back to the kisses I'd shared with her.

He smirked a little, as though he knew what I'd been thinking about. I glared at him, but that only made him laugh. "You'd better go see if she's back," he suggested. "Jacques and I can get everything put away."

I didn't need to be told twice. Paul's chuckle followed me toward the house. The carriage was back. She was back.

I found her working in the kitchen with Suzanne. Celeste pounded away at a lump of dough with such zeal that she didn't hear me come in.

"Is this about right, Suzanne?" she asked, pushing a strand of hair off her face.

"I think the dough ought to rest now," Suzanne said, her eyes flickering to me. "You should too. I'm going to see if Madame Sauveterre wants me to put dinner on early."

Suzanne's expression of guilty excitement left me without a doubt of her expectations for Celeste and me. I wondered who would be more disappointed when Celeste chose to leave, Suzanne or Aunt Inese. Then again, Carine obviously thought Celeste was wonderful too. Everyone who met her thought so.

I did.

Celeste looked over her shoulder and saw me. I wished I could paint her right there. The sun spilled through the window, giving her head a halo, and the soft smile she gave me weakened my knees. She was an angel.

"No need to scare Suzanne away," she said, abandoning her smile. "Now I'll ruin this bread for sure."

A pretty shrew of an angel. I knew she was joking, because no one could scare Suzanne.

"You should ask *me* how to make it," I said.

She turned and put a fist on one hip. "You know how to make bread?" Her tone was acid, but her eyes were laughing. The sunshine now outlined her entire form.

I managed not to stare, but it wasn't easy. "I know a lot of things," I said as my feet moved forward of their own volition.

She arched a questioning eyebrow at me, but as I drew nearer, some uncertainty crept into her superior expression.

I stalked closer, and she stepped back against the table where she'd been working. Her eyes darted around the room. I couldn't tell if she was looking for an escape or trying to make sure we were alone. Either reaction was equally interesting.

"For instance," I said, "I know how to tell if the dough is ready to bake."

"Really?"

I stood inches from her now, and my hands came to rest on the table on either side of her. I wasn't embracing her, but she couldn't move an inch in any direction without being in my arms.

She glanced at my mouth, and a wave of pink washed over her cheeks.

"The secret," I said, bending lower and dropping my voice to a whisper, "is to taste it."

I whipped one hand forward and pinched a piece of the dough behind her back, quickly jumping away and popping it into my mouth.

Celeste shrieked a surprised laugh. "Suzanne is going to get you," she said, now putting both fists at her hips. "She doesn't let dirty men touch her bread dough."

"I washed my hands," I protested, darting forward again to steal another piece.

Celeste tried to block me, but I feinted left and spun right, quickly stuffing another little piece of dough into my mouth.

"You're filthy," she said, still laughing uproariously. I couldn't help laughing when Celeste laughed. It was such an uninhibited, funny sound.

"Am not."

"You are too. Show me your hand."

I fisted my hands behind my back. "I'll bet you a kiss my hands are cleaner than yours."

Her face whipped toward mine, her eyes startled. She recovered instantly. "What kind of kiss? And with whom?"

"Winner chooses."

She eyed me suspiciously for a moment, then said, "Fine." She held out her hand for mine. I slowly extended my hand, placing it in hers. Our eyes met for a long moment before she finally looked down.

"I won," I said with a smirk. I always scrubbed my hands before I came inside. Aunt Inese insisted on it, and it was such a little thing to do to make her happy. "*Your* hands are covered in dough."

She dropped my hand to pick at the little bits stuck to her fingers. "But dough is clean," she said distractedly as she rubbed her hands together to loosen the clingy pieces.

"I still win."

"It wasn't a fair bet."

"You still have to kiss someone."

"I suppose you want me to go kiss Jacques or Maurice," she said with a haughty little sniff.

"Of course not."

"Then who?"

My hands found her elbows and pulled her a little closer. "Would it be so bad to kiss *me*?" I asked quietly as my arms slid around her waist.

Her breath caught, and she studied my face a long moment. I began to grow self-conscious under her scrutiny, but before I could take a step back, Celeste's hands travelled up my arms and to my shoulders. She paused a moment more before seeming to find her courage. She pulled my head down toward hers as she stood up on her toes. Her mouth met mine slowly, sweetly. She seemed to be saying a lot with that kiss. And I found myself really wanting to believe what her mouth was promising.

She pulled away a little to ask on a whisper, "Was that good enough?"

"That was very good," I said in a low voice, wondering how she could think one kiss would ever be enough.

My arms circled her more tightly as my lips found hers. It wasn't such a gentle exchange this time. She gasped a little, and I thought I had hurt her until I realized her hands were fisted in the hair at the back of my head, pulling me tighter.

I don't know how many minutes we stood like that in the kitchen before the unmistakable sound of Jean calling my name was heard in the passageway. I reluctantly loosed Celeste, pushing back a soft strand of hair that had fallen forward onto her face.

"I think the dough rested," I murmured.

She moved backward, her footsteps as unsteady as my heartbeat. I gripped the table for support as Jean came bursting into the room, Suzanne and Aunt Inese a few paces behind him.

"Why would I stay out of the kitchen?" Jean asked over his shoulder as he stomped forward.

Aunt Inese sent me a guilty look. She and Suzanne must have orchestrated the time I'd just spent with Celeste. I wondered if *she* had been in on their plans.

"That man was seen again," Jean said, his eyebrows a tight line. "A few miles west of here. He's a menace."

"I agree with the magistrate. We're not going to hunt him down and kill him before we know who he is," I said, less politely than I'd intended. I hadn't wanted him to interrupt what I'd been doing. Kissing Celeste was one of the best things I'd ever experienced. For the first time in almost two years, I didn't feel cursed. I just felt like a man who was lucky enough to be kissing a pretty woman. At that moment, I couldn't imagine that Jean had anything so important to say that it couldn't have waited another few minutes. Hours. Days.

CHAPTER 18

Celeste

Jean peered at Henri. "What's the matter with you?" he asked. "Don't you care that this Englishman is after you?"

Henri just shrugged. I wondered if he was still trying to catch his breath like I was. Of course, it wasn't *his* rib cage that was being crushed moments before. Not that I minded. Having Henri's arms around me like that was heaven, and I could scarcely contain the happy laughter currently caught in my throat.

I glanced at Henri. He didn't seem to be having trouble containing joyful emotions. Instead he stared resentfully at his friend.

"And what is that white stuff all through your hair?" Jean asked, leaning forward to frown at Henri.

I held my breath with realization. It was dough. It had still been on my hands when I'd sunk them into his hair. I'd never known a man's hair could be that thrilling to touch.

Henri looked everywhere but at me.

"Men do get so dirty during the harvest," I observed, wrinkling my nose for effect. "At least *your* hands look clean, Monsieur Mason. I hope you plan to stay for dinner." I kept my hands under the counter where he couldn't see them.

"Thank you," he said, though he continued to frown. "That would be very nice." He drew nearer to see what Suzanne had been making, but when he finally met my eyes, he took a hasty step back. "I say, Mademoiselle Lebeau. Are you feeling quite all right? Your cheeks look red and fevered. You're not sick, are you?"

"No, no." I managed a false little laugh. "I've only been standing too close to the stove. I ought to return to my room." I took my leave as fast as was polite.

Much later, after I had helped Suzanne clean up from dinner, I sat down to sew with Inese. Henri and Jean debated the motives of the large, blond man for some time before they brought a game of backgammon to the low table near Inese and me.

I'd hardly been able to look at Henri through dinner, and now having him so close made me nervous. I stabbed myself with my needle twice, and the second time drew blood.

Henri noticed. "What are you working on that's so important you're willing to bleed to death, Celeste?"

Jean looked back and forth between us with narrowed eyes. He must not have heard Henri call me by my given name before.

"Just a little project," I said with a dismissive little shrug. "I hardly know what it will be yet."

"Did you pick that fabric up in town today?" Inese asked.

I hadn't told her about what I was making. I didn't want to be told it was pointless, and if I failed at constructing it, I didn't want anyone to know.

"Yes, but I'm afraid I may have chosen the wrong color," I said absently as I picked at some stitching.

The men resumed their game, arguing half-heartedly about the application of a particular rule in a particular situation. I didn't follow their conversation. I was too busy studying Henri out of the corner of my eye. Over the next hour, he almost never looked toward me, never spoke to me. He finished his game with Jean, who then announced he was riding home.

"I'd hate to have to shoot that blond devil if he accosts me," he said, patting the pistol beneath his coat.

From what Henri had said of the Englishmen he'd fought, I didn't actually believe Jean had a chance of winning in a fight. I was still happy that Henri didn't insist Jean stay. Henri wasn't as happy around him, though it probably had something to do with the unpleasant memories they shared. I hoped Bertram would visit soon.

The clock on the mantle chimed the hour as I finished my seam. "Goodnight, Inese," I said. I longed to stay up late, to see if I might catch more time with Henri, but I was tired and had a lot of work planned for the next day. And I was still a little troubled that Henri kept such careful distance from me around others. I knew what that meant.

"Goodnight, dear. I'm glad you had a nice time today." Inese frowned into her needlepoint a moment before looking up at me. "I never asked who you visited with today."

A choice word I'd heard at the docks popped into my mind. I'd hoped to avoid that question, at least in front of Henri, but I never dreamed of lying to either of them. Whatever irritations Henri and I had with each other, at least we were honest about them.

"Madame Farine invited me to tea, and we had a lovely chat. She taught me a little about running a shop."

Henri had frozen in the act of putting away the game pieces. His jaw worked angrily a moment.

"Well, you'd better run off to bed," Inese said, her eyes troubled. "You've had a long day."

I thought it best to take her advice. I was too tired for an argument, and I really was trying to be on good behavior before my father came. As willing as Henri seemed to share a kiss with me, he wasn't completely convinced I should stay.

In retrospect, I should have *run* back to my room. Just as I rounded the last corner and was feet away from my sanctuary, I heard Henri's voice. "Celeste, wait."

In the moments it took him to catch up to me, I tried to think of cutting remarks about why I could do as I pleased, but my brain didn't seem to be functioning enough for sarcasm.

I turned to face him when I felt him directly behind me, but instead of anger in his gaze, there was only disappointment. "Celeste, if you knew that family, truly, you would not associate with them. Please tell me you won't go there anymore."

His gaze was so troubled, his concern so sincere that I didn't know what to say. Maybe I should have tried to soothe the worry from his brow. As it was, I only said, "I'll go where I wish," and stepped into my room, shutting the door before anything else could be said.

It was a full minute before I heard his footsteps fade away, and several hours before I could go to sleep. Henri never asked anything of me, and I had turned down a perfectly appropriate request without being able to give him any reason at all. But I had to fix this. Understand it, at least.

The next week was torturous. Henri was perfectly polite, but there were no lively conversations between us, and he never sought out my attention. He didn't take me to the lavender field, though Bertram did twice during different visits. It would soon all be gone. They were already talking of harvesting part of the distant field. I was sad about the lavender being cut, but it was only a shadow of a feeling compared to the hurt I felt over Henri. For that entire week, he never touched me and rarely spoke to me at all. I'd never needed anyone's approval before, and it irritated me to no end that I was so hurt over Henri's vague, polite attitude.

"What are you making?" Bertram asked one evening while I

sewed quietly in one corner. I sat as far away from Henri as possible so that I wasn't in his line of vision. It was just better to avoid his eye altogether.

"I haven't sorted it out yet," I said. "Something useful, I hope."

Bertram lowered his voice. "Any word from your father?" he asked with a guilty look toward Henri. "Do you know when he's coming?"

"I don't know when he'll fetch me," I said with a shrug. "I suppose that is what you get for being a merchant's daughter, but I've never known when I could depend on him."

Bertram cast another troubled look at Henri, and I soon excused myself. "Thank you for taking me to the lavender fields, Bertram," I said with a sincere smile. "Goodnight, Inese, Henri."

I was halfway to my room when I realized I'd forgotten my sewing basket. I almost didn't go back for it, but I had nearly three completed projects, and I wanted to finish off some ends, so I turned around to get them. I'd begun them long before I'd hurt Henri's feelings by seeing the Farines, and I wasn't about to give them up just because we were both acting like idiots. I heard Henri and Bertram talking in a side parlor and slowed, wondering how I could pass without them noticing, but my steps were soon arrested by my own name.

"What do you mean, what am I going to do about Celeste?" Henri asked in a harsh tone. "What is there to be done?"

"You're still waiting for her father to come?" Bertram asked.

"Of course," Henri said with finality. "The sooner, the better."

I slipped back the way I'd come, completely at a loss and hating myself for being so stupid. Those kisses hadn't meant what I thought they meant. Henri still wanted me gone.

Henri

F or a week, Celeste hardly noticed me. She never sought me out, never bantered with me, never kissed me. It pained me to no end that she wouldn't trust me about the Farines, that she wouldn't give them up when I asked. She had every right to associate with whom she wanted, but her lack of faith in me had been eye-opening. I alternated between wishing her father would come immediately and wishing he would never come. As much as I wanted him here to help clear up the large misunderstanding between us, this smaller one was horrible, and I was so afraid she'd leave when he came.

One morning when I entered the kitchen, I found Suzanne and Carine whispering together. Suzanne glared in my direction, but Carine offered me a plate of warm bread.

"Please pardon the advice if it isn't wanted, Monsieur Durant, but it seems you and Celeste really should talk with each other." She hesitated, then added, "I think she believes you are angry with her."

"Angry?" I asked in surprise.

"Yes, probably because you don't talk to her anymore."

"Thank you," I murmured, staring at the bread she set on the table next to me.

I didn't talk to *her*?

The moment Carine's back was turned, I was out the door. I didn't have much time. The workers would arrive any minute.

"She's in the garden," Carine called after me.

The kitchen garden had been transformed since Celeste came. The vegetables were trained up, the hedges trimmed back, and everything had an air of orderliness and efficiency. If I'd thought about it before she came, I would have assumed that a well-brought-up girl, if she wanted to work outside at all, would have busied herself with the flowers. We had one of the finest rose gardens in Provence. But knowing Celeste as I did now, I wasn't surprised that she chose to spend her time doing something so useful.

I finally found her behind a plum tree, digging potatoes with such ferocity that she didn't hear me approach. Not even Paul ever worked with that sort of enthusiasm.

"Celeste?"

She whirled around, her shovel raised like a weapon before she realized it was me.

I couldn't help laughing, which probably wasn't the wisest thing to do, since her eyes immediately narrowed into a glare.

"I'm sorry," I said. "I didn't mean to sneak up on you."

She shrugged one shoulder. "What do you expect of a girl when there are strange men in the neighborhood?"

"I don't expect this particular girl to work so hard," I said gently as I took in her appearance.

Celeste's hair was pulled tightly back, but the exertion of her work had loosened some of it, giving her a wild appearance that matched her dirty apron and work gloves.

"That's what I came here for." She wouldn't meet my eye.

I tried a different approach. "Would you like to walk with me to see the lavender this evening? It might be one of the last good days before we begin harvesting."

"No, thank you," she said without hesitation. "There are still so many things I'd like to accomplish before my father comes, and he could be here any day."

Carine had been mistaken. Celeste didn't fear my anger. She had too much of her own.

And she expected to leave soon.

"Have you heard from him?" I asked brusquely.

She shook her head as she turned away from me, bending to scoop the potatoes she'd dug into a basket.

"Very well," I said. "I'll see you at dinner, then." I walked away, utterly dejected.

I heard a rustle behind me, and I felt her eyes on my back, but I didn't turn around. I was pathetic enough already.

By noon, Jacques had already refilled the water jug three times. The heat was almost suffocating, and when we finally quit for the day, the men were very happy to take their pay and leave with the food Suzanne supplied them.

The dust had combined with my sweat to make my eye patch even more uncomfortable than usual, and I rubbed at it on my way to the dinner table. My hands were clean, and I'd changed my shirt, so I didn't understand the assessing look Celeste gave me. Bertram was there. He'd braved the heat in order to see Celeste and invite her to his home to see his parents' garden.

"And I want them to understand I'm not going to elope with you. They are far too anxious to see me settled with the girl they chose years ago."

Celeste grinned for the first time in days. "I'd be happy to set their hearts at ease."

I didn't like the idea of Celeste traveling alone, but when I insisted Maurice could take her to town whenever she decided to go, she only said, "We'll see," as though I was merely making a suggestion.

She was unusually quiet at dinner, as she had been for the last week, and when Bertram attempted to entertain her with vision jokes in the parlor afterward, she only gave him wan little smiles. I began to worry she was taking ill. Bertram must have thought so too.

"Should I fetch Inese? You don't seem yourself this evening, Celeste."

"I'm fine, thank you," she said, watching me rub the skin around my patch. "But you'll excuse me a moment?"

"Did you say something to her?" Bertram demanded as soon as Celeste was gone.

"What is there to say?" I said, not ready to confide all my concerns to him.

"She deserves the truth, Henri, and if you don't give it to her soon, I will."

"Don't be dramatic, Bertram," I growled.

"The longer you wait, the worse it will be."

He seemed about to press it further, but cut himself off as Celeste came back into the room, carrying a small basket.

"I'm not sure I've got these right, Henri," she said. "But if any of them work once you've tried them on, I've made patterns so Inese or Carine can duplicate them later."

I looked in confusion at the tan cloth she held out to me. Bertram understood before I did. "Brilliant, Celeste," he said. "This shouldn't irritate his skin at all."

That was what she'd been working on through the evenings. Eye patches? For me?

"You'll have to experiment to see which is best while you're working," Celeste said, waving to my old black eye patch. "It might be better at keeping out the dirt. These should be more comfortable the rest of the time, and I tried to match your skin tone so it would be less obtrusive."

I took the piece of cloth that Bertram pushed into my hand and studied it. The stitches were fine, the pattern simple. This was what she'd meant by practical sewing. She couldn't have been working all this time to make such a gift if she truly despised me. I frowned to hide my sudden giddiness.

"And when you don't want the strap to show, you layer your hair over it."

"Let's see it on," Bertram said, jumping up. "Take that old thing off, Henri."

I whipped my hand up to cover my patch. "Bertram," I said warningly. He'd seen the vile mess under the patch. Why on earth would he think I'd take it off in front of Celeste?

"I'll stand behind you and do the fastening the first time,"

Celeste offered, apparently understanding my discomfort. Could she know how difficult it was to be so close to her when Bertram was present? I didn't dare embarrass her by pulling her into my arms as I wanted to.

Once she was behind me, I took off the black patch, shielding the gruesomeness underneath with my hand as I felt her slip the new clean patch around my head. The sensation of her hands in my hair was maddening as she tied the strap and then smoothed my hair over the top of it. She came to stand in front of me and toyed with my hair a little longer before saying, "There. Go look."

I stood and walked to the mirror on the wall. I usually tried not to look in mirrors for long periods of time, but now I could hardly look away. The way she arranged my hair over my forehead hid much of her patch. It was smaller than my other, and didn't creep up into my eyebrow. It was hardly noticeable and much more comfortable.

Celeste came to stand behind me. "You can tighten or loosen it just by moving this strap," she said, reaching up to show me the adjustment. "Do you want to try the other two? See which you like better?"

I stared at her in the mirror, and she regarded me solemnly.

"This is the most thoughtful gift I've ever received," I said, my gaze trained on her beautiful eyes.

She gave me a cynical little smile. I thought it had a trace of longing in it, though for what, I couldn't guess. "Housekeepers are supposed to make people more comf—" she began.

I didn't let her finish. I spun on the spot and jerked her into a tight embrace. "Thank you, Celeste," I murmured into her hair. "You are an angel to me. Did you know that?"

She was stiff in my arms for a few seconds before she returned the embrace with a little awkward pat.

"I was glad to do it for you," she said quietly as I finally let her go.

Bertram glared at me over her shoulder. I'd forgotten about him. Celeste had a way of driving thoughts from my mind, but now I realized he must have thought my display inappropriate. I was glad he didn't know about the kisses I'd shared with Celeste on other occasions when she'd been in my arms.

"Suzanne promised to teach me another secret recipe tonight," she said, walking backward to the door. "When you try the other patches, just tell me which pattern you like best."

Bertram, possibly emboldened by my treatment of her, reached out and took her hand, kissing it very properly, though perhaps a little too long.

"Goodnight," she said with a small smile for both of us.

"Occasionally, Henri," Bertram said quietly, "just occasionally, I wish I was capable of thrashing you."

CHAPTER 19

Celeste

I left the parlor as quickly as I could. I didn't trust myself to be in the same room as Henri when my head was so muddled. I worked with Suzanne in the kitchen, but she sent me to my room for looking "peaky," and I fell into a fitful sleep.

The next morning, despite my attempts to convince Maurice to let me ride one of the horses into town, he insisted he prepare the carriage. But when Suzanne dragged him away to kill a mouse she'd trapped in an urn, I took the opportunity to saddle a horse myself. I left a note for Maurice, prayed for Henri not to know, and rode off at a dead gallop.

The livery in Aix wasn't far from the Vrais' home, and I was even a few minutes early, which I hoped they wouldn't mind. Bertram met me at the door.

"Thank you," he said under his breath. "You wouldn't believe how worried they are that I'll run off with you and leave them in a terrible spot with their friends."

I smoothed away my smile before I stepped into the Vrais' sitting room. Bertram's parents smiled when we were introduced, but his mother clutched her fan too tightly, and his father's moustache twitched at least four times. Bertram asked after Henri and gave me a pleading look. It took me a moment to understand, but I quickly recovered.

"He is such a dear," I gushed. "And always so worried when I come into town by myself." I sighed. It was a little theatrical perhaps, but Bertram's parents noticeably relaxed.

"Thank you," he mouthed at me. I tried not to smile too broadly. That I'd even seemed a potential threat to their plans for Bertram was an odd sort of compliment.

Soon Bertram's father had me laughing over Bertram's childhood antics, many of which involved Henri.

I didn't stay long. Bertram protested, but I'd grown increasingly anxious to get to the Farines'.

Monsieur Farine greeted me with a polite smile. "Mademoiselle Lebeau. My wife and Claude are both out. I hope you will not mind waiting for them. Perhaps you would like to keep me company at the counter while there is a lull in customers."

"Thank you. I confess I would love to steal your time for purely selfish reasons." I felt a small pang of guilt for the farce I was about to play. Lying was usually my father's domain. "I'm afraid I still have not come up with a good system for keeping ledgers. Could you show me some examples?"

"You must be joking, my dear," he said with a laugh. "I'm frequently told I'm overly enthusiastic about my filing and ledger system."

"I would love to learn," I said earnestly. "I need a good system if I'm to go into business for myself."

He watched me a long moment and must have decided I was serious, because he motioned me to a different counter and began pulling ledgers from the inside shelf. "See here. This is my expenditures book for the last year. It details everything I bought. And this one shows everything I've sold." He flipped through some pages too quickly for me to read anything. "And the shop accounts I keep separately in these two red books. And this brown one tracks taxes. I find the king's tax collectors to be a little more honest if they know I track every sou they take from me. Too many are inclined to line their pockets rather than return what they have to the king. It's no wonder the king's debt is larger than all of America. But here, I won't bore you with that."

He drew the first ledger toward me and flipped it open to an empty page. "I keep everything in columns. Description, price." He pointed to each as he listed them. "The name of the person who delivered it, and last is the signature of the person who sold it to me. That way, if there's a dispute or a discrepancy, it's much easier to fix."

I studied his method. Monsieur Farine was certainly a neat bookkeeper. It would be easier to call him out on the way he'd treated Henri. "That seems very well planned," I said as two young women entered the shop.

"Just one moment." He excused himself to help the customers.

I seized my opportunity while his back was turned, quickly shuffling the pages back until I reached the previous summer. I didn't know quite what I was looking for, though somehow, deep inside, I didn't actually believe I would find anything that would condemn Monsieur Farine. I suppose my feelings were rooted more in his kind expression than in any proof I had.

A lavender shipment caught my eye, and I quickly memorized the price. It was higher than the price in Henri's ledger by at least ten percent. I glanced in sad disappointment toward Monsieur Farine, who was courteously trying to explain to his wife's customers that it would be another few weeks before the next shipments of silk arrived. Knowing my time was limited, I flipped through the pages, scanning for Henri's name. I'd practically memorized Henri's ledgers, so I knew the dates I was looking for.

There it was. With my finger, I traced the name of Henri Durant, followed by the date and the amount of lavender. But when I reached the price, my finger stopped on its own. The price was wrong, *higher* than the price given the other shipment of lavender, not lower. I did the math quickly in my mind. Ten percent higher. And more importantly, it was twenty-five percent more than the price listed in Henri's ledger.

I sat staring at the entry like a complete idiot until Monsieur Farine took the chair beside me.

"Monsieur Farine," I said, before he could grow angry at what I'd done. "I beg you will excuse the presumption of looking through your accounts, but would you please answer two very important questions for me?" I asked, my heart thudding. "First, can you tell me why your price for lavender for Monsieur Durant was higher than for the other lavender you bought?"

Monsieur Farine frowned, but the sudden flush in his cheeks gave him away. "Henri has the best lavender in Provence. The Galimard Perfumery in Grasse specifically requests his lavender oil. That is reason enough, isn't it?"

"Is it?"

"Yes." He paused, and I thought I detected the slightest trace of moisture in his eyes. "But can you blame me, Mademoiselle, that I also give a better price to the son of my friend?"

"He doesn't know you gave him a good price."

"Of course he knows," Monsieur Farine said sadly. "He pushes me for a higher and higher price through all our communication."

"There is a horrible discrepancy," I whispered. "I think I will be able to explain it if you could also tell me whose signature this is."

. . .

I left the Farines' shop an hour later with our plan firmly in my mind and Monsieur Farine's ledger tucked securely under my arm. I'd promised on everything holy to bring it back in perfect shape before he would let me out of his shop with it. For a little while, I thought I might actually have to steal it when his back was turned.

Monsieur Farine, still trembling with rage at what I'd told him, escorted me to the stable before leaving me to fulfill his portion of our plot.

The mare I had borrowed from Henri wasn't overly willing to leave the comfort of her stall, but I stilled my hands and waited with a polite expression while the livery boy saddled her and coaxed her out for me. I wasn't a particularly strong rider and had purposefully chosen a sedate mount. Father had made sure we'd had lessons, of course, but I so rarely did any riding in Marseille.

I paid the livery boy and rode away, hoping the ride back would cool my anger enough that I could confront Henri without yelling at him. I think what I mostly accomplished over the next thirty minutes was to make my mount nervous. She already didn't trust me after our gallop away from the house that morning. She probably thought I'd stolen her. And now she practically danced with irritation. To calm her and myself, I loosened my hold on the reins, closed my eyes, and tried to clear my mind. The horse knew the way better than I did, so I didn't worry about getting lost.

A minute later, when I'd finally regained focus, I opened my eyes. A burst of fear had me gripping the reins tighter than ever. I just managed to choke back a scream. There, not far ahead of me in the road, was a giant of a man on a massive bay. The man's hair was almost white, and he stood his horse in the middle of the road as he watched me approach.

I pulled my mare to a slower walk, trying not to panic. The

man hadn't hurt Carine, I reminded myself, even if he had been threatening. Surely he just wanted to talk to me.

On the other hand, Carine hadn't been completely alone and hadn't had anything of value for him to steal. I realized the man could simply be waiting for me to come close so he could murder me and steal my horse.

I considered galloping back toward Aix, but there weren't any farms for the last mile, and his mount could probably catch mine in a tenth of that distance.

At that time of panic, I reverted to my most natural instincts.

I pulled my horse to a stop just close enough for him to hear my voice. "Well?" I demanded. "What do you want? I have to warn you I am not in the mood for being murdered *or* for having my mount stolen."

He stared at me, apparently taken aback by my outburst. This close, I could see that he wore a definite layer of travel dirt and that his skin was a bit loose, as though he was used to better eating.

"And it is *exceptionally* rude to stare at a woman like that. *Are* you going to stand gaping at me, or will you move aside and let me pass?" I asked, glaring at him.

He stared at me uncomfortably for a few seconds. "I hoped to speak with you," he said, almost too quietly for me to hear, but the accent was definitely not English.

"Yes?" I said, glaring him down.

"I am trying to find out about Henri Durant. You have been staying at the Durant household, yes?"

Norwegian, perhaps? Somewhere far north for certain.

"Yes," I said, growing increasingly interested in what he had to say.

"I have been told Henri Durant is alive."

"Yes, he is," I said.

He cleared his throat. "I specifically mean the Henri Durant

209

who was so badly injured during his service to France two years ago."

My fear subsided enough that a few important details fell into place. I'd never been particularly grateful for my drunken uncle, but now I silently praised his mother for naming him as she did and giving me a reason to remember Henri's friend.

"Captain Robineau." I said, my manners returning. "I am very pleased to meet you."

~

Henri

W hen Maurice came to find me in the fields late that morning and admitted Celeste had absconded with a horse, I was stunned. Had she lost her mind completely? I'd have thought the giant Englishman roaming the country would have been enough reason for her to show caution. But did she really not think that I would guess she'd gone to the Farines'? She knew how I felt about them.

I was ready to ride to Aix to look for her and lose an entire day of work, when one of the men sliced his hand sharpening a scythe. I helped my aunt see to it and was fairly certain the wound would heal without difficulty, but by then, I knew I had no chance of catching up to Celeste.

At least I could try to meet her on the return journey. Someone had to protect her from herself. But once I made it to the stable, I found Maurice in a near panic over a gelding that had suddenly taken ill. I helped him with the animal, hating the delay every second.

When I finally left the stable, it was to see Celeste riding toward me on one of my slowest, oldest mares. I probably should have been furious, but my relief at seeing her well and whole was so overwhelming that I could hardly think, let alone formulate any sort of protest at her actions.

"Hello, Henri," she said politely before dismounting and leading the horse into the stable. She was calm, but her eyes held an odd sort of excitement, as though she highly anticipated something. She perhaps expected me to be angry or... my breath caught. What if her father had come?

I waited for her at the stable door, listening to Maurice's tirade about how selfish she'd been. "I ought to put you over my knee and give you what you deserve," he growled.

I was about to intervene when Celeste patted his shoulder. "Yes, well, never mind about all that," she said. "I care about you too, and I'm sorry to cause you worry. But Maurice, can you tell me if there are any visitors expected tonight? Monsieur Vrai or Monsieur Mason?"

Maurice was normally a mild-mannered man, so his loud string of curses surprised me. Celeste *did* have an uncanny ability to make people say what they thought, probably because she took that liberty herself on a continual basis. A moment later, Celeste appeared at the door, clutching a cloth-wrapped package in one arm and looking affectionately over her shoulder, as though Maurice had paid her a compliment.

"Did you have anything to add?" she asked with raised brows when she noticed me standing close by.

I was torn between wanting to laugh and wanting to lecture her. "Maurice summed it up pretty well, I think."

I didn't offer to carry the package, since she held it like a precious box of jewels, but I did offer her my arm. She took it with dignified grace. "Are you expecting any company tonight?" she asked after we'd walked a few paces.

"Why?"

"Because *I'm* expecting a visitor."

I halted in my tracks. "Who?"

"It's a surprise," she said with an airy little wave of her hand.

Her father *was* here. Fear pricked at the back of my mind. I was so afraid of what he would say. Of what Celeste would do.

I cleared my throat. "I don't know. Bertram is leaving for Paris next week. He has a colleague there who wants his expertise. I think he'll come here before he leaves, but he knows we've been busy with the wheat harvest and haven't had much time in the evenings."

She nudged me forward, and we continued our walk to the house. "And Jean?" she asked.

"Jean should be paying the men. I invited him in for dinner, but if you have a visitor, then I can ask him to come a different time." I didn't much care for the thought of Jean being witness to what was going to happen here tonight if Celeste's father came.

"No, that's fine," she said, her eyes distant. "My guest will be coming later, and I want to talk to Jean."

"About?" They'd shared some sort of truce, but Celeste never sought him out.

"Lavender pricing."

"*I* can tell you about lavender pricing," I said, trying not to feel insulted or to panic. I had to talk to her. It couldn't wait anymore. And my family had been growing lavender for fifty years, after all.

"I know. But I still want to talk to him."

"Wait, Celeste. Come for a walk with me? I really want to talk to you. I *need* to talk with you."

She looked at me sidelong before letting go of my arm and stepping inside. "I'm sorry, but I don't have time. I promised Suzanne I would help her with dinner."

"You are not a servant here, Celeste," I growled as I paced after her.

She spun to face me, and I stopped short to avoid knocking her over. "Then what am I, Henri?" she asked through gritted teeth.

We were only inches from each other, and I stared at her, speechless. There wasn't actually a word in French to describe her role in my home. I didn't think there was a word to describe it in any language. But words weren't always the right answer, after all, and her lips were so close to mine.

I slowly pulled the parcel from her arm. It was a book, and a heavy one. I set it on a nearby table.

Her eyes flashed a warning, but she didn't have time to protest. The next moment, she was in my arms being kissed, and not at all gently.

She froze, and at first I worried I'd made a mistake. She finally relaxed and kissed me in return, but only tentatively. It wasn't the way she'd kissed me before. I held back a groan of frustration and toned down the intensity of my kiss to match. I loosened my hold on her a little, slowly winding my hand into her hair.

"I like my new eye patch," I whispered against her mouth during a pause in our kiss. "I like all three."

"I'm glad," she said breathlessly before I kissed her again. Her hands rested on my chest, and her kiss was achingly tender, but it scared me too. It lacked the confidence she'd kissed me with before, and doubt crept into my mind. Was she not sure she wanted to kiss me? Was there something going on? Was there someone else?

Aunt Inese's footsteps sounded in the hall, and Celeste quickly stepped away from me, her face a bright blush.

"Oh, good, you're back," Aunt Inese said happily before she got a good look at Celeste. "My dear, are you all right? You look overly excited, and your hair, if you'll pardon me, is rather unkempt."

Celeste picked up the parcel from where I'd put it and assured Aunt Inese she was fine, if a little windblown.

"Henri was just arguing with me over the best way to carry out a practical joke, though he's agreed to participate a little so we can settle a matter. We have a disagreement going on over who is the better bookkeeper between Jean and myself."

I snorted but didn't contradict her story.

"You see?" she said.

"What does it involve?" Aunt Inese asked, her lips twitching.

CHAPTER 20

Celeste

Henri narrowed his good eye at me, but what was he going to say? That we hadn't been arguing but instead had actually been embracing in a way most inappropriate for a landholder and his housekeeper? That he had been toying with my emotions like a puppeteer?

So he eventually went along with what I proposed, which made me glad that I had kissed him. Not that I didn't like kissing him. The problem was that I seemed to lose track of things that really mattered when he was so close to me. Things like my lack of beauty. And the fact that I was working there as insurance against my father's debt. And especially that Henri didn't intend for me to stay. My throat constricted a little at the thought, but I smiled broadly at Inese, who expressed disappointment that her part in the farce only involved taking Suzanne, Carine, and the children to the opposite end of the house.

Henri was less easy to convince. "So you're going to play a

trick on Jean, and I'm supposed to just sit in the other room, silently listening?" he asked, folding his arms across his chest.

"Yes, until you hear the end of the joke. That's when you are supposed to come in and get a good look at his face." I prayed he'd agree quickly. I was nervous enough about the entire plan, even though most of it had been my idea.

"Jean wouldn't like me playing a trick on him."

"You're not," I said, raising my chin. "You'll only listen as *I* play a trick on him."

He gave me an exasperated look.

"He will know for sure you had nothing to do with it," I said. And as soon as Inese was out of earshot, I murmured, "Then afterward, perhaps we could go back to the argument we were having before your aunt came in."

He pressed his lips together. Was he frowning or trying not to laugh? "I think I could listen for a few minutes." He looked twice at my answering smile. I must have let the evil, vindictive glee seep into it too much. I nodded at him and left the room, almost running to the front door. I hoped he was getting into place in the formal dining room like he was supposed to.

It was an age before the men left with their wagon. I hated to lose the strength of numbers they could have provided, but it was better this way. The fewer the spectators, the less Henri's pride would suffer.

It seemed another age before Jean walked around the hillside and toward the house. I waited for him by the door.

"Is Henri inside?" he asked, looking over my shoulder.

"He's gone to bed. Heat exhaustion, I'm sure. You still look energetic though." It was one of Isabelle's tricks. Pretending to compliment someone before you came to the main point.

He smirked a little but then frowned. "Well, I suppose I ought to go."

"Oh, no. Henri said you would stay to dinner, and I wanted to tell you what my sister wrote in her letter."

"Oh?" His interest was captured immediately. Invoking Isabelle was a dirty trick, but it was the simplest way to get what I wanted, so I didn't bat an eye over it. I had to get *some* benefit out of being related to her. Heaven knew there were enough disadvantages to having a "vision of loveliness" for a sister.

"You must at least come into the parlor and let me tell you what she said about you."

"About me?" he asked, suitably impressed that I carried tidings from the goddess.

Only seconds later, I was lying unrepentantly about how heroic Isabelle thought Jean had been.

"But of course, I could only tell her what Henri told me," I said, hoping that Henri would not come into the room early. I knew he could hear every word from his position, but I didn't hear a peep out of him. "What was it like? Stepping in to save him when you knew how much trouble you could get in?"

He shrugged in a false show of modesty. I wanted to hit him.

"And how you insisted on taking Henri home. That was so good of you too."

Jean gave me an odd smile but didn't comment.

"Although, I recently met the most interesting man," I said, working to keep my tone light and conversational. "He told me that you didn't actually volunteer to take Henri home, but that you were *ordered* to."

Jean's color faded.

"And that you were ordered to return as soon as he died or was well." I kept my tone light and disbelieving. "Can you imagine his nerve at telling such a lie?"

"Horrible," Jean choked out.

"But I suppose you *had* to stay here, to make sure Henri got the proper treatment. And then, because he was much too infirm, you had to look after him."

"What else could I do?" His mouth was tight, and he eyed me through a narrowed gaze.

"And then, for his benefit, because he wasn't nearly smart enough to do it himself, you simply *had* to take over his book-keeping."

He didn't say anything, only watched me.

"And of course, it was very necessary, for his own good, that you circulated through Aix the news about what a godless monster he'd become," I said more loudly. "And how anyone who worked for him chanced death or the devil's company. I think I said that right. The men I talked to in Aix might not have remembered correctly. And, in the kindest way possible, you began stealing twenty percent of his sale prices!" I was screaming by now. "Whispering lies into his ear about how buyers in Aix didn't want to do business with him. How they were cheating him, when it was *you* cheating him all along!"

Jean stood, his chest heaving with rage. "You can't prove any of that," he whispered in a deadly voice.

"How could you do it?" I asked in disgust. "How could you do that to your friend?"

"He wasn't my friend," Jean ground out in a low voice. "He was one of *them*. One of the heroic fools better with weapons than their brains. I meant nothing to him until I brought him home. I could have just taken the gold Inese offered me."

"But then you would have had to go back into the army," I taunted.

"You don't know what it was like," he whispered, his eyes wild. "Men getting butchered and shot on either side of you. The cries of the dying. You'd have to be crazy to have the stomach for it."

I agreed with him. It sounded terrible. "But you thought it was better to come home a cowardly hero where you could slowly take everything away from a man who'd been injured in one of the bravest acts ever committed in the history of France?"

He took a step toward me, but I held my ground despite knowing retreat was the safer option.

"He owed everything to me," Jean ground out. "I could have put him out of his misery. It would have been a service, but I brought him home and saved him that way instead."

I snorted.

"If he'd stayed, he would have rotted away in an army sick camp. *I* brought him home. *I* helped him through his recovery."

I noticed Inese didn't get any of the credit in his eyes.

"Became his friend when he had none."

Did he truly overlook Bertram and Paul so easily?

"I ignored the horror of his face. I dealt with that witch he calls his aunt. *That* warrants a reward."

"You think he'll reward you when he learns you've been cheating him and destroying his name?"

"What makes you think he'll believe you?" he asked with a sneer.

Why hadn't Henri come into the room yet? Had he fallen asleep?

"Funny thing. He doesn't have to believe *me*. You've been so careful to make sure Henri never wants to have any interaction with Monsieur Farine because you've seen the way he keeps his records." I withdrew Monsieur Farine's ledger from the table next to me. "Isn't his system amazing? The way he tracks the goods he purchases? I mean, doesn't his particular style strike you as interesting?"

"Where did you get that?" Jean demanded, white-faced.

Why hadn't Henri come in yet? "And the way the person receiving the payment signs right next to Monsieur Farine's name? Tell me, Jean, whose signature is *that*?" I pointed dramatically to the page I'd bookmarked. Right to the place where Jean had signed his name.

I'd been worried he might draw his pistol on me. I should have anticipated what he actually did. In two strides, he was beside me, and with all the force a small, wiry man could muster, which was quite a lot, he struck me across the face. I wish I could say that a tall, sturdy girl like myself could take it without flinching. But the truth was that the force of the blow spun my off my feet and threw me into the table. Gasping for breath, I heard Jean cock his pistol.

∼

Henri

I couldn't believe it. None of it could be true. I'd been there. I knew what had happened that horrible day. I remembered someone was ready to kill me as I'd begged them to. A pistol was aimed at my head. And I remembered someone stepping in front of me to stop them. When I'd woken from the laudanum haze, I'd taken Jean's story at full value. It all fit with what I'd experienced. But it hadn't been Jean who saved me. He'd only brought me home to Aunt Inese with the expectation of a reward, or at least, hope of avoiding military service.

And then I'd allowed him to cheat me. And to convince me that people were afraid of dealing with the disfigured man I'd become. I'd believed I was a beast with no hope of redemption. I'd lived the last two years afraid of people's reaction to me. Afraid of people. And until Celeste came, I'd gone along with all his lies and half-truths.

When Celeste taunted him about the proof that would convince me, I knew she was in trouble. Jean carried a pistol, and while he was almost the worst shot in our regiment, at this close range, he couldn't miss her. I sprinted for the door separating us. I was too late. The torment I knew in that small second when I saw him strike her and then draw a pistol on her couldn't have been any worse than the pains of the damned in hell. I yelled and dashed forward, but he didn't turn his head, didn't even seem to realize I was there. He cocked the pistol. He was going to shoot her in the back.

It wasn't that time slowed. It was more that every detail imprinted itself deeply into my awareness.

Jean's gun was level with Celeste's heart when, with a feral scream of rage, she spun toward Jean, Monsieur Farine's ledger still clasped in her hands. She slammed the book into his head, knocking him sideways as the gun discharged. The bullet shattered a vase behind Celeste as Jean staggered back, completely thrown off-balance.

That was when his face collided with my fist. He dropped to the floor and didn't open his eyes for a full three seconds. When he did, he immediately went for the knife hidden in his belt. I knew it was there and was ready.

"It took more than fifteen English soldiers to do this to me," I said as I disarmed him easily. It was hard to speak with my fury choking me, but I got the words out. "You couldn't scratch me if you tried." I punched him again and heard something crack in his nose. I held him up by the shoulder of his shirt and punched him again. His jaw made a funny popping noise. "How...dare... you...strike..." I punctuated each word with a blow to his face. "A...woman...in...this...house?"

Suddenly Celeste's hands were on my arm. "That's enough, Henri. Let the magistrate handle it now."

I looked around in surprise. My anger had tunneled my vision. I hadn't seen Monsieur Farine and the magistrate enter the room. I hadn't heard anything but the rage and hurt crashing like waves in a storm through my mind.

I dropped Jean unceremoniously on the floor and turned to inspect Celeste. I held her by her shoulders and surveyed her carefully. "Are you hurt? The bullet didn't touch you? I'm so sorry it took me so long to believe...to understand." Part of me wanted to shake her for endangering herself like that, but most of me was giddy with gratitude that she was all right.

Well, mostly all right. Her lip was split, and an enormous bruise was forming just under her eye.

She only gave me an uncertain little smile. "Good joke, wasn't it?" she whispered.

I couldn't even answer her except to bark a humorless laugh as I pulled her into a tight embrace. I loosed her regretfully in order to see to the task at hand. The magistrate shackled Jean's wrists and asked for my ledger in order to bring the appropriate evidence to trial. Monsieur Farine took turns glaring at my no-longer-friend and glancing at me with searching eyes. His hair was a little thinner than the last time we'd spoken, and I felt a pang of chagrin over the time I'd wasted avoiding my father's friend.

"It appears I owe you an apology, Monsieur Farine," I said, completely repentant. "I should not have trusted my business dealings to this man or believed what he told me about you. I assure you I will be directly managing my business affairs from now on — if you will still work with me."

Monsieur Farine beamed, deep smile lines in his face as he held his hand out. I grasped it gratefully, ignoring the pain in my hand at his tight grip. I *had* hit Jean quite hard.

"Henri," said Aunt Inese as she hurried into the room. "What's going on?"

I explained as briefly as I could and promised more details later. She didn't seem at all sorry to see Jean, still unconscious, dragged outside by the magistrate and Monsieur Farine.

"But I heard a gunshot, and a wild cry. Was there an animal in here?"

I gave a real laugh then. I couldn't help myself. "No. That was just the sound of Celeste conquering a lesser creature."

"What?" Aunt Inese turned to Celeste, who gave me a small smile.

I reached out to touch the side of her head. She was so beautiful, this tall, bruised, strong, brave, and wonderful girl. "You'd better let Aunt Inese see to your cheek while I go help the magistrate."

She held fast to my sleeve. "There is one more thing, Henri. There is someone here to see you. He should be at the kitchen door by now."

She gave me an anxious, searching look, and meekly followed Aunt Inese from the room. The meekness had to be an act. I knew what she was capable of. But how foolish she must have thought me. My own stupidity rankled painfully as I strode to the kitchen, thinking distractedly of all that had happened rather than what I was doing.

I threw open the door, almost hitting the enormous man who stood there. A jolt of battle energy hit me just before I recognized Hans Robineau. The red streaks in his hair had turned white, giving him a very unnaturally light blond look. Other than that, the last two years seemed not to have changed him. His blue eyes were just as bright, but they were anxious, as though he didn't quite know what to say.

I felt a pang for my appearance but tried to sound natural when I stretched out my hand and said, "It's about time you came to visit me. Please tell me you can stay several days."

"Henri Durant," he said, grasping my hand even more tightly than Monsieur Farine had. "You *are* alive. I should have known you could survive anything. You look so well and whole." He clapped me on my shoulder, practically dislocating it.

"Not quite whole," I said, gesturing toward my patch with a shrug. "But I am well, and all the better now you've come to visit. I'll tell Suzanne to plan on another for dinner and you must tell me what you have been doing and what has happened to everyone."

"She is the feisty red-haired woman who keeps a pistol?" he asked. His accent had improved since I'd seen him last. Having a French father and a Norwegian mother, he'd grown up speaking mostly Norwegian in his home, but he'd lived many years now in France.

"Why Hans, have you been *spying* on us?" I said, trying to contain my smile. Surely he couldn't be serious.

He shifted uncomfortably on his feet. "If you'd been chased from towns and homes at gunpoint for simply trying to ask questions about the whereabouts of an old friend, you'd be wary too. I've been shot at twice while trying to get near your house. And when I came to the back entrance of your house over a week ago to see if you lived here, I saw this Suzanne cooking with a pistol next to her on the counter. I ran away before she ever saw me." He gave a short laugh. "I didn't think it was her shooting at me, but of course, it made me cautious."

"Hans, I have no idea what you're talking about. Someone shot at you? But come inside. There are people you need to meet."

"Did your Celeste already tell you everything?" he asked.

I nodded, anxious to hear how he had met her and why he thought to call her mine.

"When I learned you were truly alive, Henri, I must confess, I was so angry with Jean that I went looking for him first. He was supposed to report back, give us news. I didn't want to face you before I learned what was going on. But the little weasel was hard to find. I'm sorry that I delayed."

I clapped Hans on the shoulder. "I'm just happy you're here."

We hurried through the house and outside to meet the magistrate, who chuckled with good humor when he saw Hans. "Ah, the English giant terrorizing the countryside is actually an honorable French soldier. I will see to it that the news circulates."

"Not as honorable as Sergeant Durant," Hans said. "But I'm sure you've already heard the story."

The magistrate eyed me a long moment. "One hears many stories, Monsieur. The trick is knowing which are true."

I tried to shush Hans, but he broke into a wry laugh. "This man took on half a regiment of English raiders on his own to save a young family from torture and death. And he succeeded, despite the evidence you see of that battle." He gestured to my scars.

My gaze snapped to Hans. I hardly heard the kind exclamations of surprise from Monsieur Farine and the magistrate. Their attention was quickly claimed by Jean, who began to stir on the ground near the magistrate's carriage.

I ignored Jean, too overwhelmed by what Hans had just said. "The woman," I whispered, my throat constricting painfully. "And her children. They lived?"

"Celeste told me you didn't know." He clasped my arm. "Henri, you saved them. They lived."

I fought back a sob of relief. How often I'd worried about what had happened to that young family.

"The mother and children pray for your soul and for your family every day."

"How could you know that?" I asked, astonished.

Hans' cheeks flushed, and he barked a laugh. "Because I married her a few months ago."

I clapped him on the shoulder, and we both laughed heartily. I didn't even think about the way my scars would pull at my mouth.

We stopped only when interrupted by Jean's cursing.

CHAPTER 21

Celeste

I nese and I spied on Henri and his friend shamelessly
through the front parlor window while I held a cool cloth to
my swollen cheek and relayed to her everything I'd learned
from Captain Robineau.

"It was that giant that kept Henri from being killed by his
own men?" Inese asked for the third time. "From being killed by
Jean? He only brought him home to me on *his* orders?"

"Yes, with instructions to return as soon as he had word of
Henri's fate," I said. "Even though the entire regiment was
honorably disbanded, Jean may still face military tribunal for
deserting his regiment and disobeying orders.

Inese nodded in approval, a fierce, vengeful gleam in her
eyes.

"Someone shot at the captain twice," I said. "We think it was
Jean trying to prevent Captain Robineau from coming here."

"Attempted murder."

"Another trial he'll be facing."

"If my nephew doesn't kill him first," Inese said with a smug smile as Henri's growling diatribe reached our ears. "Listen to Jean whimper, the filthy coward."

"We'll have to warn Carine about the captain before she sees him again. She keeps twitching and looking over her shoulder, and I can see why. The man's as big as a house."

For a few minutes, Henri seemed angry enough to reach down and strangle Jean, but his own good character, and possibly the presence of the magistrate, prevented murder being done in the courtyard. Eventually the men all shook hands right over the top of Jean before the magistrate and Monsieur Farine loaded him unceremoniously into the carriage and drove him away. Henri turned his friend back toward the house and saw us before we could move away from the window. He waved and started forward.

Suddenly very shy, I hurried out of the room, hoping to reach the stairs before Henri found me. They caught up to me in the main entryway, and I had no choice but to turn and meet them.

"Celeste, I understand you've already met Hans," Henri said.

I nodded graciously to Monsieur Robineau while he smiled and bowed. "I thank you, Mademoiselle Lebeau," he said. "I see that you are a fierce enemy and a fiercer friend. Henri is lucky to have you."

I felt a blush coming on and wondered if I should dispute the relationship he implied. Henri only smiled, so, taking my cue from him, I thanked Captain Robineau and excused myself. "I find that bookkeepers' fists are very hard objects, and I should like to rest."

They both grinned. I'd never seen Henri look so young. His actual age. I found myself in my own bed in just minutes, and despite the excitement of the day, I fell asleep instantly.

I saw little of Henri the next day as he was in the fields overseeing the preparation for the beginning of the lavender harvest. The captain went with him, leaving me free to work on whatever I wanted. I returned to the vegetable garden, a never-ending source of enjoyment and frustration, and when I heard Henri, Captain Robineau, and Paul coming back to the house, I realized I was covered in mud. I hitched my skirts up and ran for the door, hoping none of them saw.

Carine braved the captain's presence that evening, once her children were asleep, in order to be near Paul, who seemed happy to have her close. Captain Robineau amused us with tales of pranks pulled within the regiment and by reenacting the antics of his step-children.

He retired early, citing fatigue and a pleasant fullness in his stomach. Inese disappeared somewhere, and Paul, looking sneaky, asked Carine out on a moonlit stroll. The sound of her gentle laughter followed them out the door.

It was the first time I'd been alone with Henri since Jean had been hauled away the previous day, and I found myself nervous; nervous about what he would think of me, about what he would say to me, and mostly nervous he would not want to kiss me.

"What were you thinking, Celeste?" he immediately asked, shaking his head. "To put yourself in danger that way? Don't you know you might have been killed?"

I shrugged. "I wanted you to hear it from him. I didn't think it would be the same if I simply told you or even if I had the magistrate arrest him and explain it all to you."

"It wouldn't have been the same, but it would have been safer," he said, his tone grim and his brows drawn together. "Don't you know what you mean to me?" he asked.

My heart skittered.

"To all of us?"

Oh. My heart resumed its normal pace.

"I shall try to be more careful in the future," I promised. I stood to take my leave, not sure I could handle any criticism he might want to make, but Henri stood too. He drew closer to me.

"Thank you, Celeste. Thank you for what you have done for

me. You have proven yourself over and over the very best and dearest type of friend. How can I..." He paused to stare into my eyes and seemed to lose his train of thought for a long moment. "How can I ever repay you?"

To keep myself from saying anything embarrassing, I blurted out, "Well, the last buckets of lavender you gave me for other reasons. I should like you to keep to the original wager now that we know Jean made purposeful errors on every line of your ledger."

He laughed as I hoped he would. "Of course," he agreed, though his smile was a little disappointed.

"And also," I added, taking a gulp, "you could come a little closer."

The disappointment faded from his expression, and I soon found myself comfortably tight in his embrace, being kissed so enthusiastically that sometimes my feet weren't actually touching the floor. I had promised myself when he kissed me last time that it would be *the last time*, but his kisses were like Suzanne's trifle. Once you tasted it, you could never be satisfied. Gluttony really was the only option.

And so I let him kiss me. For a really, really long time. I enjoyed the feel of his hands in my hair, at my shoulders, and on my face. He was careful to avoid my bruise, which was so hideous by then that I was surprised he even wanted to be in the same room as me, let alone have me in his arms.

Henri kissed me with passion that stretched the bounds of propriety, but only by a little. He had proven himself a gentleman, and I trusted him completely, so I kissed him back, matching his intensity.

I buried the memory of the conversation I'd overheard between him and Bertram. If Henri had ever wanted me gone, he'd already changed his mind. I convinced myself I'd misunderstood, that I would be able to remain here with him. He kissed me more urgently. Perhaps he'd want me to stay forever.

I really hoped he would, because being in his arms felt more like home than home ever had.

~

Henri

Since Celeste had come to my home, she'd set the accounts in order. She'd made people laugh on a regular basis. The garden was tamed. She'd put decent food on the table when Suzanne was gone. Men weren't afraid to work for me. My friend, Paul, appeared on the verge of proposing to the woman he'd loved for years. And if I wasn't very careful, it seemed the château was going to have a complicated system of drainage pipes installed. But all this magic she'd performed was nothing compared what she'd done to me.

It didn't really have a lot to do with her discovery of Jean's treachery, nor the way she brought Hans and all his answers to my doorstep. It was simply her. She brought me to life. She didn't change who I was. She changed how I felt about it.

As I kissed her there in the dimly lit parlor, it occurred to me that I was happy. Truly happy. Happier by far than I even remembered being before I joined the army. I didn't have long to think about it because Celeste was kissing me so thoroughly that it took all my effort to keep up without doing anything I shouldn't.

For the next three days, I divided my time between Celeste and work, which wasn't work at all because Hans accompanied me around the farm, talking ceaselessly to me of happy times past and happy plans for the future. Aside from his willingness to converse, he and Paul were much alike, and the two became fast friends.

Hans had been a blacksmith before he went into the army,

and now he was starting up a smithy again, specializing in the fancy scrollwork and metal fencing that was so popular.

"And you?" he asked. "You will stay here on your farm forever, marry your sweetheart, and have a dozen babies?"

That sounded wonderful to me, though I only laughed at him. "What girl would want to have a dozen babies?"

Every time I saw Celeste, that dream seemed better and better (though perhaps with a smaller number of children), and every day in my mind I asked her to marry me, but it never seemed the right time to say the words aloud. If she said no, she wouldn't want to stay under the same roof with me till her father came. If she said yes, I don't think I could have waited for her father before I married her.

I spent as much time with her as I could. I had to convince her to love me before it was too late, but I couldn't bring myself to tell her about her father's treachery. I couldn't tell her why I'd originally wanted her sister to come. I tried a few times, but she turned those big brown eyes on me, their concentric rings of green almost glowing, and I lost my nerve.

"Henri, are you all right?" she asked after I'd done this for the third time in the same day.

"Yes. Yes, of course. Wouldn't you like to walk down to the lavender fields with me?"

Every evening, that is what I did: walk with Celeste, laugh with Celeste, and as often as possible, kiss Celeste.

The morning that Hans left, I stayed home from the fields to see him off.

"Some parting advice, my friend," he said before mounting his horse. "You are waiting too long. If you don't act now, you may lose your chance with her."

"Did you ask your wife after only knowing her a few months?" I asked.

"Yes," he said.

"What? I thought you were only married this spring."

"She said no the first ten times I asked her. Perhaps it was eleven. It would have only been five or six if I'd been able to resist asking until she was done mourning her husband, God rest his soul. But I couldn't wait. I loved her from the first time I met her."

I smiled. "The first time I met Celeste, we despised each other."

"She is not…overly timid," he said, grinning. He'd already told me about her encounter with him on the road.

I laughed, thinking of the way she'd slammed Monsieur Farine's ledger into Jean's head. "No. And I am never bored around her."

Hans gave me an understanding look before pulling me into a bone-crushing hug. "Come visit us soon," he said. "Maude and the children would love to meet you."

Celeste came to the door to wave him off, and when his horse was out of sight, I turned to her. "You look very pretty," I said. And I meant it. Her hair was swept softly back from her face, and she wore a flattering fawn-colored dress.

"Thank you," she said, her eyes downcast. I suspected Celeste was not accustomed to many compliments. That was something I intended to change.

"But you are not dressed for the garden," I said. "Will you be sketching plans for some new outbuildings for me today?"

She wrinkled her nose at me. "Not today," she said. "I'm going to Aix with Inese and Maurice. I promised your aunt I would help her pick out some fabric for a new gown she's starting. And Suzanne wants to make a new pinafore for Marie for her birthday next week and needs some cloth as well. Would you like me to carry a message to Bertram? He's leaving in the next few days, and you might not see him for months."

"No. Though perhaps you should remind him to come see us when he gets back."

Celeste smiled and nodded, turning back to the house to

finish preparing for the trip to town. She either agreed with my use of "us" or misunderstood it to mean Aunt Inese and me. I had every intention of Celeste being my wife by the time Bertram returned from Paris.

She was one step through the doorway when I snagged her hand and spun her back into my arms where she allowed me to steal a kiss. I didn't want to let her go. I was jealous of Aunt Inese, jealous of Bertram for sure. But the look she gave me over her shoulder when she scurried off made me think I might be kissed again when she came back. Thirty minutes later, I stood on the hill behind the house, watching the carriage pull out of the drive and onto the main road. Someone waved out of the window at me. Celeste. My heart felt light. I'd never been so content. Once the carriage was completely out of sight, I turned and walked back to the lavender field, completely unaware of the misfortune about to befall me.

CHAPTER 22

Celeste

Once I saw Inese safely to the cloth warehouse, her favorite place in the world, I walked to Bertram's parents' home to wish him good luck on his trip.

His eyes widened in shock when he met me at the door. He glanced behind him and immediately suggested a walk in the little garden behind the house.

"I probably shouldn't have come into town with my black eye," I said, laughing. "But I wanted to see you before you left for Paris."

"What happened?" he demanded.

I quickly relayed the story, pretending not to notice when he swore under his breath several times.

"I wish I'd been there," he said when I'd finished.

"So you could say 'I told you so'?"

"No. So I could have had a turn hitting Jean. The little weasel. I should go to the magistrate's office to see if they'll let me have a go at him."

I smiled and shook my head. "Henri probably had you covered."

Bertram's angry look faded, but he watched me with a troubled expression. "I'm glad you came. There's something I need to tell you before I leave for Paris."

"Are you all right?" I asked.

"Yes, yes." Bertram paced back and forth while I watched him, my unease growing.

Finally he stopped, leaned against a wall, and dropped his face into his hands. "Henri is going to kill me."

"Why?"

"But you have to know," he said. His hands fell from his face. "It isn't fair. You're my friend too."

I smiled. "Thank you, Bertram. That means a lot to me."

"It means a lot to me too," he said, clenching his teeth. He paused one moment more, then burst out, "Did your father explain to you why Henri wanted your sister to come?"

I was expecting him to say something about Jean. How did he know it was Isabelle that was first wanted? After a startled moment, I said slowly, "He never actually said much about it. I knew that Henri had wanted Isabelle to come, not me. Father made me leave the room when he told her about it. She insisted that I come in her place, and I was very ready to get away from Marseille. This seemed a good way to do it. I was lucky."

"I wonder if you were," Bertram said, his eyes uncharacteristically mournful. "Have you ever wondered why Henri keeps that bedroom locked? The one that joins the family rooms?"

"Yes. I thought maybe it was his mother's room, that it was perhaps a sad place for him. He didn't seem to want to talk about it."

"No, Celeste," he said quietly. "That room was prepared for someone. He's been saving it for her."

I stared at him while he waited for me to catch up. It took a moment for me to make the connection. "You mean for Isabelle," I said. "That room is for Isabelle?"

He nodded, a troubled look in his eyes.

"So he planned a larger room for my sister, but when I came, he didn't want me there," I said, not understanding the significance.

Bertram just waited, watching me process it.

"Well, I suppose he thought a great beauty needed a larger room," I said with an attempt at indifference. "What I still don't understand is why Henri thought he needed a beautiful house-keeper in the first place. It's the silliest notion, really—" I broke off as the most horrific thought took shape in my mind. "He didn't want a housekeeper," I whispered.

Bertram didn't have to say anything. The pitying look in his eyes confirmed what I'd guessed. I hated pity. Despised it. It was one of the things my life had taught me to abhor. I really shouldn't have minded it coming from Bertram, but even from a friend, I couldn't stomach it. It was almost painful, the ripping sensation in my mind as I tore my outward reaction away from my true feelings. Those I buried deep inside.

I put a fist to my hip and arched one eyebrow. "Do you mean to tell me that Henri bargained with my father to send Isabelle to be his bride?"

Bertram nodded, some uncertainty obvious in his expression. "He thought a beautiful wife would help people see past his scars. It would be good for his business dealings. She was to come to see if they could get along well. Part of the debt was to be forgiven if she came, the rest if she married him."

I snorted in a very unladylike way. "That is the stupidest business transaction I could imagine. He'd never even met her," I scoffed. "To commit himself like that. The girl ruins every-thing she touches, though she certainly has ornamental value, so perhaps it would have worked out. It may have helped his busi-ness dealings at first. It still might."

"What do you mean?"

"Oh. I thought you knew. She may be coming here."

It was a bluff, but I hoped he would buy it.

"Really?"

"It's been the plan all along." I considered a moment. "She knew about all this from the start, so I suppose she just needed time to get used to the idea. She really does enjoy society. It will be hard for her to leave Marseille. She'll grow to like Aix, I think." Or possibly not. There weren't enough men to fawn over her.

"Please don't tell me you're leaving us," Bertram said, the sadness in his eyes almost pulling tears from mine. But I couldn't cry about this in front of him. Not in front of anyone.

I smiled at him. "You are too kind. You know I only came for a visit, to help Inese. I may have been tricked into it, but I can't change the plans now. Once my father comes, I go back to Marseille."

"What will you do?"

"Well, that hasn't changed," I said with a laugh. "I'll continue the path I set for myself." I couldn't help the wistful note in my voice when I added, "You will write to me, though, won't you Bertram? I don't have so many friends that I can afford to lose track of any."

He covered my hand with his. "I don't know what I'd do if you didn't keep me updated. Here." He took out a fancy little card and pressed it into my hands. "It's my friend's office address in Paris."

"I'll miss you, Bertram. And thank you."

"You're not leaving immediately?"

I laughed. The sound pained my ears. "I don't think so. But with my father, you never can tell."

I quickly took my leave and almost ran to Monsieur Farine's shop. I couldn't bear not to say goodbye to him and his wife. Thankfully the shop was empty.

I repressed the pain that threatened to eat its way to the front of my mind and hurried to them. They kissed my cheeks, but I didn't give them time to ask me any questions.

"I recently learned my visit is almost over. How I will miss you."

They made all the proper protests as I gazed around their shop, taking it in. I don't know how I managed to even think, but my intellect hadn't abandoned me completely. Yet.

"You have inspired me to follow through with my dream. I am going to take my savings and open a shop."

"Where?"

"I haven't decided yet. Probably in Provence, but maybe as far north as Paris. What I really need is a supplier, someone I can purchase my wares from, someone who already has a tightly run business and knows the industry."

"Oh, Mademoiselle Lebeau. You must use us," Monsieur Farine cried. "We will not even charge a percent."

I laughed at him. "Of course you must. Don't be silly. But there is something I will require of you."

They leaned closer.

"Secrecy," I said.

"What?"

"You know that a woman in business has a more difficult time, so I will contact you under a man's name. You will know it is me, of course, and you will tell no one, absolutely no one at all of our arrangement." I held up my hand to stop their protests. "Don't you see it? I will become successful on my own. My triumph will be my own, and then I can share it. But if I fail, then no one will be the wiser, and my pride will not take a completely fatal blow."

Their faces relaxed into smiles again.

"But you must promise that you will tell no one I am in contact with you. Not anyone, ever."

"Of course," they said in unison.

I hugged them both and hurried out, making it to the fountain just in time to meet Inese and Maurice. Luckily, Inese was tired and promptly fell asleep. I didn't think I could have pretended for long around her.

I quickly succumbed to my mental fatigue, drooping against the window and into a numb stupor. I knew what had to come next, but I couldn't mentally face it yet. I might have lost consciousness a few times. I couldn't tell. The miles went past at a blur. My eyes had difficulty focusing on objects.

When we arrived home, or rather, at Henri Durant's home, Inese startled awake. "My dear, are you ill?" she asked, looking closely at me.

I tried to smile and failed. "I might be. You don't mind if I skip dinner, do you?"

She insisted on tucking me into my bed before she went down to dinner to meet Henri coming in from the fields. I quickly put on my slippers and then waited by my door. I heard Henri speak to Paul outside my window. His cheerful voice shook the emotional wall holding back my pain and tears. I gave him time to get to the dining parlor and greet Inese, and still I waited.

I'd been right to. A few minutes later, I heard his tread in the hall. He stopped in front of my door, while my heart pounded in my chest. "Celeste?" he said in a low whisper. Inese probably told him not to bother my sleep.

I waited breathlessly until I was certain he was gone down to dinner. Then I slipped out of my room and around the corner to the bedroom where Henri had retrieved the white gloves I wore to the dance. I only hesitated a moment before putting my hand boldly to the knob and turning it. He must not have ever remembered to lock it again, because it opened easily. I quickly slipped inside and shut the door behind me.

I stood in the most elegantly decorated, beautiful room I'd ever seen. Thick carpets softened my footfalls, and intricate tapestries hung from the walls. An enormous, silk-draped bed took up an entire corner of the room, and in another corner was a dressing table covered with enough jewel cases and perfumes to satisfy any princess. There was a bookshelf against one wall, full of costly leather-bound volumes. I didn't think any of them detailed the finer points of drainage systems.

I walked forward as though in a trance. Trances were for melodramatic heroines in books, but I was no heroine. I'd only been the comic relief until she could arrive on the scene and claim what was hers. He'd been saving this room for Isabelle. He'd been saving *himself* for Isabelle.

I traced the bed frame and bookshelf with my fingers. I opened the wardrobe and took in the bolts of fabric waiting to be turned into dresses. I opened beautifully decorated boxes of jewelry and gloves. I peeked in hatboxes. I even smelled a few of the perfumes. It helped convince me that this horrible scene was all very real.

This entire time, Henri had been wanting Isabelle, dreaming of her, waiting for her. He'd been a friend to me, had even been confused enough to kiss me a few times, but he'd wanted her all along.

Leaving the room just as I'd found it, I closed the door and went back to my own quaint bedroom. I changed into a night-dress and slipped under my lavender-scented blankets. Then I let myself remember.

I remembered every fool thing I'd said. Everything I'd done. Every mortifying detail. All the kisses I'd initiated. I'd thought he cared about me, perhaps even loved me. And all that time, Henri had only been humoring me while he waited for Isabelle. Nothing had changed. I was still in her shadow. I hadn't gotten far enough away. I turned my face to the wall, no longer able to hold back the sound of my despair.

∼

Henri

B efore I went to bed, I convinced myself I'd see Celeste at breakfast. I'd find an excuse to go on a walk with her, and then I would confess everything. She needed to know all of it. I couldn't wait any longer. Her father could stay away forever for all I cared. I would tell her myself.

I had a troubled night's sleep, despite the many hours I'd spent helping with the harvest, and when I woke, I hurried downstairs.

The first thing I saw in the main entry was a traveling trunk. Celeste's trunk. I swallowed back a wave of fear and began to run.

I tried the parlor and sitting rooms first, then the kitchen. There was no sign of her, no sign of anyone.

"Celeste?" I called. My heart thudded painfully in my chest, but I hoped my anxiety wasn't evident in my voice.

"We're in here," Aunt Inese called from the dining room.

I found Aunt Inese and Suzanne talking seriously with Celeste, who didn't turn to look at me when I walked in the door.

"You can't leave *now*," my aunt said.

"I'm afraid I must. I delayed too long as it is. Who knows what I'll find when I get home?"

"You're leaving?" I said, my voice too loud.

Aunt Inese and Suzanne stared at me, but Celeste only nodded without turning my way. "I took far too long to read my sister's letter. I must hurry home to help her."

I could only imagine the horror on my face. Suzanne nudged Aunt Inese. They both murmured excuses and left me alone with Celeste.

I stared at her for a long time, my mouth opening and closing like a startled fish.

She finally lifted her chin and turned to look at me, her eyes

241

wary.

"Why?" I finally managed. I think my voice broke.

"I'm needed at home. I never should have stayed so long. I just—" She took a deep breath, and I realized she truly was in distress.

"What happened?" I asked, but at her mutinous look, I added, "I'm so sorry. How can I help? I see Maurice is readying the carriage to take you to Marseille."

"Oh, no. He is just taking me to town. I'll get a hired carriage for the rest of the journey."

"You'll do nothing of the sort," I said. "Maurice could get you there in a day and then back just as quickly. He has a brother he can stay with in Marseille until you're ready to come home." I didn't realize until several minutes later that I'd just implied her home was here with me, rather than in Marseille.

She stared out the window, her lips a thin line as she considered my offer.

I took in her bloodshot eyes and pale skin. "Are you well, Celeste, truly?" I asked, stepping nearer and gently tracing the side of her face with my fingers.

"Stop," she said in a strangled whisper, stepping away. "I am *fine*, Monsieur Durant," she said irritably. Her jaw trembled. Did I dare pull her into my arms? I took another step toward her, but she moved back again.

"Of course you are," I said. I wished I could help her, but she obviously didn't want to talk about it. I suspected she did not want to cry, and she looked on the verge of it. "But I'm not sure *I'll* be fine without Mademoiselle Lebeau," I said, mimicking her formal words. It was true though. How could I stand for her to leave?

She turned her back to me and said drily, "I assure you, Mademoiselle Lebeau will be here as soon as I can possibly arrange it." The light from the east window illuminated her outline, and I quickly admired her form while I had the chance.

I wished she would look over her shoulder at me, so I could see the angle made by her chin and neck.

"Then I will trust you to Maurice," I said. On a sudden impulse, I closed the remaining distance between us, rested my hands on her shoulders, and lightly kissed the back of her head. "Godspeed, Celeste."

"Goodbye, Monsieur Durant," she whispered.

I left her there, my mind troubled and anxious. I forgot about breakfast entirely as I went out to meet Paul and Jacques, but I couldn't focus on my work. I climbed the small hill behind the house in time to watch Celeste approach the carriage. Carine, Suzanne, and Aunt Inese each embraced her. She looked up then, and I thought she saw me. I raised my hand in farewell, but she turned away and allowed Maurice to assist her into the carriage. She must not have seen me.

That first day without Celeste felt an eternity, the second even longer, especially when darkness came, and she didn't. True, whatever she needed to fix in Marseille might take a while. She hadn't told me what it was, but I had taken it for granted that she'd be back within the week. I didn't mind the work in the stables. Maurice always kept things orderly, and it was easy to pick up where he'd left off. Carine's son, Martin, liked to feed the animals, and after I'd threatened him with all the appropriate hazards to his life should he get in the stalls with the horses or even the cow, I allowed him to help with that task. He almost never missed anything, and was so enthusiastic about it that I wondered how I'd take the job away from him when Maurice came back.

Bertram should have left Aix days ago, so I was surprised when he showed up the morning of the third day of Celeste's absence.

"Where is Celeste?" he asked without preamble.

"Gone home. Something came up. Why?"

Bertram had always been entirely too interested in Celeste.

"You let her go," he said, shaking his head. "You are the biggest fool I've ever encountered."

"What?"

"She knows you wanted her sister, and not as a housekeeper."

I stared at Bertram while the life Celeste had put into me slowly ebbed away. "You told her." I should have been furious with him, but I was too shocked.

"Someone had to," he said, almost shouting. "You strung her along for months. I'd thought better of you, Henri. If you didn't like her, that's fine. But you never told her. You let her think you cared for her. "

"I do care for her." I had trouble breathing. She hated me. Despised me. She'd been desperate to leave.

"You have a great way of showing it," Bertram said, pacing in front of me. "She was the best thing to ever come your way, and you only toyed with her. And why? For the dream of a pretty girl you've never met."

"No," I choked out. "I love her, Bertram. I was going to tell her."

His scowl softened. "Truly?"

I practically fell into the nearest chair and put my head in my hands. I should have told her weeks ago — that her father had lied to her, that I loved her. Everything.

"You should go get her."

He was right. I should. I stood up. I would go this minute. Paul and Jacques could manage the harvest. Then I remembered. "She said she was coming back."

"She did?"

"Yes." Hadn't she?

"Are you *sure*?"

"Yes."

"Well, you don't deserve her," Bertram said, "but for both your sakes, I'm glad."

CHAPTER 23

Celeste

W hen Maurice pulled up in front of my father's house, he hesitated before opening the coach door. "It doesn't appear anyone is home."

"That's quite all right," I said. "I know my way in the dark. My sister and her chaperone are probably out with friends."

He didn't look convinced, but placed my trunk inside the door anyway and promised he would be back the next morning.

"I will need two days at least," I said. "You don't mind staying with your brother?"

"Of course not, but—"

"Thank you," I said, trying to smile. I might have succeeded. I was too spent to tell. I waved at Maurice and closed the door, staring around in the darkness. I recognized the outline of every table and chair. I knew each room inside out. But it didn't feel like home. The place that felt like home was miles and miles away, and I would never go there again.

I might have sat down on the floor right there and cried my eyes out, but a scraping noise from the direction of the kitchen distracted me. It sounded like a door opening. I thought uneasily of burglars, and wished I'd let Maurice look through the house after all. I walked on tiptoe toward the back of the house, finally spying a light under the kitchen door. I paused long enough to grasp a heavy ornamental vase before I threw open the door, ready to do battle.

Isabelle jumped up from the table and screamed. And then she sobbed. And then she rushed forward and threw her arms around me.

"You got my letter," she cried, half hysterical. "Oh, Celeste, I knew you would come back." Her grip tightened and she cried so passionately, that my anger with her lessened by a degree, enough that I could ask her what was the matter.

It took another ten minutes for her to answer me. I suspected she'd been saving up for this dramatic display and wasn't willing to give it up too quickly.

"He d-doesn't love me," she finally said, clasping her hands together.

"You know very well I don't know what you are talking about," I said, exhausted and without any patience for her theatrics. "And why are you here alone? Where is Madame Shepherd?"

"She abandoned me." Isabelle sniffed. "T-two days ago."

It showed that she'd been alone here. The kitchen was a terrible mess, and there was no fire. Isabelle didn't know how to start one. It was amazing she had candles lit.

"Abandoned you? Why?" I demanded.

"She must have read my note," she said, a trace of guilt in her tone.

"What note?" I asked with forced patience.

"I told her not to come back because I was eloping." Isabelle's eyes filled with tears again. Real tears. It was probably a good thing, because I may have slapped her otherwise for being so stupid.

"And with *whom* did you plan to elope?"

"P-Pierre Monard," she said, weeping. "He's a c-captain."

"What were you thinking?" I demanded. With brains like hers, she was lucky to be alive after two days alone. "Do you know the kind of life sea captains live?"

"But Celeste, he's not like them. He's young and so handsome. We met at a dance at the Allertons'. I think I actually loved him. I never thought I'd ever love someone."

I believed her. Isabelle's flirtations to this point had largely been staged to gratify her vanity and manipulate people.

"And what did you plan to do when he was off at sea?" I growled.

"H-he was going to give it up, was going to become a merchant. I told him Papa would help him."

"So what happened?" I asked through gritted teeth, not really wanting to know.

"He saw Papa's letter," she said, stamping her foot. "Papa never should have written such a thing. If he hadn't, I'd be married to Pierre right now instead of living in this horrible, dark house, penniless. I've had to eat old bread for the last two days. There's nothing else in the kitchen." Eating peasant fare seemed to rank right alongside losing her fiancé.

"Where's the letter?" Father was usually more straightforward in his letters than in person. Perhaps I would get some answers.

Isabelle waved at the counter but continued to cry, though now into her pocket cloth. I found the letter and read it through.

My darling Belle,

I hope you will not be too disturbed to hear that I am on foot now, all my money gone. I was able to pay the Italian bankers with the last of the silk shipment, so I'm sorry there will not be any extra for the new gown you wanted. I am glad to be alive and not confined to an Italian prison, however.

I make my way home now, my little flower, and expect I shall be there in about a month considering the slowness of my travel and the work I have to do to support myself along the way. I should not have trouble finding a buyer for the house and furnishings, and I'm sure that I can quickly reverse my misfortune once I've a little capital again. In no time at all, we shall be able to buy back your jewels and trinkets. Until then, I'm afraid we'll have to rent a place in a different neighborhood.

If you still refuse to go to Monsieur Durant's, I shall have to have you come with me when I travel, as I have no more money to pay Madame Shepherd for chaperoning you. I would avoid telling her this until I arrive.

Your loving father, etc.

"He sold your jewels?"

"Yes." Isabelle sniffled. "The day you two left. I told him they were mine, and he couldn't, but then I went out to meet Pierre. When I came back, they were gone."

Isabelle was such a ninny. She probably would rather have seen Father in prison than give up the gifts he couldn't afford even when he bought them for her.

I put a hand over my eyes.

"You needn't worry," she said, sniffling. "He didn't take any of *your* things."

"None of my things are valuable enough." I dropped my hands to the counter, staring at the letter and trying to clear my muddled thoughts.

She leaned forward and peered at me in the candlelight. "You look different. New glasses." Her tone was accusatory, as if I had betrayed her by wearing something new when she was in such dire circumstances.

"My other pair broke."

"And your hair is nicer, too," she said, obviously begrudging the compliment.

"I've been traveling, not working. I didn't need it up so tight."

She stepped closer. "But you have something on your face." Her eyes grew wide with shock as she realized the mark on my cheek was an enormous bruise. It was still quite purple and blue. If she hadn't actually had real tears in her eyes for once, she probably would have noticed it sooner.

She gasped, looking frightened. "Did Monsieur Durant…"

"Don't be ridiculous, Isabelle," I snapped. "Of course he didn't do this to me. He is a complete gentleman, which is more than you deserve."

"What?" she screeched.

"He still wants you," I said, my tone harsh as I spun away from her. I couldn't stand the sight of her. "I fell for your little joke and worked in his beautiful home as his housekeeper. I even grew to be friends with him, but it's you he's wanted from the beginning. I don't know why you didn't want to go."

"But he's supposed to be so…so *ugly*," she said, not bothering to apologize for what she'd done to me. She had no idea, not of how happy I'd been, nor of how miserable I was now.

"Ha," I scoffed. "He has some scars on his face and wears an eye patch, but the way he earned them made him a hero."

"A hero?"

"And I'll bet your little Pierre, who captained, what? A merchant vessel? I'll bet he didn't have shoulders as strong as an ox."

"He's strong?"

"You'd probably swoon if you saw him with his shirt off."

"You saw him with his shirt off?"

"You don't have to." The image of Henri with his shirt off appeared, uninvited, in my mind. He'd been showing me his scars, but I hardly remembered them when I thought of how he looked. "That's what a man gets for actually working, you ninny. The soft-handed men you string along—"

"Wait." She cut me off. "You say he has a beautiful house?"

"A classic country château," I said through gritted teeth. I wanted to hit her in the face, maybe give her a bruise even better than mine. I resisted, with effort. "And the town of Aix is beautiful. You'll love it."

"I will? What do you mean?"

A day and a half later, Isabelle stepped up into Henri's carriage, assisted by Maurice. I'd accomplished much, and though I'd hardly slept, the work had been a therapeutic break from my own thoughts. And from my sister. After that first conversation, she'd flown into a flurry of activity, and practically all her conversation with me centered on her complaints that she didn't have enough room in her trunks for her clothes. She'd eyed my small trunk in evident design before I hid it from her. Mostly, I had avoided her. I still loved her, but I couldn't bear the sight of her, *and* I'd had renters to find, the house to put to rights, Nicole to contact, and my own plans to set in motion.

Maurice protested vehemently when I'd first told him he was taking my sister home instead of me. His protests died on his lips when Isabelle walked into view.

"Monsieur Durant will understand, Maurice. He's planned this all along."

Maurice didn't say anything. He only stared at Isabelle, who preened as she pulled on her gloves, a smug little smile at her mouth. She loved the attention she received any time she met someone new, even if it was someone she considered beneath her.

After shutting the carriage door after my sister, Maurice ducked his head at me. He'd finally recovered enough from beholding the goddess to speak to me. "I hope you'll be back soon," he said. "It won't be the same without you there."

For an answer, I could only grip his hand tightly before he moved to secure the luggage.

"Isabelle?" I waited for her to lean to the window. "I promise you," I said with a sweet smile. "On everything holy and then some, if you do *anything* to make him unhappy, I will find you and cut off your hair and eyelashes while you sleep." There was not a worse threat I could make to her, and I meant every word.

Her smile was instantly replaced with a glare, but I turned my back and walked into the house. I still had a lot of work ahead of me, and maybe it could keep me from crying all night long, but probably not.

~

Henri

I waved off Bertram and spent the rest of the day preparing the distilling equipment for the lavender harvest. Paul helped me, and it was a good thing, since I almost made two critical mistakes with the sensitive equipment. I couldn't blame it on my nightmares. They'd been noticeably reduced, probably starting around the time Celeste first kissed me. The last few nights I'd had trouble getting to sleep but only because I'd been staying up worrying about her. And just now when I should have been focused on my task, I could only think fondly of the way Celeste had smashed Jean's face with Monsieur Farine's ledger.

"I think you're doing more damage than help, Henri," Paul said, tightening a ring I'd loosened and giving me a funny look. "I think you'd better go back to the house. I'm sure Celeste will come tonight, and you should be there to meet her."

I hesitated a moment.

"She won't be impressed if you lose your fingers trying to work with your mind elsewhere." he said.

I nodded my thanks and hurried back to the house where, to my surprise, Monsieur Farine was waiting.

"I was just coming out to meet you, Henri," he said with a jovial smile. I was again grateful for the way he'd forgiven over a year of stupidity on my part. "I had a small parting gift for Celeste, but your dear aunt just told us she's already left."

His son, Claude, stood nearby looking dejected. I swallowed my anger. It wasn't the boy's fault for liking her.

"You knew she was going?" I asked.

"Yes, of course. Inese tells us she left the morning after she visited us. We hadn't expected her to leave quite so soon." He waved a handsome new leather-bound ledger at me. "She'll need this, won't she? I'll have to just have it shipped once she sends her address."

"Why would she need that? You're expecting a letter from her?"

"What? Why, why no. No, not necessarily," he blustered. "But of course, we hope she'll write. Charlotte will be despondent if she doesn't." He lowered his voice. "Claude too, I'm afraid."

"I do expect her back any day," I said.

"Oh? That's wonderful. She'd said she wouldn't be coming back when she talked with us. I'm glad she changed her mind."

"She said she wasn't coming back?"

I didn't realize I'd been shouting until I registered Claude's startled expression.

"She said she wasn't coming back?" I repeated more quietly.

Monsieur Farine only smiled at me. "Women do change their minds, don't they?"

He and Claude bid me good day and rode away, apparently oblivious to the wound they'd inflicted.

She wasn't coming back. She didn't intend to come home to me.

I walked into the sitting room and collapsed into a chair, the shock sinking into my system.

A long time later, hours probably since the sun was starting to sink toward the horizon, a rumbling noise in the distance pestered my mind for attention. It was several minutes more before I recognized the sound as a carriage coming closer. A carriage. I sprang to the window, almost knocking over a small table in my haste. It was *my* carriage, Maurice in the driver's seat, and more luggage on top than when Celeste went away. She was back, and she planned to stay a long time. I was nervous, giddy.

I ran outside, flicking my hair over my patch, and trying to straighten my shirt. I was going to see her.

Maurice gave me a look full of some sort of warning, but I didn't pay any attention. Celeste had come home to me. I was going to tell her everything.

Maurice opened the carriage door, and assisted down...a woman. Not Celeste.

My happiness careened to an abrupt end. It wasn't her. I looked beyond the newcomer and into the carriage, but it was empty. In deep disappointment, I turned back to our visitor. She blinked once, obviously taking in my scarred appearance. Other than that, there was no impolite reaction from her. I, on the other hand, gawked like an imbecile. Now that I actually paid attention, the girl standing before me was the most beautiful person I'd ever encountered.

Her stylish blue traveling gown was the height of fashion, and the hat perched on her head was a complicated concoction of feathers, lace, and ribbons. But all this had nothing to do with it. The girl, herself, was exquisite. There was no other word for it. Her large eyes were pale blue and long-lashed, her skin creamy perfection. She had a dainty nose, a perfectly proportioned forehead, and the most beautiful hair I'd ever seen, glossy dark brown curls spilling from some sort of knot just under her hat.

I opened my mouth and shut it again as she smiled coyly at me, flashing a tiny dimple in one cheek.

She was shorter than Celeste, with a fuller figure, and aside from the shape of their eyes and chins, you would have never guessed they were sisters.

"Mademoiselle Isabelle Lebeau, I presume?"

She dipped a little curtsey. "Monsieur Durant, I am so pleased to meet you." Her voice was unexpectedly high compared to Celeste's mellow tones.

"I was not expecting you," I said, still a little dazed by the turn of events.

"I'm sorry I couldn't come sooner," she said with a demure little smile. "But my commitments have finally been fulfilled."

"Did your father explain the, er...nature...of your visit?"

"Of course," she said, fluttering her eyelashes at me. I suspected that most men became her willing slaves when she did that.

"I only ask because Celeste hadn't known."

She giggled. "A sisterly prank. Celeste is so fun to tease. And I'm sure she was very helpful around your *beautiful* home." She stared at the house. "She did not do *it*," her eyes flicked back to me, "nor *you*, enough credit in her descriptions." Her eyes widened, as though she'd suddenly realized what she'd said, and she glanced down, a faint shade of pink infusing her cheeks.

"Where is Celeste?" I asked.

She turned startled eyes on me. "Celeste?" She quickly recovered her smile. "She's probably still in Marseille."

"Probably?"

"Well, of course, I don't know for *sure*. All day yesterday she was in a whirlwind of preparations for her trip and for leasing the house out. It was all I could do to get packed without her help." She gazed longingly over my shoulder toward the general direction of the ornamental gardens. "Won't you tell me about your roses?"

"Trip? Leasing?"

Maurice had already lugged one trunk inside and now was hoisting a second off the back of the carriage.

Isabelle tore her eyes away from the rose beds, a hint of confusion in her perfect features. "It is nothing to be concerned about. Celeste has decided to do some traveling. I think that's what she said. And since neither of us would be in the house, and Papa might not be back for another month, she decided to rent the house out."

"She just left without telling you where she was going?"

Isabelle's lower lip pursed in a dainty pout. "Celeste does what she wants. I can't be responsible for her." She took a tiny step nearer and gazed up at me through thick lashes. "It's sweet of you to worry about her, but I'm here now, and she can take care of herself."

It was true. She was here. I couldn't believe it. She was everything I'd wanted.

CHAPTER 24

Celeste

Two months later -

I set aside my bookkeeping as Madame Trenet sailed into my shop with her entourage of friends. I was fond of her, but not her questions, and she *never* failed to ask me questions.

I welcomed her, hoping to stave her off her inquiries. "What can I help you with today, Madame Trenet?" I asked. "And how do you like your new perfume?"

I owed half my success so far to her immediate interest in my beautiful shop. She'd pronounced the place charming and sophisticated, and she'd told her friends and everyone else in town. I was grateful, as it had taken all my savings to get started here, even with my old friend, Monsieur Descanfort, backing me and renting the location to me. No one knew it was my shop, as I couldn't legally own it, and that should have made me nervous, but Monsieur Descanfort was as honorable as a merchant could come. He knew better than to do business with my father, but was more than happy to do business with me. With his solemn promise, I didn't have the faintest concern he'd tell Father where I was, despite their long friendship. Now I was well on my way to making back my initial investment.

"The perfume? Why, it is a dream, but I came in today for more of your lavender oil." She turned to her friends without the tiniest wobble of her enormous coiffure. "Even Marcus says it's the finest we've ever had here. Where did you say you get it, my dear Madame Renault? Was it Morocco?"

I mentally waved away a vision of Henri standing by his lavender fields at sunset, and instead I laughed. "Why, goodness, no. Provence itself has the finest lavender in the world."

I didn't own a trace of unease over the name I'd chosen for myself. It was one of the many steps I'd taken to ensure that even if Father or...anyone else...did actually want to find me, they wouldn't be successful. It took surprisingly little to bribe the official who created my new papers and identity. He was an acquaintance of Nicole's cousin and came highly recommended. And the name wasn't completely a lie, I suppose, since Renault was my mother's maiden name. It was a common enough name that not even Father would think twice of it.

"And I only buy from the most discerning supplier," I assured Madame Trenet. Thanks to Monsieur Farine, my shop had been stocked in almost no time.

Madame Trenet's friends scattered around the shop, but she leaned closer, dropping her voice. "My dear girl, how are you doing? Running this shop must be exhausting. At least you don't have anyone to care for when you go home, but I still worry for you." She paused, but as all I did was smile and clench my teeth together, she went on. "Is there really no chance that you will reconcile with your man?"

When I'd arrived in town, Jean's handiwork had faded to a horrible green. By the time I'd opened shop, the bruising was gone, but enough people had seen it that it couldn't be forgotten. Most assumed I had run away from an abusive husband.

"He doesn't want me any longer," I said. I didn't want to talk about Henri, and I didn't want to be caught in my half-truth. He didn't want me, but he never actually *had* wanted me. I'd only thought he had.

Leaving Henri had been like ripping out pieces of my insides and hanging them up on fence posts every few yards, and I'd had to act quickly to keep myself from going back and begging him to choose me. So I'd arranged things with Monsieur Descanfort, retrieved my hidden savings and my most precious possessions, things of my mother's that Isabelle and Father had forgotten I had, and then traveled until I could think straight. Or at least, almost straight.

It was good I'd had this planned for a couple years already, and that I'd been able convince my friend, Nicole, to come with me. Her family had only consented because they knew she was miserable in her current position. She tended the store when I needed to be away and had already attracted a few potential suitors, men who'd fallen for her peaceful smile and dark eyes. She assured me she was thrilled.

I wanted to be happy for her, and I was, but I still couldn't believe what a fool I'd been. How could I have misunderstood what was going on? How did I not realize Henri wanted to marry Isabelle?

I told myself every day, many times every day, that I didn't need Henri's love to be happy in my life. I already knew I didn't need my father's or my sister's. I'd existed without *their* love for as long as I could remember. I knew that in time, even if it took years, I would get over the hurt I felt. Then I would contact Isabelle or Father and tell them where I was. But until then, I was happy to have a fresh start somewhere new. Aix had taught me what my life could be like, far away from a beautiful sister and a father whose business practices were less than ethical. That, and I was too cowardly to face the announcement of the wedding. It would be better for me to hear about it years after the fact.

I occasionally felt a twinge of guilt for leaving before Father came home, but there hadn't really been a choice. I knew he'd need the rent money when he got back, and I didn't think I could hide my plans from him if he'd been in the same house.

"I can see that your thoughts are elsewhere, my dear," Madame Trenet said with a kind smile. She wasn't such a bad soul. She gathered up her friends, and they made their purchases before bustling out the door and into the plaza.

I sighed and slumped against the counter as I watched them meander across the cobblestones. The view from my shop couldn't have been more beautiful. Gusts of wind swirled autumn leaves around the little plaza where a few dozen people still shopped. The afternoon light filtered through the trees, scattering golden patches everywhere. I had chosen an amazing location.

I inhaled deeply, trying to settle my mind. I think half the people that came to my shop did it for the smell. I had French and imported oils and perfumes, luxury goods of almost every sort, and common little items that every shop in town carried as well. Not so many of those that I would compete with the other shops, but enough that I met my customers' expectations. It was a beautiful, wonderful shop with potted plants and elegant artwork behind the displays. It actually rivaled the perfection of Madame Farine's shop. I was already working to become a supplier to shops in three different towns. It was the fulfillment of my dream.

I should have been much happier. Every night I went to sleep in my own apartment over the shop. I cooked for only myself. I had no one to please and all the freedom I could wish for. I had new friends, no one close, though perhaps I'd done that on purpose. I wasn't ready to confide in anyone yet.

A commotion at the other end of the plaza caught my eye, and I straightened, walking nearer to the window. A tall, dark-haired man had jumped down from a carriage and was moving

ROXANNE MCNEIL

from person to person, gesticulating forcefully. He seemed quite wild.

Trying to get a better look, I adjusted Bertram's glasses and squinted. A small crowd had gathered around the man now, and they didn't look pleased with him. He turned toward the shop, and I gasped, instantly stepping back from the window.

Henri.

He pointed toward my shop and began walking toward it, but a shout from within in the crowd stopped him short. He spun around and spoke urgently to someone, and I wished I could hear the exchange.

Henri's form slumped a little, and he moved back toward the carriage, getting in and slamming the door before Maurice could get down to help him. I watched the carriage roll away, my heart in my throat. A few children ran along after the carriage, throwing rocks. I wanted to knock their heads together.

Madame Trenet almost ran back to my shop, fluttering her hands nervously as she came. I schooled my features, but the moment she entered the shop, she exclaimed, "Celeste Renault, how pale you are." Her tone was all kindness, but there was triumph in her eyes. "You'll never believe the scene I just witnessed."

I wanted to shake her into faster speech, but said, "I hope everything is all right, Madame Trenet."

"Well, I hardly know," she said, tilting her head to the side and appraising me shrewdly. "You see, the oddest man just came to town. He was so haunted-looking, you'd almost feel sorry for the devil."

"Oh?" I hoped my voice didn't betray interest, but I would have tied her to the counter rather than let her leave without telling me everything.

"He was looking for a girl. He told anyone who would listen that he was worried sick for her, that he loved her, that he had to find her. It was terribly romantic, even if you could see when you got close to him that he wore an eye patch and had horrendous scars."

I shrugged. "France is always at war, her men always being injured."

"So true," she said, before pausing to study a box of hairpins. I wanted to pinch her for toying with me.

"I suppose she looked like a princess, with long golden hair and sapphire eyes," I said, leaning over to adjust a display.

"Not quite, but he did say she was very beautiful."

I stood up straighter. He'd lost Isabelle. Disappointment warred with worry until she added, "But right away, he corrected himself. He seemed confused for a moment, said she was beautiful to him but that we would probably think she was just an average sort of pretty with brown hair and green-brown eyes."

I sat down, hard, before recovering enough to wave my fingers. "That describes about half the women in town, including you and me."

She laughed with good humor. "My eyes are blue. And I am very certain he isn't looking for *me*. Imagine what Marcus would say." She glanced at me. "Can you believe the man has been searching for her for months? He seemed beside himself with worry. He was particularly interested in looking for her in *your* shop, but when I told him it belonged to a Madame Renault, he jumped right back into his carriage."

The air was too dry to breathe properly, and I wished I'd left the windows open. The heat was making my head spin. Could this be true?

I managed to hurry Madame Trenet on her way and then pressed my back to the closed door. I slid slowly down to sit in a heap on the floor, my heart pounding and my eyes oddly wet.

～

ROXANNE MCNEIL

Henri

Maurice clapped me on the shoulder consolingly as I left
the stable. We'd been on the road for a week again, and
without a hint of success. I looked up at the house. The place
had ceased to feel like home without Celeste there. I'd felt so
sure, in the second to the last town we'd visited, that I'd found
her shop. It had an elegant and functional appeal to it, exactly
the sort of place she would own, and the town had been on the
list Claude Farine had given me. But when I'd asked about the
owner of the shop, I was told it belonged to a Madame Renault
or Renore or something similar.

I'd thought I was onto something when Claude had admitted
his parents had been making shipments to Celeste. I thought
that if she was alive, she would have a shop somewhere, and that
confirmed both. I didn't know if I was more furious with the
Farines for pretending not to know where she was, or more
relieved that she had someone helping her.

I'd tricked Claude into his admission, hinting that if I could
find Celeste, I would be sure to arrange a way for him to meet
Isabelle. Every single man in Aix who met her thought themselves in love with the horrible brat, and I would have loved to
send her off to any of them. For simply arranging two meetings
with her, Claude told me everything he knew, which wasn't
much but did include a list of new towns the Farines sent shipments to.

As it was, we'd had to house the little banshee for two
weeks before her father came to pick her up. He'd evidently
come home to find his house rented and his favorite gone.
Luckily, his fortune had reversed again, and he was well
enough off to take Isabelle home with him, as well as make a
payment on his debt. If Aunt Inese hadn't felt sorry for me, she
probably would have been insufferable. Isabelle was ten times
the spoiled ninny Aunt Inese had claimed she'd be. Whatever

had induced me to send for *her* had surely been a form of madness.

When I'd informed Isabelle, not so gently, that I was in love with her sister and had no intention of allowing her to stay at my house, let alone of courting her, she'd flown into the most ridiculous hysterics I'd ever seen, and only Aunt Inese's constant insistence on smelling salts had kept her in check. My aunt could be very formidable when she chose to be.

She had insisted we keep the girl until we could find suitable arrangements for her, and for Celeste's sake, I knew we couldn't turn her out, but it had been a near thing a few times. Carine and Suzanne had both come close to throttling her on several occasions.

"I don't *work,*" she'd wailed when Aunt Inese suggested she help with some of the duties Celeste had assumed.

"Aren't you going to take me to any parties?" she'd whined at least twenty times a day, despite frequent reminders that we were in the middle of the lavender harvest.

And when we pressed her for ideas about where Celeste could be or how we could find her, the stupid little creature just cried, "Celeste's friends are below my social level. I don't know any of their *names.*" I think that was the first time Aunt Inese had to prevent Suzanne from doing the girl bodily harm.

The only thing that saved our sanity, and possibly Isabelle's life, was the girl's devotion to roses. She spent hours every day out among my rosebushes.

Celeste did send a letter to tell Aunt Inese she was all right and to wish us all well. I'd practically ripped it in my haste to take it when I learned what it was. By the next day, I had it memorized.

Dear Inese,

Thank you for your kindness during my stay. I was able to correct the mistake that sent me instead of my sister to you over two months ago, and I hope you will not bear me any ill will for not understanding the situation. I never would have imposed on you so. I will not be coming for the wedding as I intend to follow through with my original plans, but I will try to send word to you once I am established. I am so grateful for your friendship, and for Suzanne's and Carine's.

I wish you all very happy and well,

Celeste Lebeau

She had not mentioned me once, had not addressed me at all in the letter. I'd already been frantic to see her, but the letter certainly made it worse. She'd run off on some harebrained adventure and hadn't even told her father where she'd gone. He'd hardly feigned concern when I confronted him about it. I think the coward was glad not to have to face her for now. At least he'd taken Isabelle away. I could be grateful to him for that.

And now, arriving home from what must have been the fifteenth trip to search for her, I was no closer to finding her than I'd been when I'd first read her letter. In some towns I was treated as a leper, and sometimes I just received pitying looks. Five months ago, I would have hated their reactions, wouldn't have dared visit new towns where people weren't used to my scarring. But five months ago, I hadn't been in love with Celeste Lebeau. I slumped into a chair in the parlor and sank my face into my hands. The gesture didn't keep me from smelling the sweet rolls Suzanne was making in the kitchen. Why did she have to make them like Celeste did?

A tear leaked from my eye. I think the pain of losing Celeste was just as excruciating as the pain of my burns and wounds two years ago. And there was nothing to ease this pain. How had she not understood that I loved her? Why hadn't I told her? And why hadn't I told her about her father's, really her sister's, unkind trick? She'd been right here in my home, and I'd wasted my chances to ask her to marry me.

I wrote her father almost weekly, but he never received any

news from her. He'd been extremely surprised when I told him I intended to marry Celeste if she'd have me. Of course, I think I threatened him with dismemberment in the same sentence, so he may have just been reacting to my threats.

My breath caught on a sob. Where was she? How had I been so foolish to drive her away?

"Henri, are you ill?"

At her voice, I jumped up from my chair, overturning it. Celeste stood only a few feet from me, her brow furrowed in concern. I would have thought I was dreaming if she hadn't been holding a broom in one hand. In my dreams she held *me*, not brooms. Her hair was tied back in a cloth, and she was wrapped in one of Suzanne's large aprons. A smudge of soot marked one side of her forehead. Her eyes held a touch of defiance.

I uttered her name in a low, disbelieving whisper, and her expression softened.

"If you aren't ill, you'd better change. You're filthy, and we just cleaned in here."

"Celeste?" I whispered again.

She leaned forward, as though she wanted to come to me but was uncertain of her reception. She shook herself a little, crossed her arms, and regarded me with an insufferable little lift of her eyebrows.

"Where have you been?" I managed.

"Running my shop," she said with little shrug. "It's doing quite well." She watched me, waiting for something.

My voice returned to me with volume I think I'd never before managed. "What were you thinking?" I shouted. "I didn't know where you were! You might have been dead for all I knew! You never told us what you were doing! You said you were coming *back*!"

She sighed and set her broom against the wall before advancing on me with her fists on her hips. "*That's* what you have to say to me? *Those* are the words you greet me with?" she demanded, drawing disturbingly near.

A strangled moan of anger, longing, and frustration escaped my throat before I could catch it back.

"Well, Henri Durant, I have words of my own," she snapped. She peered up at me, glaring. "*Would* you sit down? *How* can I argue with someone who looks down at me so easily?"

I dropped onto the nearest chair in shock, and without a moment's hesitation, she seated herself on my lap, gripped my head in her hands, and pressed her lips to mine. I wondered again if I was dreaming before I decided it was impossible. She smelled of lavender and dust and household cleaner. It made my nose itch. She was real.

She sighed contentedly when I enthusiastically returned her kiss, wrapping my arms tightly around her. "I love you, Celeste," I said when we paused for breath. "I'm so sorry I didn't tell you about everything. I didn't know how. I've miss—" Her lips caught mine again.

After the most pleasant five minutes I'd ever experienced, she pulled away a little to look at me. Her head scarf had been discarded within seconds of her sitting on my lap, and her hair was definitely mussed by now. It was difficult to keep my hands out of it, so I didn't.

I searched her beautiful eyes as she said quietly and deliberately, "I love you, Henri Durant. I'm sorry that I made you look for me. I wouldn't have wasted that time if I knew you cared for me."

"I was an idiot not to tell you," I said.

She kissed me again.

"Marry me, Celeste?" I asked. "*Please.* I love you. I never want to be without you."

Celeste leaned her forehead against mine. "Henri, I adore you. Of course I'll marry you."

My laugh might have sounded like a strangled cry, but it was the happiest sound I'd ever made.

"Well, it's about time, Henri." My aunt stood in the doorway, looking extremely pleased.

Celeste blushed crimson and tried to get up, but I held her tight. "You'd better send for the priest, Auntie. Promise him we won't throw him bodily from the house."

She smirked at us and walked away.

After another few minutes, I released Celeste to arm's length. "What about your shop?"

"I'll manage it from a distance. My friend, Nicole, is going to run it for me. I've got so many other business ventures starting up right now that it's a relief." She toyed with a bit of hair at my temple, making it extremely difficult to concentrate. "And then, of course, I'll be reworking your lavender products."

"You won't have to hide in the basement to experiment," I said, grinning like an idiot.

Celeste's lips turned up in a smug little smile before she buried her hands in my hair and pulled me closer again. She paused an inch from my lips and said with a little frown, "And then I'll start on my plans for that washroom. Why, the piping alone—"

I closed the distance between us and kissed her again, fiercely, happily — until the dust all over her made me sneeze. Twice.

EPILOGUE

Celeste

One year later -
I almost hit my face against the door when it didn't give way. I pressed the handle again, but it didn't budge. Why was the princess room locked? A month after we were married, Henri had helped me empty the entire room. We sold almost all the perfumes, jewelry, and books, and with the money, paid for installation of pipes for waste and wash water from the kitchen and the washroom. Suzanne had been almost delirious with happiness. I kept the beautiful gloves with lavender embroidered up the wrists that I'd worn to the dance in Aix, and of course, all the family heirlooms as well. I was extremely glad Isabelle had never seen that room. She would have never let them send her home with Father.

I sighed, thinking of the pair of them. I'd finally written to them six months after I was married. I didn't want them to hear it from someone else. I was sure to wait until after Father had finished paying his debt to Henri, of course.

I tried the door again and grunted in frustration. At the

sound of Henri's voice, I let go of the handle and hurried downstairs. I couldn't help but smile at the sight in the entryway. Little Marie sat on Paul's shoulders, laughing delightedly while Paul turned in circles, speaking seriously with Henri of hiring more farmhands. Martin stood between them, obviously fascinated by the conversation. Indeed, his admiration for Henri seemed only eclipsed by his admiration for Paul, though that was as it should be.

Possibly emboldened by my sudden marriage to Henri, Carine married Paul just a month afterward. Suzanne had sniffed fiercely into her handkerchief at their wedding and had baked a cake the size of a large lavender bush for them.

Now, as Carine joined her husband in the doorway, they shared a look of quiet happiness that had me grinning. My happiness was not so quiet. Henri and I bantered relentlessly. Inese told me we only ever paused our arguments to kiss indecently in any room in the house. I silently agreed. Henri's kisses were indecently passionate. I couldn't get enough.

Paul and Carine took their leave before I could shake myself from my thoughts.

Henri closed the door, but before turning around asked, "Eavesdropping, Celeste? Will you never give up the habit?"

He turned to grin at me as I approached him. He never tried to hide his smiles from me anymore.

"I didn't want your guests to hear you scolded," I said primly, adjusting my glasses.

His brow furrowed. "Did Suzanne tell you I ate the last of the meringues?"

I glared at him. "You didn't."

He laughed heartily and gathered me to him. "No, I didn't. There are at least three left."

I relaxed into his embrace but wasn't deterred. "Could you possibly tell me *why* the spare bedroom is locked again?"

"Oh."

"Oh?"

"Well, I suppose you might as well see it."

"Might as well see what?" I asked, instantly alarmed.

Henri only sighed and led me back up the stairs, ignoring my tirade of questions. He pulled a lone key from his pocket and inserted it into the lock. He made a show of the lock sticking, but I knew he was only doing it to irritate me.

Finally the door swung open, and he gently pushed me forward. The spare room was unrecognizable. The wall hangings had been done over in pale green, and a beautiful crib stood in the middle of the room. The wardrobe doors were open, displaying several baby gowns.

"I hope you like it all. Jacques built the crib for us, and I asked Bertram ages ago to bring some things from Paris. Carine made everything pretty." He paused. "Do you like it?"

I couldn't help laughing as I flew into his arms. "We still have *months* left, you know."

"Well, yes, but Bertram is getting married in a few weeks, and who knows when he'll be able to bring things back from Paris again."

I shook my head. "I love you, Henri Durant. And it is perfect."

He grinned triumphantly down at me, but after a moment of looking into my eyes, his expression changed, and he pulled me more tightly into his arms. He bent his head toward mine. "I can't believe I didn't see how perfect you are the first day you showed up at the door," he murmured.

I laughed aloud. "I should have seen it in *you*. Maybe if you had kissed me."

He laughed. "You weren't wearing your glasses. You couldn't see me at all." And then one of his hands slipped around my neck, pulling me in for a kiss, while his other hand drew me closer to him. "I love you, Celeste," he murmured against my mouth before kissing me gently. And then not so gently.

I buried my hands in his hair and retuned his kiss with enthusiasm. Kissing him, *life* with him was exactly what I wanted, better than any fairy tale ending, better than anything I'd ever imagined. And even though being so ridiculously happy with him still felt new, I knew with absolute certainty that I would never tire of it.

I hope you enjoyed *Sister to Beauty*. Please consider leaving a review. For occasional announcements, free content, and information on future releases, eventually including another fairy tale centered around Bertram, sign up for my newsletter at https://roxannemcneil.com/newsletter/. Turn the page for other books by Roxanne McNeil.

ALSO BY ROXANNE MCNEIL

LOVE AND SORCERY: DISILLUSIONED

An unwanted bodyguard, an underestimated sorceress, and their
powerful, mutual dislike.

∼

LOVE AND SORCERY: BAITED

An arranged marriage to a dangerous man calls for an escape plan. Too
bad his kisses are completely addictive.

∼

LOVE AND SORCERY: DISGUISED

His heart belongs to someone else. She's a danger to all around her.
They have no business falling in love.

ABOUT THE AUTHOR

Roxanne writes sweet, chemistry-driven romance. Her bookshelves are full of happy endings, and she would never consider writing anything else. Roxanne loves the Pacific Northwest and has a long-standing relationship with See's chocolate. She lives with a sweet, 45-pound ball of fur named Queenie, who is much more of a princess than Roxanne is.

Made in the USA
Monee, IL
31 December 2022

24126257R00163